STAR-CROSSED HOLIDAY

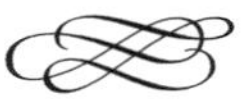

SARAH DEEHAM

CHAPTER 1

93 DAYS TO CHRISTMAS

Poppy

I ADMIRE ANY PLACE THAT WILL UNIRONICALLY LEAN INTO Christmas in September. Perhaps to honor its name, the owners of Holly Hill Inn do not believe in harvest festivals or autumn decor. Nope, they go straight from summer to mantels filled with garland, with nary a pumpkin in between. It makes my Christmas-loving heart happy, and I revel in any opportunity to stay here in the historic mansion.

I stab the elevator button a few more times, then decide the elevator is as antique as the inn itself, which does not instill confidence. But it's better than taking the stairs to the fifth floor in my froth-filled nightmare of a dress and torture-chamber heels. I curse my sister for suggesting a 1980s prom-themed bachelorette party. "The tackier, the better" was her instruction, so I spent the entire night dressed like an extra in a teen-scream horror flick, corralling drunk women, singing bad karaoke, and itching all over from layers of tulle.

Normally, I'm the queen of theme and costume parties. I'm wicked with a glue gun and feather boa. I even own a Bedazzler. But being dumped by my fiancé two months ago is causing my maid-of-honor duties for my sister's wedding to lose their luster. Even singing "Dancing Queen" couldn't perk me up, and ABBA is my jam. My heart hurts watching my sister, who never wanted to be tied down, prepare for the wedding I'd been dreaming of my whole life. I'm happy for her. But sad for me. All I want is to go back to my hotel room, cry myself to sleep, and then wake up fresh for the wedding tomorrow.

I stab the button again in rhythmic bursts.

"That won't make the elevator come any faster," a man says behind me.

Normally, being snarky is way outside of my people-pleasing comfort zone, but I turn to say something, and all thoughts fly out of my head.

I can only see the man before me. A man with the eyes, face, and body of a Norse god. My gaze tilts up, up, up to his granite jaw, made softer by stubble, to his pale blue eyes and sexy smirk. His long blond hair is caught in a man bun. Viking looks good on him.

My heart flips and tumbles to my toes.

His thick, corded arms hold a sleeping child snuggled against his broad chest. I don't blame the small girl. That chest looks as if it could protect all manner of children, women, and even a forest animal or two.

And they have, I realize with shock—at least on the big screen. I know those eyes, face, and chest. They belong to Ronan Masters, Hollywood's most famous action star. And here he is, at Holly Hill, in a small lake town in upstate New York.

My mouth opens. But nothing comes out.

Ronan doesn't seem surprised by my expression. He probably stuns women to silence daily. Hourly.

A ding sounds. "Elevator's here," he prompts me. "Are you sure that dress will fit?"

"Oh. Um. Yes." That's me—all quick wit and clever rejoinders. I stumble into the elevator, tripping on my ridiculous dress.

He shifts the blond-haired angel in his arms and ambles in behind me. It's remarkable that someone as large as him can amble.

Once in the elevator, he brushes past me to press the button for the fifth floor, sending shivers of tingling awareness through my body.

I sneak a glance, trying to be cool, but knowing he sees me checking him out. He's larger-than-life, just like the action hero he plays in the movies, complete with a rescued child. Maybe he saved her from a burning building or a terrorist cell. At least in my imagination.

My soft sigh attracts his attention. His icy eyes squint in silent reproach, reminding me I shouldn't ogle a complete stranger. But it's not my fault he's so ogle-able.

I sigh again.

He looks away, staring at a fixed spot on the doors. I imagine he's wishing himself anywhere but in here with me.

He shifts.

The elevator groans and then comes to a creaking, croaking, crashing stop. I fall back against the rear wall of the elevator with a thud, and my wide eyes meet the intense gaze of Ronan Masters, action star.

A grinding sound comes from above us.

“Oh shit,” I whisper before the floor falls out from under me. As quickly as the descent starts, it stops with the sick scraping of metal on metal.

When conscious thought resumes, I realize I’m clinging to Ronan Masters like a limpet. I let go of his solid muscles, resisting the urge to give them a farewell pat.

“Sorry. My bad.”

There’s that eyebrow of his rising again.

I clear my throat and press the button for the fifth floor. Nothing.

I press it again, harder, then pound all the buttons in desperation.

The grinding starts again, and I freeze, afraid to move, afraid to breathe. I don’t dare touch another button for fear of plunging us to our deaths.

My panicked gaze takes in the mountain man next to me. When I say mountain, I don’t mean a glorified hill. He’s of an epic variety: Mount Everest or the Himalayas. Perhaps the elevator couldn’t handle his heft. Or the weight of my tulle.

“Sooo… Ha-ha… This is freaky. I’ve never been stuck in an elevator before.” I bite my lip to stop babbling. I don’t want to seem more unhinged than I already am, what with the ogling and the grabbing. And now the fear of imminent death.

“It’s a first for me, too,” he says. The depth of his voice echoes through me.

“Unless you count *The Escape*,” I whisper, so as not to wake the sleeping child. *The Escape* is one of his most popular blockbusters.

“Except that wasn’t real. You do realize I didn’t climb thirty-nine floors through an elevator shaft?”

“You didn’t do the stunts yourself?” I eye the way his navy-blue Henley hugs rock-hard biceps.

"I did all the stunts myself. But we were on set, not in an actual elevator."

"Still," I say. I can't let this go. Hollywood led me to believe he can fix any situation with just his muscles and a quip. But in real life, he has no quips, and he's exchanged his famous grin for a grimace.

Why be stuck in an elevator with the most famous action hero on the planet if he won't do anything to get us out?

"Are you sure you can't force open the doors? Fix it with duct tape?" I stare pointedly at his powerful forearms.

He rolls his eyes. I'd be offended, but I suspect he's only pretending to be annoyed. The questions I'm asking are valid.

"I could try to force the door open, but it might trigger us falling again."

I shake my head. "Oh no. That would be bad."

"And I'm all out of duct tape."

"You really should plan better. Ronan Masters in the movies always has duct tape," I grumble.

"Noted," he says, as dry as the Sahara.

I crane my neck to admire his strong jaw. If we don't sit down soon, I'll have a neck cramp.

"Perhaps, and this is just a wild idea here," he says, "but we could press the emergency button and call for help? Disappointing as that may be—"

I'm already on it. Before he can finish his sentence, I break eye contact with the sexy beast and leap toward the elevator's control panel. Perhaps I should be the action star. I'm hitting the call button, the emergency button, and every button that's there. But…nothing.

"Why are none of these working?" I whisper-cry.

My actions anger the Elevator Gods. There's a splintering sound full of evil and malice. I'm not stupid. I throw myself back onto the star, trying to avoid the sleeping girl, while burrowing myself into his side. It doesn't take much to be encased in his arms, what with the space being so tiny.

I resist the urge to grope his granite abs. Even without duct tape, his presence is comforting.

I'm not sure if it's my banging, the groaning elevator, or me jumping Ronan, but the little girl in his arms opens big blue eyes and, with a wide yawn, looks around.

She doesn't seem alarmed about the stranger-danger situation.

"Hello," she says shyly. She turns away, burying her face in Ronan's shoulder, but then curiosity seems to get the best of her, and she turns back to me. "Who are you?" she asks with a slight English accent.

Given that we're both clinging to the same man, it's a fair question.

"Pleased to meet you," I say. "I'm Poppy."

Ronan snorts. "I should've known."

I shoot him a chastising glance for interrupting. And for insulting my name. It's a good name. It suits me. Everyone says so.

I decide to ignore him and the scary elevator. I focus on the girl because little people are also my jam. "What's your name?"

"I'm Belle."

"I love your name!" I exclaim. "You're a princess."

"I love yours, too," she says. "You're a flower. And I love your dress." Her face scrunches in confusion. "But why are we in here? Why aren't we moving?"

"We're stuck," I say as cheerfully as I can manage. "But we're super safe, so don't worry, Belle." I say that to reassure her, as well as myself. I try to push away any anxiety that we might be stuck for hours and thank the saints that I went to the bathroom before I left the bar.

"Oh." She nestles into the big guy's chest. "I'm not worried. Father will get us out," she says with calm assurance.

So he's her dad. Interesting. I've never heard that Ronan Masters is a baby daddy. I rarely follow celebrity gossip, but I peek at the tabloids at the checkout stand. Especially when he's on the cover. For academic interest, of course.

"While I have supreme faith in your dad," I say with a grin, "we could play a game to see who can scream 'Help!' the loudest. I bet you'll win. You seem like a girl with good lungs."

Her eyes light up. "I can yell loud. My last nanny complained I hurt her ears."

"I hate to interrupt the fun, but maybe we should try a phone first? Do you have one?" Ronan asks.

Of course! A cell phone. "Do you?" I shoot back.

He shakes his head. "Mine's out of battery. But given the size of your bag—" he points to the enormous bag I've dubbed the Party Rescue Kit for all the times it's come in handy tonight "—you've got room for a phone."

He looks so hopeful. I hate to break his faith in me and my purse. "I was at a bachelorette party. The whole wedding is unplugged." I use finger quotes for the word unplugged.

"What the hell is that?"

"Unplugged. You know, no phones allowed."

"That's the dumbest thing I've ever heard," Ronan grumbles.

"Don't be such a hater," I sniff. "It was my idea. All the wedding blogs advise it. Camera phones and bachelorette parties are a terrible combination. There's too much risk of photo blackmail from bad choices, fashion or otherwise."

Belle shifts, and Ronan turns his attention back to her, his eyes softening in a way that goes straight to my uterus.

"Is it okay if I yell with Poppy now?" Belle asks.

"Of course," he agrees, brushing a strand of hair out of her face.

I don't want Belle scared, so I say, "It will be fun. It's called the yelling game."

Ronan snorts, but when I glance at him, his expression is bland.

"Ready?" I ask Belle. She nods.

"Three. Two. One." I count down then wink at Belle. We scream at top volume.

Ronan doesn't join our yelling fest until I shove him in the ribs with my elbow, and then he joins in halfheartedly.

"You have a big voice," Belle says to me in admiration when I take a screaming break.

"You too, kiddo. Big voices, small bodies," I say, pointing between her and me. I offer her a high five. She slaps my hand and giggles some more. I probably shouldn't call myself small, not with having inherited the O'Brien hips, but I'm short, so I take linguistic license with the word. And I'm far, far smaller than the big guy next to me. It's all relative.

"Are you saying I don't have a big voice?" Ronan's growl is as deep as the ocean.

"I'm not sure," I tease. "I can't tell because your yelling is wimpy."

His eyes skim over me in a way that heats my skin, but his expression remains, as ever, inscrutable.

I turn to Belle. "What do you think?" I give the thumbs-up sign, then the thumbs-down sign.

Belle shakes her head. "Poppy is right." Her thumb turns down.

"You're a traitor," he grumbles, looking wounded. But he doesn't fool me. Or Belle. She giggles.

"It doesn't matter. No one can hear us anyway." I sink down to the floor and try to rein in the tulle of my skirt as best as possible. I pat the empty spot next to me. "We might as well make ourselves comfy."

Ronan Masters eyes the floor dubiously, but he sits with surprising grace. Good core muscle control does that for you.

"At least the lights are still on," I say.

Ronan frowns. "You had to say that. You've cursed us."

We go silent, waiting for the lights to dim, but they don't.

I stick out my tongue. "See, Mr. Doom and Gloom?"

"Did you just stick out your tongue at me? What are you? Seven years old?"

"I'm seven and a half. What's wrong with being seven?" Belle asks him, affronted.

"Yeah, what's wrong with being seven?"

He shakes his head.

I look away from his too-handsome face because it does things to me. I'm annoyed at myself for being so affected. He probably has girls throwing themselves at him all the time. I refuse to be a cliché.

"I'm hungry," Belle says, on the edge of a whine.

"It won't be long." Ronan wipes his daughter's glistening forehead. It's getting hot in here.

I dig through my oversized handbag. Bright yellow and decorated with pom-poms, it's hideous. But it was a gift, and I'm sentimental that way. Plus, it has a fabulous number of pockets. I'm not saying I'm a hoarder, but if there's ever an apocalypse, my ugly bag and I will have what we need to survive.

"What are you looking for?" Ronan asks me.

"Reinforcements," I say. "Aha! I knew I had snacks!" I pull out two granola bars and wave them in the air.

"Can I have one, please?" Belle asks.

"Of course, little one. Here's one for you and one for your dad."

I swear his stomach rumbles, but he holds up his hand. "You can have it. Or save it for Belle, in case she's still hungry later."

I shrug and put it back into my purse with a small smile. So he's not selfish. My ex would have devoured that granola bar in a hot second, not worrying about who else was hungry.

I open the package for Belle and hand it to her. My smile widens at the way she attacks it, daintily, but with enthusiasm.

"What do you say, Belle?" Ronan prompts.

"Thank you," she says between bites. It sounds more like, "mrph phew."

"Thanks for the snack," he says grudgingly. "She didn't have much to eat tonight. We'd planned on ordering room service when we got back here."

I shrug, trying not to get caught up by the blue of his eyes and the long sweep of his lashes, so much darker than his golden hair. "I always carry food. 'Cause food is great. Drink?" I pull out a stainless-steel water bottle.

"What else do you have in there?" He leans over to look.

I peek up at him. "That's for me to know and you not to find out."

He shakes his head again. He does that a lot, as if he's not sure what to make of me, which is silly, because I'm not that interesting. I'm just a small-town girl with a simple life. I'm no famous Hollywood star.

Belle wiggles in Ronan's lap.

Now that she's eaten the granola bar, and the excitement of being stuck in an elevator is gone, boredom will follow. Overtired and bored is a dangerous situation for a child, even one as sweet as Belle.

Ronan shoots me a nervous look. Great minds think alike.

"My magic purse to the rescue," I say, rooting through it. He touches the edge of the bag as if to open it farther. I swat his giant hand away and find the object I'm looking for.

"Ta-da!" I say, pulling out a small cloth pouch. I empty it on my lap.

Belle gasps in delight. "Glitter pens! And a sparkly notebook."

Pretty pens and stationery are a particular weakness. Occupational hazard.

"Would you like to color?" I draw a series of flowers and pass her the set of pens and a book.

Belle looks at the flowers with reverence. "I wish I could draw those."

I smile. "I can teach you. Here, watch."

Ten minutes later, I'm showing Belle how to draw a rose, and we're crooning the lyrics to one of the *Frozen* songs.

Ronan watches us in bemusement.

Next, I show Belle how to draw a butterfly. She works in concentration while she watches me sketch each line. When we color the last bit, she beams.

"It's so pretty!"

"Something is missing." I reach into my purse and pull out a small plastic bag of colorful tubes from one of the inside pockets. "Ahh... I thought these were in here." I present it to the girl like a gift. "*Voilà*."

"Glitter glue!" she breathes. "Perfect!"

Ronan stares at me as if I'm from another planet. "Glitter

glue? Are you for real? Who has glitter glue in their purse?"

I blush. "A girl who likes sparkles?"

"Who are you?" he asks, as if *I'm* the green alien, not him.

"Poppy O'Brien, kindergarten teacher, at your service."

He barks out a laugh. "That explains it. Everything's become clear."

"Explains what?" Should I be offended?

"You," he says, pointing in my general direction. "Your magic bag. You're like the Pied Piper. Belle doesn't usually warm up to strangers."

"Poppy isn't a stranger," Belle interrupts. "She's Poppy. And she's awesome!"

Belle reaches up and pats Ronan Masters's famous stubble, playing with the scruff on that sharp-as-a-blade jaw.

I envy her. I'd give up the break period in my school schedule just to run my hand over his jaw. Or his chest. Or his arms. Or his—

Ronan tilts his head, giving another abrupt laugh. "My point exactly." At first, I'm confused at what point he's referring to, my mind having gotten so off track. And then I remember Belle called me awesome.

"Thank you." I gently boop her nose with my finger. "You're awesome too."

Her dad is also kind of awesome, if a little grumpy. But I keep that information to myself. He doesn't need to know. I'm sure his ego is big enough.

We sit coloring for a while. It's probably only ten more minutes, but it feels like forever. Not a bad forever—a peaceful one.

Eventually, Belle crawls from Ronan's lap to mine. I'm not surprised. It's a scientific fact that little girls can't resist tulle. It's as if a troop of ballerinas and a dozen princesses threw up in my lap. I am tulle-erific.

Ronan takes advantage of his freedom to get up and try the call button again. He bangs on the door and yells, but it's quiet outside. We're in our own little world.

Belle stretches and yawns. If I know anything about seven-year-olds—and I know a lot about seven-year-olds—she's about to fall asleep. Her eyelids waver, then close. A few minutes later, she gives a slight snore.

My smile is bittersweet as I run my hand over her silky blond hair, my heart melting at the feeling of the girl asleep in my arms. I want a family and a child of my own. I thought that time was nearing. But now, after being dumped by my fiancé of twelve years, that dream has never felt further away. I know all the bachelors in my small town, so trust me when I say the odds are not great.

Belle's breathing deepens.

"She's asleep," I whisper to Ronan.

"It's late for her."

A more practical concern pops into my head. "When did Belle go potty last?" I whisper in horror.

He raises an eyebrow.

"The bathroom. The toilet. Tinkle," I hiss.

He grins. "Worried?"

I glare. He quirks up one side of that sexy mouth. That I'm noticing his sexiness when I could be minutes away from being peed on only shows how lethal he is.

I feel his chuckle in my very core.

"You're safe. She went right before we left the set. It hasn't been long."

"Thank God," I breathe in relief. As a teacher, I've been peed on before. I don't recommend it. "We got lucky. And at least we have light."

And that's when everything goes black.

CHAPTER 2

93 DAYS TO CHRISTMAS (STILL)

Poppy

"YOU HAD TO SAY IT," RONAN GRUMBLES.

"What? You're crazy. The lights going out is not my fault." I defend my honor in a fierce whisper.

He sits back. "You jinxed us."

"How can you be superstitious?" I retort. "You're Ronan Masters."

He sighs. A sound that's loud in the dark.

Belle stirs in my arms. "Wha—" she mumbles, still half asleep.

I don't want her to wake up and be scared. I admit, I'm freaked out too. The dark is so thick it's a tangible presence, like drowning in black ink.

With my sight blocked, every rustle of fabric, every shift of position, every breath is magnified. My sense of smell is enhanced as well. Belle's lavender shampoo reaches me, as does the fresh scent of laundry detergent and something deeper from Ronan. Something that reminds me of walking through the woods in the winter. It has to be pheromones because it makes me want to close the scant distance between us and see if he tastes as good as he smells.

Rocking Belle to distract myself, I hum a familiar lullaby. I'm used to singing with kids. Every routine in my classroom has a song, from welcoming the day to cleaning up, from washing hands to saying goodbye. So I have zero self-consciousness with the under-ten crowd. But singing in front of the Sexiest Man Alive? That's different.

Despite my nerves, I forge on with the tune as I rock the girl in my arms. Soon enough, she sinks back into a deep sleep. I shift until a mound of tulle supports her head.

"Sorry. I'm aware I'm not Taylor Swift."

"It's fine," he grunts. After a minute, he adds, "Are you sure you want to hold her? She's heavier than she looks."

I die a little at just how rich his voice sounds, like sinful chocolate. And I'm a hot-chocoholic.

"I'm afraid if you take her back, she'll wake. Is she scared of the dark?"

"She likes to sleep with a night-light. Don't tell me you have a flashlight in there."

"No..." I drawl. "But..."

I reach into my bag with my free hand, twisting like a pretzel so my movement doesn't disturb the sleeping girl. I knew yoga would come in handy one day.

"Yes," I huff in triumph when my fingers feel the familiar shape.

With one hand and my mouth, I rip open a package, pull out a small plastic stick, and bend it until there's a soft snap and then a green glow.

"You have a glow stick," Ronan says as if I have a tail or three eyes.

I open another package in the same awkward way. "No. I have *two* glow sticks," I say, more than a little gleeful. The diffuse light makes the elevator not so scary. I can now make out the details of his darkened form.

"I'm almost afraid to ask why."

"One of my students had a birthday last week, and a mom brought goody bags. Everyone got one, including the teacher."

Ronan mutters something under his breath.

I push him with my elbow, then regret it, because now I know just how hard his abs are and, *damn*. "Don't knock goody bags till you've tried them. They have candy. Games. Glitter glue. Slime. Glow sticks. Bouncy balls. And candy. Did I mention candy? If you're not nice, I won't share."

"I stand corrected."

Is that amusement in his voice?

I pass him a chocolate. I'm nice like that. The wrapper rustles as he opens it.

"Smart man." I suck on my own sweet treat.

I should try to yell for help again. Or pound the useless buttons on the elevator panel above me. But it's peaceful sitting in the dark with Ronan Masters. This is a once-in-a-lifetime opportunity, and I'm not fool enough to hurry it along. They'll discover the elevator is stuck eventually. Someone will come looking for us. Or not. There isn't much else we can do until then.

Plus, I'm with *Ronan Masters*. Even if he weren't world-famous, I'd still be crushing on him for the eye candy. I'm going to enjoy this.

"So..." he says, crossing his arms over that broad chest.

I wait for him to continue.

"Nice dress. Is there a story behind it, or is this your usual outfit choice?"

I laugh. "Thanks." I pluck at a tuft of tulle. "This thing could launch a thousand ballet recitals. The bachelorette party I was at had a prom theme. The bride thought it would be fun to show up at the bar in bad prom dresses. We had a contest for the ugliest one. News flash—I won."

"It somehow works on you."

I blush. Blushing easily is one downfall of being a freckle-faced redhead.

As sad as it sounds, his half compliment is more than I've gotten from anyone in a long while. And I'm not sure if it's Ronan's presence, the dark, or that it's the first time in this shitty whirlwind of the last few months that I've got nothing to do, but the adrenaline I've been running on leaves me, and I'm wrung out. Normally, I'm an optimist, a doer. The one who everyone relies on. But right now, all I want is to stretch out and fall asleep, just like Belle has, trusting that everything will work out.

I'm not sure what Ronan sees in my face, or if it's in my sigh, but he leans toward me. "Are you okay?"

I shake my head and laugh, trying to surreptitiously wipe away a tear that I'm surprised to find is making its way down my cheek. I'm not usually a crier. Not at all.

"It's nothing. Really. It's just been a long day. A long few months."

He's quiet for long minutes. I don't say anything either.

"Go on."

I bite my lip. I haven't unburdened myself to anyone. My sister lives in New York and just came back home to get married, so I wasn't going to ruin her happy vibe by complaining to her. My parents have been so focused on preparing for the wedding I haven't wanted to distract them.

Plus, I hate to bother people with my problems. I'm the one people go to for advice. Not the other way around.

There is no way Ronan Masters wants to hear about my woes. But there must be something about him because I find myself unraveling more in his strong presence. Maybe it's his broad shoulders. He seems big enough to carry any load.

I open my mouth to tell him how I lost my job teaching art before the new school year started due to a lack of funding. I was dumped by my fiancé two weeks after that. And since we lived together in the house we rented, I had nowhere to go, so I moved back in with my parents. The words are there, wanting to flow out of me, but they stick in my throat.

I've worked so hard to pretend to be upbeat, to not complain, to act as if I'm fine. And it's mostly worked. Another tear slips down my cheek and, frustrated, I swipe it away. Why won't these tears understand that I'm not a crier? I don't want the first celebrity I've ever met to think I'm unhinged.

He keeps watching me steadily, and somehow that intense gaze draws the words out.

"I kinda lost my job, my fiancé, and my house all pretty close together," I say as lightly as I can. "But it's fine. It really is. It just feels like my life has unraveled, and I need to figure out how to tie it back up. In a bow, of course."

"That's shitty," he says eventually.

"Yeah." I take a deep breath. "Yeah, it is shitty," I acknowledge for the first time. What a relief, not having to deny that it does, indeed, suck. "Don't feel too sorry for me, though. I really liked my job. But I'm not sure I liked the house. It was in a development where all the houses look the same. It had no character. I always imagined living somewhere historic, with charm—you know? So that probably wasn't too much of a loss."

"What about the guy?"

"What do you mean?" I ask.

"How big of a loss was he?"

"The jury is still out on the guy," I say with an awkward laugh.

Another pause. He slides a glance at me. I can't read it. His face is a smooth mask, as it's been for most of the short time I've known him. I look away.

We don't say anything for long minutes, and the only sounds in the elevator are Belle's quiet snores and the rustle my tulle makes when I shift positions slightly.

"Belle is wonderful." His perusal makes me as uncomfortable as my uncharacteristic self-disclosure, so I change the subject. I want him to talk, not me.

His face softens in the dim light of the glow sticks.

"She is." He hesitates, but I keep watching, willing him to say more, to tell me the things I'm too shy to ask. Like, why didn't I know you had a daughter? How long has she lived with you? Why does she have a slight English accent when you don't?

"Go on," I tease, parroting his earlier words.

"She's spending a few months with me," he volunteers. Hurrah. It's not much, but my prolonged silence trick works again. I use it whenever I need children to admit to minor wrongdoings, and I have a ninety-five-percent success rate.

"You're filming *The Wanderers* around here, right? Some teachers at school are fans." Some teachers, as in some teachers and I, but I'm not sharing that. *The Wanderers* is one of the most popular franchises in the world. It's a time-travel adventure story with action, comedy, and romance. Part of why the movies are so popular is this Viking god sitting next to me, as well as his other costars. The movie's hot quotient is off the charts.

He nods. "Yes."

He doesn't elaborate, and I don't want to pry further.

Though we're strangers and he's not exactly the chatty type, I still have an odd feeling of familiarity. I wonder how much of it is because I've spent hours watching him on a big screen, building a connection that's not actually there. It must be weird to walk around with people imagining they know you, imagining they have this one-sided relationship with you.

Which makes me wonder, what *is* the etiquette for being trapped in an elevator with last year's Sexiest Man Alive?

I can't figure it out, so I give up trying and use one more trick of the kindergarten-teacher trade. It's to be used only in cases of extreme emergencies. I reach into my bag and pull out two more treats.

"Lollipop?" I offer.

He nods and takes one.

And I could be crazy, but he seems to watch me extra carefully as I lick mine.

Ronan

I HATE SMALL TALK. I HATE CHATTING WITH STRANGERS. AND I'm not into tiny, tight spaces. So being here, trapped in this elevator, with a strange but compelling woman, is sapping my reserves to appear like the cool, collected action star she obviously expects me to be.

I tilt my head so I can check out my elevator companion. Her short, curvy frame is caught up in a mound of fabric.

Poofy sleeves. Poofy skirt. Fuchsia pink. She should look awful, especially given her freckles and copper curls, but her eyes are large and hazel, and she has this one dimple that flashes at the corner of her mouth every time she smiles.

I clear my throat and try to say something for a change. "Thanks for being so sweet to Belle. She doesn't open up to many people."

Poppy's grin is warm and genuine, not traits I see often in my line of work. Genuine people are few and far between in the shark tank called Hollywood. And I'm happy to see her smiling again, with no trace of the tears she tried to hide earlier. I have no idea how to handle a crying woman. I can barely handle a crying little girl.

"She's adorable. And what can I say? Kids like me."

"How long have you been a teacher?" I ask.

"For about five years." Her smile falters for a split second before it appears again. "I'm actually an elementary art teacher, but my school's art program closed down. That's when I lost my job. So I've been substituting for a kindergarten teacher on maternity leave, but she's returning soon. What about you?" she rushes out, as if uncomfortable having the attention back on her. "How did you get into your...line of work?"

"I started as a stuntman."

Her eyes twinkle, even in the diffuse light.

"Don't say it," I warn, tamping down a laugh and trying to look stern.

"But you started out as a stuntman!" she exclaims with a laugh. "Why can't you get the elevator open?"

"Are you going to do a tell-all about how useless I am in a crisis?" I ask, only half joking.

"It would serve you right. All those muscles." She tsks. "False advertising."

"If the crisis required bench presses to save us, I could help."

"If only."

"You're mean for someone so small."

"I'm not small. You're just a giant."

I smirk. "If the shoe fits."

"It wouldn't, 'cause you're so *large*."

Her laughter is infectious. I've smiled more while stuck in an elevator for less than an hour than I have all month—hell, probably all year. There's something effervescent about this girl. Even in the dark, she shines. It's in her teasing eyes and her smile and, once she relaxed, her lack of self-consciousness around me. No one dares to tease me. People are either too intimidated or afraid to piss me off.

When her laughter fades, the elevator goes quiet again. In the dark, all I hear is the rhythm of our breaths. The occasional rustle of clothes as we adjust our positions. It's strangely intimate.

Poppy moves and stretches out one leg, careful not to wake Belle. "Sorry," she says as her movement causes her soft breast to brush against my arm. "My leg fell asleep," she whispers.

"Do you want me to take Belle?" I offer again.

"No. I'm good now. Just had to stretch. She's a heavy sleeper," she remarks.

I nod. "It's been a lot for her, with the traveling, and now with my rehearsals starting."

"I'm sure I'm prying, so you don't have to answer. But I didn't realize you had a daughter."

I debate what to tell her. She's right. She is prying, and I don't owe her any explanation. But there's something about her that makes me want to talk, which is not like me. I realize

I have to get used to talking about Belle and her presence in my life. This is as good a time as any to start.

"It's complicated. She grew up with her mom, mostly in London. This is the first time she's ever stayed with me. We're getting to know each other," I admit.

Belle didn't complain when she was left with me, a father she barely knew. She was withdrawn, but she didn't complain. How chaotic had her life been to make her so adaptable? And how would she—how would we—adapt when her mother returns to take her back?

"How are you holding up?" Poppy asks me gently, as if she can read the turmoil on my face.

"We're managing," I mutter.

"I'm sorry. I shouldn't stick my nose into your business. But I feel like it's only fair because you know about my problems. You may not realize it because I'm such a hot mess right now, but I'm really good at advice. I'm a fixer."

"I'm not much of a talker," I grunt out. I don't share my business with anyone. It's the way I'm wired. And being famous has only made me that much more guarded, that much more wary.

"I get it," is all Poppy says.

Silence stretches like a rubber band until it can't stretch anymore, and I—who normally love silence—break first.

"Belle's mom left her with me unexpectedly. I had to start this movie, but I didn't feel right leaving her in Los Angeles with a nanny." The words tumble from me. "We're here for a few months to shoot. I have to rent a house, hire a nanny, and try to give her a normal routine. Something she deserves."

Poppy beams at me, and the horror that I've said too much, that I've put my trust in a stranger, is replaced by a feeling of rightness. It makes no logical sense, but in my years of doing stunts, I've learned to lead with my intuition.

Poppy places one hand on mine and squeezes. She's petite, but there's a gentle strength in her touch. "You're doing exactly what you should do. I can see your bond with her already. A house and some stability are just what she needs. You're doing really well."

I feel like one of her students, getting a gold star at the end of the day. But it works. A weight lifts, and I'm dizzy with the lightness of it. I hadn't realized how heavy the load I carried was until I shared it. I've been concentrating on surviving each day, praying I don't fuck up this fatherhood thing too badly, praying that I, with a million flaws, can do right by my daughter and give her what she needs.

I have people in my life—a manager, costars, acquaintances—but no one I confide in. Yet somehow, in this dark elevator with this girl, I'm spilling my secrets.

If we stay in the elevator much longer, I fear I'll tell her the rest. How I hadn't even known I'd had a child. Then six months ago, Claire, my ex, called to tell me I had a daughter. We confirmed it with a DNA test, but I already knew the truth the second she sent me a photo of Belle. She had my hair, my eyes, even the same small cleft in her chin. The resemblance is undeniable.

Claire and I dated for only a short while, but my simple lifestyle wasn't flashy enough for her. She set her sights on a better prospect who would give her the designer life she wanted, and when she found out she was pregnant, she told him the baby was his. But when that marriage eventually ended in divorce, the truth came out about Belle's paternity. With Claire now single, her latest billionaire boyfriend isn't interested in playing dad to a seven-year-old.

So she finally told me the truth. I was in the middle of

shooting a movie, but I flew to visit Belle on the breaks I could get over the next few months, trying to get to know her, trying to figure out how to relate to a little girl who was shy and withdrawn around me.

And then just when I finished my shoot, Claire showed up in LA with my daughter, said she would be spending several months traveling with her new boyfriend and needed me to take care of Belle. And then she left without telling me exactly when she would return, as if Belle were nothing but an afterthought.

I can't share any of this, though, and risk the tabloids finding out the truth. The public relations spin on this is delicate. I never want Belle to know how cavalierly her mother lied about her for all those years. My manager only recently leaked the fact that I had a daughter to the press, sharing a photo of us and inventing a much simpler backstory. I've always refused to play any PR game before, but if this is spun wrong, it would result in a media-feeding frenzy and Belle would be the loser.

"It's obvious how much Belle trusts you," Poppy says, pulling me out of my deep thoughts about my ex and the mess she created by lying for all these years.

I look away, avoiding my elevator mate's keen gaze, trying to remind myself that she's still basically a stranger. I don't want her to see the guilt in my eyes. The uncertainty. If I'd been a better father, I would have somehow known about Belle. I could have found her, made sure she was okay, years ago. Instead, I have seven years of wasted time, seven years of Belle being shuttled between an endless succession of nannies, according to the few stories she's shared.

"Don't worry. I won't tell anyone the big, tough action star isn't so tough after all."

"And what about you?" I ask, needing to turn the tables.

"What about me?"

"You got me to talk, something that no one does. So now it's your turn."

She looks away. "I already told you way too much. And, I'm the listener. I'm the helper."

"So no one listens? No one helps you?"

Her smile shifts but doesn't falter. "I've lived in the same town my whole life. If I need something, I have plenty of people I can call. But I prefer being there for others, not the other way around."

"Because…"

"Because I don't know." She lifts her hands in an exasperated gesture. "It feels good to be useful. I like doing things for people and making them happy."

"You're one of those people who can't say no."

"I can too. I could say it all the time if I wanted. I just choose not to." She huffs.

"Bullshit." I bite back a smile. "You should try it sometime. It's satisfying."

She rolls her eyes to the ceiling and makes a surprised sound. She squints. "Is that…?"

She points her glow stick up high, and I make out some sort of foliage hanging on a ribbon or string.

"It's mistletoe." She laughs. "I can't believe I didn't notice that before."

"It's September," I say disbelievingly. "Who puts mistletoe in an elevator? *In September*?"

She grins. "That's the Holly Hill Inn for you. Any excuse for Christmas. And it's almost October. Wait till you see this place in December. If you have any Santa phobias, stay far, far away."

Her wide smile draws my attention to her lips, which makes me think about the mistletoe and kissing. Even in her garish dress, Poppy exudes a fresh-faced loveliness, with curly red hair, a wide smile, laughing eyes, and a smattering of freckles across her nose and wide cheeks.

She must sense the direction of my thoughts because her eyes flicker to my mouth, and she licks her pink lips. I become hyperaware of just how close we're sitting together. My brain lists all the things that are wrong with this scenario. I've just met her. Hell, she's holding my sleeping daughter in her lap.

But everything else fades as she shifts closer, her breath catching in a small, sharp inhale. Longing shoots through me as slowly, silently, unbidden, we inch toward each other.

What would one kiss hurt? I'll never see her again. In this tight, warm, hushed space, who would know? Who would care? *Besides all those people on social media she could tell.*

We're poised there. Only a breath apart. She smells like berries, and I need to know if she tastes like them as well.

At first, I think the banging is my heart.

But then the voices start.

And I wonder why my conscience has to be so loud.

And I wish it would shut up.

But it won't be quiet.

The ringing starts.

And the floor starts to move.

"Um, Ronan?" Poppy says.

I freeze and pull away, shocked that I almost kissed a stranger in an elevator with my daughter sleeping next to me. This is why I'll never win a father of the year award.

She sounds breathless as she says, "I think the doors are about to open."

And fucking hell. They do.

CHAPTER 3

93 DAYS TO CHRISTMAS (STILL)

Poppy

THE ELEVATOR OPENS, AND I BLINK LIKE A GARDEN MOLE emerging from her tunnel. The night manager, a grumpy-looking repairman, and an older couple stare at us in surprise. Which is fair. We're a motley crew to be trapped in an elevator together. A little girl in a rumpled princess gown, a lady in a prom dress, and an action superstar.

Ronan leaps to his feet in the smooth motion of an athlete and bends to lift Belle from my lap. Belle rouses slightly, opening her eyes before closing them once again. I clamber to my feet after Ronan.

The night manager wrings his hands. "I'm so sorry, Mr. Masters. This has never happened before! We didn't know the elevator was stuck." The manager grovels to Ronan and ignores me.

“I wasn’t the only person trapped,” Ronan says, looking meaningfully at me.

The manager glances my way. “Yes! Of course. I’m sorry, miss.”

I nod, pleased that Ronan spoke up for me, even in this small capacity.

“No harm done,” I say. “It was an accident. These things happen.”

“Is the elevator fixed now?” the older gentleman asks. “My wife’s hip can’t handle the stairs.”

We turn to the repairman, who fiddles with his tool belt. “It might take a while.”

“I think we’ll take the stairs,” Ronan says quickly, as if another stint in the elevator would be one of Dante’s circles of hell.

Meanwhile, for me, our elevator time had been a top-tier life experience. Marriage. Firstborn child. Trapped in an elevator with Ronan Masters. It might rank even higher on the list if I count the almost-kiss, which I totally do.

“Are you sure I can’t do anything else for you, Mr. Masters?” the night manager asks.

“No. Thank you.” Ronan turns to me. “Are you waiting for the elevator?”

“No. I hear stairs are great for the thighs.”

Ronan glances at my voluminous skirt, which hides any evidence of how toned my thighs are—or, more truthfully, are not.

“I’ll have to take your word for it.”

We walk to the staircase. He tries to let me go first, but there’s no way I’m going to have him watch me as I huff and puff and wheeze up the stairs, so I insist he go ahead. By the time we hit the fourth floor, I’m regretting my lack of fitness. I knew I should have joined my mom’s

Zumba class more often. Ronan, even carrying Belle, isn't winded.

When we make it to level five, I blow the hair out of my eyes. "This is my floor," I say.

"Ours also." He opens the stairwell door for me like a gentleman.

I blush and murmur a breathless, "Thank you." We walk in silence until he stops in front of a room.

"Here, let me take her," I say as he attempts to reach into his pocket while carrying the groggy child.

With a nod, he passes Belle to me. "Shh, little one. You're almost to bed," I say when she stirs.

He opens the door, and I follow him in. Instead of taking Belle back, he clicks on the lights as he makes his way through the spacious suite. It's got enormous windows overlooking an expansive lawn leading to the lake.

"Wow. This is way nicer than my room," I remark, looking around the entryway and living area decorated with an elegant mix of modern and vintage furnishings.

He considers the room as if noticing his surroundings for the first time. "We haven't been here much. But Belle loves it."

I follow him into a rose-pink room. A four-poster bed, too large for a small girl, takes up most of the space. I can see why a princess enthusiast like Belle digs it.

"It's very..." I struggle with the right words. "Floral. And pink."

His mouth quirks. "It's enough to give me nightmares, but Belle likes it."

"Well, I'm not surprised. She likes my dress."

He pretends his laugh is a cough, but I know it's not.

"She especially likes the miniature pink Christmas tree in the corner," he says.

"And what girl wouldn't?"

"It's only *September*." Every time he says that word, he growls it. And that growly sound makes me wish we were alone so he could growl other things into my ear. Like, "Kiss me again," and "I want you." And "Climb me like a tree so I can make your wildest dreams come true."

I give a little whimper.

"What?" he asks.

"Nothing. Do you want her awake so she can change and brush her teeth?" I say.

"She's fine."

He pulls the covers back, and I slip off her shoes and place her in the middle of the crisp sheets. She opens her eyes.

"Poppy." Her voice is slow and sweet, on the edge of dreams.

"Hey, Belle." I smile down at her. "It was great meeting you. You were very brave in the elevator. I'm glad you and your dad were there to keep me company."

She rubs her eyes and yawns. "He's a hero in the movies. It's good he was there to keep us from being scared," Belle says.

"He was quite the hero," I agree solemnly.

"Exactly. That's what I've been saying." Ronan pretends to grumble, but his eyes are filled with amusement. "Not all heroes carry duct tape."

"Did you make a joke, big guy?" I can't help the warmth of pleasure that runs through me. Something tells me that he doesn't joke with many people.

A slight smirk is his only answer.

And that's when it hits me. I'll likely never see him again, at least not in person. This sense of loss is illogical. But he's so handsome. And adorable in a burly action-hero way. And how his mouth quirks up when he's amused just does it for me. Me and a million other ladies.

"So—"

"Well—"

He inclines his head. "You go first."

I have no idea what I was going to say.

"Oh, um. Just goodbye, I guess. I'll leave you to it and see myself out."

I look into his inscrutable eyes and will him to say he's fallen for me and that he wants me for all eternity.

Or something like that.

Instead, he just watches me, giving away nothing.

I nod, swallowing back the disappointment.

"Bye, Poppy," Belle says on a yawn.

"Bye, Belle. Remember. Princesses can slay dragons too."

"I don't want to slay dragons. I want to help them be happy."

I grin. "Wise girl." On impulse, I brush my lips to the top of her head. "Sleep well, sweetheart." Her eyes close.

"Night," she mumbles.

I step aside, and Ronan leans down and kisses her as well, brushing her straight blond hair back from her forehead.

"Good night," he says gruffly.

"Night." Her mumble is less distinct now. She rolls over, her hands clasped beneath her chin.

He steps aside, and I make my way to the front door of the suite. To my surprise, he follows me.

"Well," I say. "It was interesting meeting you." I can't hold back my shy smile.

He hesitates. "Do you, um..." He stops and shakes his head.

"Do I what?" I ask, hoping, praying, for him to continue.

"Nothing," he says after a beat.

What did I think? That he was going to ask me to stay? I'm hot for him, yes, because he's Ronan Masters, a superstar. But that doesn't mean *he* feels the same. This is nothing more than a fangirl crush.

"It was nice meeting you." I try to hide my dejection behind a perky smile.

"Nice?" he queries.

I laugh. "Well, like I said, interesting. And, yes, nice as well."

We reach the door, and I linger, loath to leave, yet knowing it's inevitable.

He leans against the door. An electric current runs through my veins. There's no mistletoe this time. But could I hope for a kiss goodbye?

"Good night."

"Good night."

I step back, out into the hall, still facing him, not able to break his gaze. "Bye."

"Bye."

Bye. I silently mouth to Ronan. I'm such a dork.

He nods, breaking the spell.

I turn and float to my door at the end of the hall. I hear his door click shut.

When I slip into my room, I latch the lock to keep from vaulting back down the hallway and begging Ronan to spend the night with me, though I've never had a one-night stand in my life, having been with my former fiancé since high school.

I lean against the door, eyes closed, knees still weak, remembering everything he said. Everything I said. Every word. Every movement. Every smile and laugh. Every little moment between us. Committing them to memory with a fangirl sigh.

CHAPTER 4

92 DAYS TO CHRISTMAS

Ronan

THE NEXT NIGHT, I WALK THROUGH HOLLY HILL INN, STILL thinking of the girl in the elevator.

Even if I could forget her, my daughter hasn't let me because she's asked about Poppy every hour.

This morning, while I was brushing the tangles from Belle's hair, she said, "I wonder what Poppy is doing right now." And, "I bet Poppy can braid better than you."

As we were eating breakfast, she said, "When we move into our house and have a proper kitchen, can you make pancakes instead of your healthy shakes? I bet Poppy makes pancakes. And she probably lives in a yellow house. Or maybe a pink one. A pink house would be nice."

And as we were driving to set, she said, "That dog is so

cute! I wonder if Poppy has a dog. Maybe she could teach me to draw one?"

If Belle hadn't gone back to the hotel hours ago with her temporary babysitter, a grandmother-like assistant on set, she'd still be talking to me about Poppy.

Is the woman a witch? Because she's transfixed my daughter. She'd be a benevolent one, of course. Like Glinda. Or Samantha from *Bewitched*.

But her magic has me under her spell as well. Even when Belle wasn't reminding me about Poppy today, she was in my head. There was something about the way she smiled, the way she teased me, that I can't shake.

So when I walk through the doors of the hotel and see a wedding reception in progress, I'm reminded of her.

Is this the wedding she was attending? She said she was at the inn for one. Why hadn't I pried details from her? For the first time, I regret not talking more.

I walk past the wide doors that open onto the patio where the sounds of music and laughter stream in. Though I don't slow down, I can't keep myself from casually checking things out. What I see causes me to freeze in the doorway.

Poppy.

Looking radiant.

In a wedding dress.

She walks toward me, and my mouth opens. And closes.

Unnerving disappointment courses through me, which makes no sense. She's almost a stranger.

A stranger whom I shared pieces of my life with that I haven't told even my closest friends.

A stranger with kind hazel-green eyes, the most adorable fucking dimple, and curves I can't forget.

I replay the conversations in my head and realize she never said she was a guest at the wedding. She never said she was the bride either. But she hadn't said she wasn't. She told me she broke up with her fiancé a few months ago, that her life was a hot mess. Had she lied? Had she rebounded to someone new, and that's why things were so messy?

Talk about burying the lede.

Poppy sees me. Her eyes widen, and she stops in front of me.

"Hi." I burrow my hands into my jeans pockets.

Her breath catches, but she says nothing, just stares.

I realize how out of place I must look. I'm dressed casually, in jeans and a T-shirt. My hair is wet and hanging around my face. I'm sure I still have remnants of makeup and fake grime on me, despite the quick shower I took before leaving my trailer.

I'd been in a hurry. I told myself it was because I'd hoped, in vain, to be early enough to say good night to Belle. But I also hoped I might bump into Poppy again.

This sure as hell wasn't what I'd expected, though.

"Hi?" Her voice turns up at the end as if in question. I can't blame her. She must be wondering what I'm doing here, crashing her wedding.

I try to come up with something. "You, uh, look beautiful." It's the truth. Beautiful but different. Tonight, she's wearing heavy makeup. Her wedding dress is glamorous and ornate, in a way that seems wrong for her. But what would I know? I remind myself that I obviously don't know her, and what I thought I knew was wrong.

"Thank you." She blushes and pats her gravity-defying hair. I pray Belle won't ever ask me to do one of those styles.

"Sorry for interrupting," I say, feeling off-balance. I forge ahead anyway. "I wanted to thank you for your help with Belle. In the elevator."

"Oh." She looks confused. Her eyes widen. "*Ohhh*. You're welcome." She laughs.

I step back, feeling strangely deflated. "Anyway. That's all. Have a great wedding and...everything." I turn to walk away.

"Wait!" She grasps my arm with another throaty laugh. "Please. Wait here."

Maybe the stress of the wedding is making her act strangely.

"Fine." I don't really want to wait, not anymore, but I owe it to her after how sweet she was with Belle. And I'm not in a hurry to get back to my room. Belle is already asleep, so all I have planned is a quiet night with my script for company.

She flashes me one last smile and disappears.

Five minutes later, I hear voices around the corridor.

The bride appears, leading another lady by the arm.

My eyes widen. "Shit. There're two of you."

"Yep. I'm Rose," the bride says. "This is my sister, Poppy. I believe you've met."

Poppy is wearing a gauzy peach-colored dress that makes me want to take a bite out of her.

"You're not getting married." I fight a smile at that revelation but lose the war. I outright grin. Poppy is not taken. She's not a liar. She didn't fail to mention she was getting married while flirting with a stranger.

Her hazel eyes go wide. "No. My sister is... We're twins." She waves her hand between the two of them, then lets it drop.

It hits me. "Poppy and Rose?"

Rose laughs. "Our mom is a gardener. If we were triplets, there'd be a Violet."

They are identical. And not. Rose is bolder, more confident in her speech and movements.

But it's Poppy I can't stop watching. I want to see her sweet smile. That pop of dimple.

I can't tear my eyes from her.

After the gut-wrenching disappointment when I thought she was married, I don't want to force myself to walk away yet.

Her sister finally breaks the silence. "Ooookaaaay. I gotta get back to my wedding. Poppy, don't do anything I wouldn't do, which means you can do a lot." She turns to me and winks.

Poppy watches her go. Then she hiccups. And sways a bit.

I was so shocked there were two Poppys that I missed the signs.

She's clearly enjoyed the wedding champagne. A lot. She takes a deep swig from her glass.

"I'm going to need more of this. Keep 'em coming." She hiccups again. And giggles. "Sorry, sorry."

"You might want some water instead."

"Nope." She sighs. "I need gallons of wine to get through this wedding." She raises an eyebrow. "Though, it *is* looking up."

I rub one of my shoulders that's sore from a stunt I rehearsed today.

"Do you often need gallons of wine?" I ask warily. My mom had addiction issues, so I keep my distance from people who drink a lot, which means I keep my distance from half of Hollywood. "You weren't drunk after the bachelorette party."

She lowers her voice and leans toward me. "Not usually—but the ceremony's done, and I've officially completed my duties, so I'm free. I only had two glasses. Three. Plus, it helps with the hiccups." She hiccups to make her point. Or perhaps to belie it.

She sighs and sways again. I put my arm around her to keep her upright.

"Did you know that Rose never wanted to get married? All she ever wanted was to leave Snowflake Harbor and dance on Broadway. *I* was the one who was supposed to be planning my wedding this year."

She drains the rest of the glass and frowns into it when it comes up empty. She sets it down, then looks at me. "But that was before Derek the Dick dumped me. He brought a date to the wedding and told our friends that he's in love. In love! We broke up two months ago. How can he be in love again?"

I shuffle, not sure how to answer.

She hiccups. "I need another glass of champagne."

"I'm not sure you do."

"I'm absolutely sure that I do, and I'm absolutely sure that whether I have another glass of champagne is my decision and my decision alone, Mr. Ronan Masters, international movie star."

I grin. "See, you're not such a pushover. You can stand up for yourself."

"Thank you. I'm practicing. But it's not easy." She hiccups. "Damn hiccups."

"We'll get you something to drink. But if you insist on champagne, have a water as well. You'll be glad tomorrow."

She tries to wave me away. "I'm sure you have better things to do than hang out at my sister's wedding. And, while I'm super glad to get reacquainted with you and your lovely muscles, I'm wondering why you're here. I mean, don't you have big and important things to do?"

I cross my arms. "Most people want me at their events. And you look like you need some help."

She smiles, a real one this time. There's that dimple. Why is it the same, yet so different from her sister's?

"I do. I do want you." She gives me a slow once-over that heats my blood and makes me want to taste those full lips, makes me wonder if she still smells like berries.

"But you don't need to feel sorry for me," she continues. "I have my friends and family here."

"Are they okay that your ex is at your sister's wedding?"

She slumps a little at that. "Yes. But to be fair, Derek and I dated since high school, and they consider him to be part of the family. We have so many friends in common, and we even teach at the same school. My parents thought if they invited him, he might decide he was lost without me. Instead, he brought his new girlfriend, the French teacher."

I clench my fists. What an ass.

She hiccups again, then looks around, this time more wildly. "I really need that drink now."

"I'll get it for you. Stay here."

I wander into the reception and walk up to the bar.

"Holy shit. You're Ronan Masters!"

I tilt my head in assent. I'm not even wearing a hat or sunglasses, the most basic of disguises. It's pointless to pretend.

"Ronan fucking Masters!"

I nod again and rub my jaw, wondering how long this will take.

"Ronan Masters! You're a badass. I can't believe it!"

"Yup. Still Ronan Masters. Champagne and a sparkling water, please." I don't drink when I'm filming. Being an action star known for my eight-pack means I have to have one-hundred-percent discipline and zero-percent wasted calories.

"Coming right up. I loved *The Escape*."

He pours two glasses and presents them with a flourish. "Anything else you want? I'll hook you up with the top shelf, dude. Anything, just ask," he says, as if he's tending bar in a high-end LA nightclub and not a cash bar at a small-town inn. I have to admire his hustle.

I put a generous tip in the jar and grab my drinks.

"Anything at all, you got it!" he calls after me.

When I get back to Poppy, she's standing with a beefy guy and a girl.

"Hey." I hand her the champagne.

"Thank God." She takes it and drinks deeply.

"I've been called that a time or two," I say, hoping to get any reaction from her besides "hell-bent-on-drunk."

It works. She rolls her eyes at me, and her dimple peeks out.

The couple next to her are staring at us in open shock. I can tell they recognize me.

I take the champagne away before she can finish the rest and hand her my water.

"Aren't you going to introduce me to your friends, Poppy?"

"Ronan. This is Derek. And Monique."

"So these are—" I don't continue my sentence.

Poppy's tight expression and quick nod confirm that this is her ex-fiancé and his current flame.

"Oh my God! You're Ronan Masters," the girl simpers, gazing at me with star-struck eyes. She looks like every other girl in LA—tall, blond, stacked—but she stands out in this small town in upstate New York.

Derek doesn't seem happy about the attention I'm getting from Monique. He puts his arm around her. He's tall by normal standards, but I tower over him. Hell, I tower over everyone except professional basketball players.

If I made even the slightest effort, Monique would leave good old Derek so fast, his head would spin on his thick neck. Not that I want her. Who would be idiot enough to be with this girl when he could have Poppy?

"Why are you here?" Derek asks me with sullen curiosity.

Again. Can't a star crash a wedding these days without all these questions?

The amusement drains out of Poppy as she watches her former boyfriend, the man she was going to marry, act possessively toward another girl.

That's it. No one puts Poppy in a corner.

I take the drink in my hand, set it on a table and pull her to me.

She's so short that, tucked into my chest, she only comes up to the top of my abs. I put my hand possessively on her hip. She looks up at me with a dazed expression. The sadness in her eyes is gone. Good.

"I'm Poppy's date."

Poppy's glass slips from her hand, but I catch it midair.

She opens her mouth. Will she deny my claim? Laugh at me? Play along. She closes her mouth. Opens it again. And...

Hiccup.

Poppy

IT TAKES ANOTHER GLASS OF CHAMPAGNE TO GET RID OF MY hiccups.

You might think my irresponsible drinking caused the hiccups. But nope. They're a nervous habit. I get them when I'm stressed, and alcohol helps.

This theory was tested when, before my first performance as a ballerina at Mrs. Bellamy's Dance Academy, I got a horrible case of hiccups. My mom gave me a shot of sherry, apparently a family cure, and both my hiccups and nerves vanished.

Perhaps it wasn't the best of life lessons—giving alcohol to minors to solve their problems—but it worked. I don't like hard alcohol, so I've been trying champagne.

Unfortunately, it's led to the side effect of being a little tipsy.

But in addition to getting rid of hiccups, I got rid of my sadness over Derek the Dick, and my inhibitions and self-consciousness around my new fake date/boyfriend, Ronan Masters.

I made up that part about him being a fake boyfriend. No one truly believes that. But everyone has been shocked into silence that he's here with me, so I'm thinking it's the best idea ever.

Although Ronan is the strong, silent type, I feel surprisingly comfortable around him. And let's be real, he doesn't need to talk much anyway because I nervously chatter enough for both of us. He's also an excellent slow dancer, which is another surprise. Derek's been staring at us with an annoyed look for the last hour, and all the people who were once watching me in pity are now watching in envy.

Because even in jeans and a T-shirt, Ronan Masters is just...more...than any other male present. Any other male anywhere. He's ten times bigger. Ten times more masculine and ten times more ruggedly handsome. And, for the night, he's all mine. Sort of.

I don't fool myself into thinking he's here for any other reason than he feels sorry for me. He's kind beneath his stoic silence. And maybe he had nothing better to do, what with this being Snowflake Harbor and all.

But somewhere between the dancing, Ronan's protectiveness, and the champagne buzz, I'm beginning to wonder if maybe he could be my rebound. My one wild rebellion in a lifetime of playing it safe as the girl next door. My passionate indiscretion. My first and probably only one-night stand.

Do I have the guts to proposition him? Could I live with his rejection?

I'm still mulling over these nerve-racking, butterfly-inducing questions when I take a quick makeup check in the bathroom. A girl has to have fresh lipstick if she's going to hit on a movie star.

I'm staring into the mirror, giving myself a pep talk, when my best friend, Sadie, and my mom find me.

"There you are. You better explain yourself, young lady," my mom says, her toned arms crossed in front of her.

I gulp.

"You bring a *movie star* to your sister's wedding, and you don't tell your best friend?" Sadie says, equally outraged. Sadie owns the artsy general store, Miracle on Main Street, where I rent space for my art lessons. She's the only person I talk to about my ex. The rest of my family and friends still want me to get back together with Derek, despite his dick-ishness. But Sadie is always one-hundred-percent Team Poppy, for which I'm grateful.

"I can't believe you didn't say a word. Where did you even meet him?" Sadie asks.

"And why in heaven's name is he at your sister's wedding?" my mom adds.

I hold up my hand. "I'll answer your questions one at a time. First, he's staying at the hotel while he looks for a house in town. You know they're filming *The Wanderers* here."

They both nod. This is the biggest news our town has ever seen.

"After the bachelorette party last night, I got stuck in an elevator with him," I rush out.

"You got stuck in an elevator with Mr. Big, and you didn't tell your own mother?" My mom is not happy.

"Mr. Big?" My mother has a *Sex and the City* nickname for Ronan. Of course she does.

She shrugs. "What? You don't think the girls at the senior center talk? You should have seen all of us when his Sexiest Man Alive cover was released. Whew." She fans herself.

My mom is a fitness instructor for seniors. Before retiring, she was a middle school teacher. But she got bored with all her free time, so she started teaching Zumba. She channels her inner Jane Fonda with a unitard and a headband. I tease her, but my mom has firmer abs than I do, so I'm secretly jealous. And the irony is that my dad is the world's biggest couch potato.

I close my eyes in pain. I love my mom. I really do. But she's extra-extra.

Sadie, the traitor that she is, encourages all my mom's extra-ness.

"I'm going to forgive you for not telling me because I understand it's been a busy day," Sadie says. "But only if you give us all the deets now. What happened? Did you invite him to the wedding as your date?"

"No!" I whisper-squeal. "That's what's so surprising. Okay, maybe we had a moment the night we met. But I thought it was just *my* moment. Not a moment he cared about, if you know what I mean, because I'm, well, normal. And he's, well, look at him. Anyway, we went our separate ways, and I thought I'd never see him again. But he showed up at the wedding, and he met Derek—And I guess Ronan felt sorry for me because one thing led to another, and now he's my pretend date."

"That's so romantic!" my mom exclaims with clasped hands. She loves books and plays, especially romances. In *Romeo and Juliet,* she doesn't see teenagers making questionable decisions and killing themselves. Nope. She sees starry-eyed romance. And in *Gone with the Wind,* she swoons at the so-called love story buried deep beneath that pesky, problematic behavior.

I hate to admit it, but I was once a romantic as well. BDA. Before the Derek Apocalypse.

I put my hands on my hips and frown at my mother. "Are you trying to set me up with Ronan Masters now? I thought you were rooting for Derek and me to get back together."

"Oh, pish." She shrugs. "That was before he showed up at your sister's wedding with that woman. No. Ronan Masters is a much better option. I 'ship' you two. You need to jump him. Because if he's that big, can you imagine—"

"Mom. Stop!" My face heats in mortification. "You can't 'ship' me with Ronan Masters. How do you know what that means, anyway?"

"Sure, I can. Isn't that the phrase the kids use nowadays? I've seen it on social media."

"What social media are you on?" I groan.

She pats her Jane Fonda-esque hair. Eighties Jane Fonda-esque. "I started an Instagram for my Fabulous Fit Ladies. We have over one hundred thousand followers on IG."

Sadie gasps. "How do you have that many followers? I only have a few hundred for my shop."

"I'm happy to give you some tips," my mom says. "And I've just started on TikTok. Maybe we can make a video with Ronan to post. Can you talk to him, Poppy dear?"

Before I can respond, two bridesmaids stroll in.

My mom's protective genes kick in, so she hustles me out of the bathroom. Sadie follows, citing urgent wedding business.

"Wait!" my sister's best friend from high school calls after us.

"Are you with Ronan Masters?" her former roommate from college cries.

I wave at them, pretending I don't hear.

We burst out of the bathroom to find that the man we've been discussing is holding up the wall in the narrow hallway.

He unfolds his long, broad body in slow motion, which has me awestruck.

"Hey." It's his evergreen greeting, apparently good for all occasions.

"Hey," I return, feeling shy now that my champagne buzz has started to wear off.

"Hi!" My mom eyes him up and down.

"Hello." Sadie looks fierce in a body-hugging pale-pink dress and wild head of blue curls.

Ronan doesn't smile. He seems wary. It must be tough to never be sure how someone will react around you.

"I have your magazine. The one where you're shirtless on the cover." My mom fans herself. "Aren't you just the whole snack."

"Mother!" Red suffuses my cheeks. Again.

"Thanks." He's fighting a smile.

"I'm sorry. Ronan, please meet my mother, Sandra, who is obviously quite well acquainted with you and your abs. And this is my friend Sadie."

He tips his head in greeting. "Hey."

I stare at my mom and Sadie, but they don't get my subliminal message.

"Don't you both have somewhere else important to be?" I say as sweetly as I can muster.

"It's obvious we're not wanted here," my mom huffs. "Dear, please make sure to ask Ronan about the video. My followers are counting on you."

"Okay. That's it. You two need to go. Now." I turn to Ronan when they leave. "My mom is a little eccentric. And she has more energy than anyone I've ever known."

"You're kind of like her."

"Ha. I'm not social media famous like she apparently is."

"You're young. You have time."

"So..."

"So..." he repeats. "Do you have to stay here any longer?"

I shake my head. "No. I've done everything. My duties ended, and my sister and Brad left."

"Don't look now, but your ex is on his way toward us again."

I turn and see that Ronan is right.

Derek is being led by Monique, who is striding toward us.

I'm suddenly tired. I don't want to talk to them. I don't want to see the woman who's sleeping with the man I thought I'd marry. Any magic had faded from our relationship long ago, so we were closer to old friends than passionate lovers, but it still hurt. It destroyed my youthful hopes and dreams and dented my pride.

I want someone to make me feel wanted.

I want someone to make me forget.

I want someone to take me outside of myself.

I want Ronan.

I only have a few seconds before Derek and Monique arrive at our side, and maybe it's the diminishing effects of the champagne or the sadness of the last few weeks or just a level of fucks I no longer have to give, but I grasp onto Ronan and say, "I need to leave."

"Be ready to run," he whispers in my ear. "We're making a getaway."

He puts a hand on my back and navigates me around a column to block us. I turn to see Monique looking around for us. When it's safe, he grabs my hand and leads me toward the stairs. He opens the door to the stairwell and pulls me in, shutting it quietly behind us. I'm not sure if I'm relieved or disappointed he didn't choose the elevator. I wouldn't mind getting stuck in there with him again, this time with the two of us alone.

I take off my heels, and we run up the stairs. Or, more accurately, I run to match his casual stroll.

When we make it to our floor, he continues to follow me until we reach my door.

I turn but can't look him in the eye. I fiddle with my key card.

"Do you—do you want to come in?" I ask, sure he will say no. The request can only mean one thing. A woman doesn't ask a man to come back to her hotel room to chat or play Pictionary. Even as the words leave my lips, I want to swallow them back in a gulp of embarrassment. But I don't. I force myself to meet his light blue gaze.

He leans down, way down, and brushes the hair out of my face.

He watches me.

When I first met Ronan, his lack of words was unnerving. But now, there's something about his steady silence that I crave.

His eyes say what his mouth does not.

His eyes are storm clouds of heat. They're glaciers on fire. They're rivers of ice and flame.

His frozen words and hot gaze speak volumes.

I only hope I'm hearing him correctly.

I'm both hesitant and unbearably excited, waiting for his answer. Nerves dance in my belly. My face feels poker-hot.

Without speaking, he takes the key card from my hand and opens the door with one smooth swipe. He steps aside to let me slip through the doorway first. When I turn back to him with a shy glance, he stands at the threshold.

Is this his answer? I can't tell.

Shaking, I hold out my hand, and he takes it.

There's something about Ronan's watchful presence that emboldens me. I'm rarely shy, but the idea of propositioning a celebrity seems out of the question, as unlikely as a trip to the moon. And here I am, touching a literal star.

I know there's nothing beyond this night, but he makes me feel safe and cared for.

He follows me into the room, and we reach the bed in only a few strides. I'm not in a suite like he is. There's no plush sofa. No coffee table or side chairs. Just an ornate king-sized bed that keeps drawing my attention. We stand at the foot of it.

The only place we touch is where our hands are clasped, his so much larger than mine, with his thumb brushing back and forth over the sensitive skin of my palm.

Still, he doesn't speak.

Still, he doesn't make a move.

I want him to take me in his arms, to kiss me until the doubts and insecurities that bubble up in my head pop. I want to be ravaged, ravished. But he doesn't do any of that. He waits.

The only way I'll get what I want is to ask for it boldly. He's letting me have control. It's as scary as it is heady.

This knowledge thrums in my brain, clearing any remnants of fuzzy-headed feeling from the champagne.

Can I do this?

Holding hands is electric. I imagine what else those large, calloused hands can make me feel.

Just dancing with him earlier made my panties wetter than they've been in years. Maybe ever.

I clear my throat. The sound is loud in the silence. "I don't do this. I've never done this." I don't explain what "this" is.

"I know."

There's no coercing. No false flattery. Just "I know" in that deep voice that's as rough and raw as a storm-swept ocean.

He inclines his head, and I catch a slight smile before it disappears. He's not expressionless as I first thought. He has his tells. They're just subtle. A softening of the eyes. A quirk of the lips.

"What?" I ask.

"I didn't say anything."

"I know. But you're thinking something."

"I'm just trying to make sure you're not drunk."

"I'm fine. The coffee, water, and time helped. I'm just—" I search for the right words. "Just a little smoothed out around the edges."

His gaze rakes over mine before sliding down my body. "You say you don't do this. But do you *want* to?"

My breath whooshes out. "Yes?"

His eyes meet mine. His smile doesn't unfurl as I hoped it would. Instead, his frown deepens. "You don't sound certain. And even if you're not drunk, I'm not sure you're completely sober either."

I want to deny it. I can't imagine I'd ever regret sex with someone as perfect as Ronan Masters. But my head is still swimming. Maybe a little from the champagne. Mostly from being near Ronan. And from the emotions of the day. My breakup with Derek was so recent. I can't erase twelve years as easily as he has. Acknowledging that I'm torn and realizing that Ronan Masters is too much of a gentleman to sweep away my doubts and ravish me, is one of the greatest disappointments of my life.

It's my fault for being so unfamiliar with one-night-stand etiquette. If I had more experience, maybe Ronan would be less reluctant to do all the things I desire. All the things I need. And all the things I'm nervous about.

"Ugh. You're probably right," I say with a deep, disappointed sigh. "But it sucks." My grumpy frown matches his.

Then a slightly mollifying thought occurs. Maybe I could have a little treat? Just a taste of what naughty feels like. "Can I have a kiss, though?" I rush out. "I've only ever almost kissed a movie star once."

That small, sly smile of his is back. I'm getting addicted to the quirk of his lips.

"You better be talking about me," he growls, almost sounding jealous, which is divinely thrilling.

Unlike earlier, he moves with swift surety.

One moment, I'm asking to be kissed, and the next, he's the lord and master of my lips. Demanding and worshiping, commanding and revering.

With tongue.

He's good at this—of course he is—is my last coherent thought.

CHAPTER 5

82 DAYS TO CHRISTMAS

Ronan

THE STORE IS CALLED MIRACLE ON MAIN STREET, WHICH makes sense because the shop window looks like Christmas threw up all over it.

I know with absolute certainty that Belle will beg to go inside.

It's ridiculous—it's only October. Apparently, the town is famous for its Christmas celebrations, which may explain this fetish for holiday decor. It may explain it, but it doesn't excuse it.

The sight of all that Christmas makes me think of mistletoe, which makes me think of Poppy and the devastating kiss we shared in her hotel room.

I managed to stop us at just kissing. *Barely.* Though it was hard. *Literally.*

There was just something about her. It wasn't only her freckles and red hair. Her sparkling green-gold eyes. It was more than that. It was the way she dared me to laugh and got me to smile. It was her sweetness with Belle. She radiated… goodness and positivity. Traits that are rare in the world I normally inhabit.

"Look at all the angels! And Rudolph!" Belle cries. "May we go in? Pleeeeasssse?"

Belle puts her hand in mine and pulls me into the shop before I can answer. Not that I would say no. I haven't seen her this excited since Poppy taught her to draw flowers. Belle rarely asks for anything. She stays in the background, assessing the mood of the surrounding adults before making any move, so I'm glad she's comfortable enough to ask for what she wants. It warms me more than the inviting glow of the shop on this crisp day.

The inside is just as over the top in seasonal decorations as the outside, but instead of selling only Christmas decor, it's cluttered with nostalgic toys, books, art supplies, gifts, stationery, and the classic sweets I remember from my childhood.

Basically, it's a lot. My senses on overload, I want to run for the exit, but Belle is in heaven.

"Maybe they sell those sparkly pens like Poppy had?"

"Let's see."

Her wide smile is my reward for being forced to listen to Christmas music.

Christmas music. In October. It's an assault on the senses.

Belle stops in front of a colorful display of watercolor sets, gazing at them as if they're sweets in a candy shop.

"Can I help you? It looks like we have a young artist here."

I turn and see Poppy's friend, the one I met at the wedding, smiling down at Belle.

I adjust the brim of my ball cap. She looks up at me, and her eyes widen in recognition. She seemed cool at the wedding, but after years of being famous, I've learned that you can never tell about people.

My fears prove unwarranted. Her surprised expression turns into a wide, welcoming smile, but there's no fangirl glaze in her eyes. "Nice to see you again." She turns her attention to Belle. "You look like a girl who knows her own mind. What are you in the mood for? Markers? A painting set? Colored pencils? Pastels?"

Belle scrunches up her forehead and twists her mouth to one side in intense concentration. "Yes, please," she breathes.

I laugh, shaking my head. "She was asking you to choose one thing, Belle."

"I can't choose. They're all perfect," she says, touching a set of small potted paints with reverence.

I nod to the shopkeeper. "We'll take one of everything."

Sadie points to several tall shelves. "But there are more than a dozen different sets."

"Give us an assortment." I know I'm spoiling Belle, but she's had a hard time. I figure she's due for a little spoiling. And I want to keep that smile on her face for as long as I can.

"You don't need to do what he says. I don't need *that* many things," Belle says to Sadie.

Sadie grins down at her conspiratorially. "But I do need to do what he says! Because I might need him to rescue me from bad guys, and if I annoy him, maybe he won't. And then where would I be?"

"Oh, he'd always rescue you," Belle says with earnest, wide eyes. "He rescues everybody."

I lay a hand on her shoulder, careful not to mess up her French braid. That simple style took twenty minutes to get right this morning.

Every morning, I get a little better at doing her hair, but it's deceptively hard. For *The Wanderers,* it's in my contract that I have to keep my hair shoulder-length, so I know how to do a simple ponytail or man bun.

But Belle doesn't want simple. I'm not sure if it's just a stage she's going through or a result of having nannies who have always done her hair. Either way, it's nearly brought me to my knees. Last week, she wanted me to do an intricate bun that was designed by the devil. In the end, I found a dad video on YouTube that explained it step-by-step. Mastering pigtails is next on my agenda. They might look easy, but they're impossible to get even.

My big fingers are good at a lot of things, but tying a girl's hair into fussy styles is not one of them.

Belle looks up at me. "Thank you," she says with big a smile.

Worth it. All of it.

Sadie places an assortment of art supplies in a cloth bag. "I'll get these ready while you browse. There's a children's book section over there." She points to a cozy-looking corner of the store with towering stacks of books, beanbags, and stuffed animal displays.

As I watch Belle skip away, I wonder how I can live up to her trusting innocence. I'm terrified I'll fail at the immense job of parenting her.

But the longer I spend with her, an even bigger fear is emerging, heavier than the weight of responsibility, bigger than the worry of messing up. It's a boulder with the potential to crush me—this fear of what will happen when her mom returns and wants her back. I try to steel myself from getting too attached because she is not mine permanently. She's like an unexpected gift that I'll have to return at any moment. But I can't seem to control how much I care, no matter how I brace myself.

"She's adorable. And clearly loves art," Sadie says with a warm smile toward Belle.

I nod but don't elaborate. I learned long ago not to volunteer information. Even the most innocuous of comments can end up as tabloid gossip.

I debate asking about Poppy, but there's something about this lady's knowing, mischievous smile that holds me in check.

"We have a painting class starting in our art room that would be suitable for Belle's age. Would you like to sign up your…?"

"Daughter," I acknowledge after a moment's hesitation. The word is rough and unfamiliar on my tongue, but I won't pretend my daughter isn't mine.

"She'll love the class," Sadie says with a grin. "The teacher is fabulous, and they're making a fun holiday project. It's full, but we can squeeze in one more child."

Holiday? "Please don't tell me it's Christmas-themed. What's the deal with Christmas around here?"

She laughs. "No. It's something with fall leaves. But you're right, Christmas is big here, and we start it earlier every year. It's our claim to fame. Visitors come from all over to experience our historic Dickens Christmas Festival and all the other activities leading up to it. We only have two seasons. Summer, with our summer vacationers and sailing regatta, and Christmas."

"Can I take the class? Please!" Belle asks, appearing around the corner with a giant stuffed dog that looks vaguely like a Labrador. Belle is obsessed with dogs.

I still have lines to memorize for tomorrow. "How long is it?" I ask Sadie, with a quick glance at my watch.

"Just an hour, from four to five p.m."

Belle had to hang out on set all day while I had costume fittings. An assistant helped her complete the work her tutor in LA gave her before we left. Her new nanny hasn't started yet, and it's been tough to juggle rehearsals while keeping Belle entertained with a revolving door of babysitters. She deserves fun with kids her age.

"That's fine," I say, hoping I can tackle the new script revisions while she's at the class.

"Great! I'll take these things to the register and sign you up." Sadie points to the bulging bag she filled. "This won't be cheap."

I shrug. Some might call this buying my child's love. I just call it using what few advantages I have. "This also." I point to the stuffed animal Belle holds.

A few minutes later, we've paid and registered for the class.

"So," I say with an uncharacteristic bout of nerves. "How's Poppy?"

"She's good." Sadie smiles but provides no more information. "Just go through that door. It leads to the back room where we hold the art classes. It should be ready to start."

Belle grasps my hand and gazes up at me, apprehension evident in her eyes. I squeeze her hand in silent support and force an unnaturally enthusiastic smile, which makes my face feel like it's going to crack. Her uncertainty brings back uncomfortable memories of my own shyness when I was younger. I rarely had anyone to hold my hand and tell me everything would be okay. I want to give that gift to her, more than any bag of toys or art supplies.

Children of varying ages mill about two long tables set up with paints, canvases, and an assortment of autumn leaves. A group of moms chat in the corner. I adjust my hat low and pull out my sunglasses. I don't want a group of fans pushing Belle further back into her shell. She's already nervous standing at the edge of the doorway, coming in as the new girl in a room full of children.

A lady with her back facing us stands on a chair, reaching for a glass container filled with paintbrushes at the top of the highest shelf. As she reaches farther, her chair tilts. In three strides, I'm there just as she topples over with a cry and lands in my arms.

Wide hazel eyes, more green than gold today, stare into mine.

"You!"

"Poppy!" Belle runs up as I let the bundle of womanly curves slide to the floor. My gaze runs over her, from her tall, high-heeled boots—no wonder she tipped on the chair—to her faded jeans and long-sleeved green T-shirt that matches her eyes. Wild reddish curls are tamed in a messy bun. My fingers ache to brush back the soft tendrils of hair escaping around her face. She smells like sunshine and...yes, berries. I want to know if it's her shampoo. Her shower gel. Her lotion. Or just her.

"H-hi." Poppy's face suffuses with pink, causing her freckles to stand out in relief.

Meeting those wide eyes, I struggle to find my voice.

In lieu of a greeting, I reach up and grab the container of brushes she'd been trying to reach. When I hand it to her, our fingers touch.

Her breath draws in, making me wonder if, like me, she feels the spark of electricity.

I can't seem to break free from her gaze until Belle tugs at my shirt.

"Yes?" I ask, without looking away from Poppy.

"All the mommies are staring at us."

"Oh!" Poppy says as her gaze finally breaks free. I turn to find the parents staring, their mouths open, eyes as wide as Poppy's had been.

Shit. So much for making a quiet entrance and exit.

Poppy comes to life in a flurry of agitated movement. "Children, take your seats. We'll get started in just a few minutes."

Belle is bouncing in pleasure, all her shyness gone. "Are you really the art teacher?"

She grins at Belle. "I certainly am, little one."

"I thought you taught at the elementary school," I say.

"I do. Also. When our school stopped teaching art classes, Sadie helped me start these lessons after school and on weekends. It's small, but we're hoping to make up for a little of what the children lost. Art is so important."

"We came into the store and bought paints and books and Biscuit, my new puppy," Belle says.

Poppy's eyes widen.

"Her new *stuffed* puppy," I clarify.

"Ah, got it." She grins.

"Sadie, the nice lady with the mermaid hair, told us about your class."

"Hmm. She does have awesome blue hair."

As if on cue, Sadie sticks her head into the doorway.

"You doing okay in here?" she calls out cheerily.

"All good," Poppy says.

Sadie winks, then disappears back to the main shop.

"You better make your escape before you start a riot with the parents." I turn to see several women taking photos. The others are looking on with glazed eyes. Several dads seem to be gearing up to approach.

Normally, the attention doesn't bother me. Much. I've learned to block it out. But I don't want it to impact my daughter.

"Are you sure you'll be okay?" I ask Belle.

"Of course. I'll be with Poppy."

I nod and pat her shoulder awkwardly. She tugs at my shirt. I lean down, and she surprises me with a kiss on my cheek. In the last month, she's taken to hugs, but this is the first kiss I've gotten. I swallow a fiery ball of emotion.

"See you in an hour, Belle." My voice is gruffer than usual. "Be good."

"If you need to work and want to stay close, the café next door has decent coffee, Wi-Fi, and some private tables in the corner," Poppy says.

"That sounds great. But I'm not sure how private it will be with an audience." I tip my head at the people still milling about and staring from the back of the room.

I shouldn't complain. My life as a celebrity could be worse. Perhaps because I didn't get my start as a teen idol, I don't have the same rabid fan base as my pretty-boy costars, Chase James and Sebastian Blake. If they showed up in a bookstore, it would turn into a riot. My admirers tend to be calmer. More chill. And because of my action-star status, I have as many male fans as women. The men ask me about my workout routine. The women ask me to take off my shirt.

"Go out the door behind us. There's an alley that leads to the coffee shop," Poppy whispers, stepping close to me so she isn't overheard.

"Thanks for the tip," I murmur, swallowing hard against the urge to take her in my arms. "Do you do private art lessons?" I ask on a whim.

My question is practical. If Belle wants to take these classes regularly, I'd prefer not to deal with the other parents every week. It's not because I want to see Poppy again. At least that's what I tell myself.

She tilts her head. "I do on occasion. How often?"

I scratch my jaw. "We could start with once a week and go from there? We'll be in town for a few months. I can call you and make arrangements."

"Oh! Sure," she says, flustered. "Let me find my card." She turns and rummages around on her worktable.

"Aha! Here it is!" She hands me a paint-smudged card with a bright, whimsical logo.

"Great! So call me," she says when I take it. Her face turns pink. "About a lesson, I mean. Or…don't. Either way."

"Ms. Poppy, Johnny is painting his leaf. And he's also painting Caroline," a girl interrupts us. I look up and am both proud and appalled that I know her hair is in a bow bun. I attempted one two days ago. It didn't end well.

"I am not!" a curly-haired boy says. But the paintbrush in his hand and the orange evidence on the arm of the girl next to him would say otherwise. Her hair is hanging messy and straight. She has no bun, braid, bow, or clips. I'm jealous of her parents.

"Are too!" the bow-bun girl retorts.

"I better start this class before they revolt," Poppy says, stepping toward the arguing children.

Belle is sitting in the front row, shyly talking to a girl with pigtails—which are crooked. Naturally.

A loud crash echoes from the back of the class as a boy knocks over his paints.

"The parents are distracted. Quick, go now," Poppy urges.

As I slip out the back door, I put the card in my pocket, trying to identify this feeling. Excitement. Anticipation. It's been so long since I've felt anything for a woman besides occasional lust. I remind myself that I'm here temporarily. And I'll have my hands full juggling the movie and the demands of fatherhood. I don't have time for anything else.

So I'm going to have to forget about the pretty art teacher.

CHAPTER 6

81 DAYS TO CHRISTMAS

Poppy

THE NEXT DAY, THE DOOR JINGLES AS I WALK INTO MIRACLE on Main Street. Yesterday, I escaped Sadie's interrogation after my class because she'd been busy with customers. But today, I know I won't be so lucky.

I'm right. Sadie appears before me, wearing corduroy pants and a hunter-green turtleneck. She crosses her arms. "Poppy O'Brien, you aren't going anywhere until you tell me what's going on with your movie star stud."

I laugh. "Don't call him that. It's so objectifying."

"You'd like to do more than objectify him. Just admit it."

"Fine. I admit it. But he's way out of my league. There's nothing going on." *Much,* I think. Normally, I share everything with Sadie, but ever since I broke up with Derek, things are different. My heart's more fragile. My emotions tilted off-center. I'm not heartbroken, not anymore. But I realized after Derek left me that I'd hung onto him and our relationship more out of habit and a fear of change than anything else. Before, I knew exactly what was in store for me. I was a teacher. I would marry my high school sweetheart. And we'd start a family.

My life was once an open book that I knew by heart—but now it has pages torn from it. It's been trampled on. Tossed aside. But Ronan Masters, with his inscrutable stares, barely there smiles, and intoxicating kisses, makes me feel as if I've finally turned a fresh page, one that's for my eyes only, and I want to keep that feeling to myself for just a little longer. I don't want anyone else's opinions to intrude on my fangirl crush.

Sadie narrows her eyes at me. She doesn't buy what I'm selling.

"You're lucky I have something else I want to talk to you about, so I'll let this go. For now. We can circle back to the town's celebrity later. Do you have a few minutes for a coffee?"

With a quick glance at my watch, I decide I do.

Sadie makes our coffees with her fancy machine in the back of the shop, and we sit on stools behind the counter with our drinks. A few people are browsing, but it's a quiet morning.

"So, what do you want to talk to me about?" I ask, blowing on my coffee.

"You know the hardware store next door?"

"Of course. It's only been there my whole life."

"Well, did you know that Mr. Madeiros is retiring and will be selling the building?"

"What? No!"

"Yes! His daughter, who lives in California, has a new

baby, and her husband skipped out on them. Mr. and Mrs. Madeiros are moving to help her out as soon as they can. Do you know what this means?" Sadie asks with an excited gleam in her eyes.

"Uh, that Mr. Madeiros's son-in-law is a jerk, and I have to find somewhere new to buy a hammer?"

"There is that. But also, you can buy the building and have your own art studio on Main Street! We'd be neighbors. Storefronts never open up here. I love having you rent my back room, but we both know it's not big enough for you."

"I can't buy a building."

"Why not? I know you've been wanting to purchase a house. You've been saving forever for it. The building comes with an apartment upstairs, so you wouldn't need to have two mortgages. Plus, you have all that money that you were saving for your wedding. Don't look at me like that. It's true, Poppy. You can use the money for something better. For your own studio. With the space next door, you could give lessons, classes, even have a gallery to sell your work. Maybe this is meant to be."

"A gallery? What work would I show, Sadie? I barely have time to paint." My thoughts are racing. The hardware store is similar to Sadie's shop. They both have the same beautiful high ceilings and big windows. And the hardware store isn't dusty or dated. Thanks to Mrs. Madeiros's perfectionism, I've never seen it without fresh paint and gleaming hardwood floors. Sadie is right. The space *is* perfect.

I've been saving since I got my first job. But I don't know if it would be enough. Could it be?

"I thought your substitute teaching job ends next week. You'll have the time to paint then," Sadie says.

"But I also won't have a steady income. I'm thinking about taking that fourth-grade position in January."

My parents and my former principal are pushing me to be practical and take the job. It's the only way to keep teaching at Snowflake Harbor Elementary. Otherwise, I'll have to move to a school district that hasn't cut its art funding yet, but those schools and positions are far rarer now. I'd likely have to move towns, possibly even the state. And I can't imagine living anywhere else or leaving my friends and family.

The problem is, though I've always loved teaching, my heart is in art, not the regular classroom.

I've often daydreamed about having a studio. And here it is, the type of space on Main Street I'd always dreamed of. It would get lots of tourist foot traffic to sell my paintings and perhaps to feature other artists. In addition to the gallery, I would have a place to hold art lessons. Maybe I could even expand the free classes I teach at Kids Creativity Center for at-risk youth. The center doesn't have the space or equipment for me to do all the lessons I'd like to offer.

"You could make it work," Sadie urges. "And that upstairs apartment would give you a reason to move out of your parents' house," she says with a grin.

I laugh. "That's very tempting. I love my parents, but I'm going to lose my mind if I live with them much longer."

I can just imagine what they would say about this idea. They want me in a secure job with benefits, not long-term substitute teaching like I've been doing since school began again. Or risking it all on a start-up business.

Here it is—the fear of making a wrong choice. The regret of a missed opportunity wars with the risk of making a stupid financial move and failing. I know what my heart wants, but I also know what my brain is telling me.

"If you can't get the loan on your own, maybe you could

take on a partner. Your parents could help. I've got a little saved that I can lend you."

I frown. "You know I can't do that."

"You'd do it for any of us in a hot second."

But that's the thing. *I'm* the giver. Not the other way around.

"It's so risky," I hedge. "To make the mortgage and the business expenses, I'd have to have full workshops, as well as steady private lessons and sales."

"But you'll love it. Your workshops are more popular than you can handle. My place is way too small for you. And if you don't snap up Mr. Madeiros's building when it hits the market, someone else will. If I have a CrossFit gym next to me, it will be all your fault." Sadie shudders.

She levels me with another hard look. "You could find the time to make this work if you stopped doing every favor anyone asks of you. And if you raised your lesson prices above dirt cheap."

"I'll think about it," I say noncommittally and take a sip of coffee. I know I should raise my prices. When I factor in the costs of my equipment, I'm not making what I should, even at the cut-rate rent Sadie gives me on her old storeroom. But I also know that so many of the town's families can't afford to pay more. And then there are all the workshops that I do for free. I would never stop those.

My phone rings, and I'm thankful for the distraction. Butterflies take flight in my stomach when I look at the screen.

"It's an unknown number," I hiss. "Maybe it's *him*."

"Him?" Her eyes get big. "As in *him*? Ronan Masters has your number?"

"Yes." I shake my head. "I mean, no. Well, kind of. He wanted to set up art lessons for his daughter."

"Hurry. Answer your damn phone."

"H-hello?"

"Hey, Poppy." I'd know that voice anywhere. My heart rate kicks higher.

"H-hi." I try to sound breezy, as if celebrities call me every day, but my stuttering gives me away. "What's up?"

Sadie makes swooning gestures. I shoot her an exasperated look and turn away so I can concentrate.

"I want to schedule that art lesson for Belle. She won't stop talking about it."

"Oh, sure." I strive for boss-babe vibes. Unbothered and professional. Making an appointment for a Hollywood superstar? No biggie. "When would be good?"

Yes. Nailed it.

"How are Sunday mornings at ten? My schedule is chaotic now, but that's the day I most often have off. Unless you don't work Sundays, in which case I understand."

Sundays are wide open for me.

"No, Sundays are fine. I can...rearrange a few things on my schedule," I lie. Rearrange things like sorting my laundry. Or color-coding my pens. Or baking large quantities of cookies and eating most of them myself. But I don't want him to know that my social life is pathetically lacking.

"Great. We're not in the hotel anymore. I'm renting a house on Lake Road. It's number fifteen. It's the—"

"The big historic white house with the wraparound porch on the lake." I try not to sound too besotted. If I weren't swooning for him, I'd be swooning for his temporary digs.

"It really is a small town." He sounds disconcerted.

Great, now he thinks I'm a stalker.

"Sorry. It's big news when a celebrity rents the old Hastings estate. It's such a large place, but I imagine you need privacy to keep all the ladies away," I tease. "The women in town are disappointed that it's not an easy location for snooping."

I hear a commotion in the background.

"I've got to go. They're calling me to set," he says. "See you Sunday."

"Okay. Bye—" But he's already hung up. He didn't ask how much I charge. Though I suppose with people as rich as he is, it doesn't matter.

"Bye," I repeat into the phone, even though the line is now dead.

Sadie stares at me, hanging on every word.

"You're going to Ronan Masters's house! *Oh my God.*" She shakes her booty, making sexy swivels with her hips.

I roll my eyes. "Relax, Shakira. I'm teaching his daughter art. He might not even be there."

But I can't help the burst of excitement at the merest chance that I might see that big, burly beast of a man again.

CHAPTER 7

77 DAYS TO CHRISTMAS

Ronan

IT'S THE DAY OF THE PRIVATE ART LESSON WITH POPPY. AND IT begins with another elaborate hairstyle request. This time, Belle wants two bun circle things at the top of her head that remind me of Princess Leia. I curse whatever nanny she had in the past who gave her ridiculously high grooming standards. But mastering this has become my challenge, my point of pride, my own white whale. I didn't master jujitsu, mixed martial arts, Muay Thai, and earn a black belt in karate because I'm a quitter. The ability to dedicate myself to a single goal is one of my biggest strengths.

Plus, I'm good with hand-eye coordination and following complex instructions, which are important for both martial arts and following YouTube hairstyle tutorials. Who knew the two topics intersected so well?

When I'm finished, Belle looks in the mirror, turning her head this way and that to judge how well I've executed the style. "It will do," she pronounces.

Joy and relief run through me at her grudging approval, as if I've passed a critical test. This hobby is getting out of hand.

When the doorbell rings at 10:00 a.m., I'm doing bench presses in the makeshift gym I set up in the large and airy downstairs guest room. Belle runs down the stairs, screaming, "I've got it!"

Belle yanks open the front door as I walk out of the gym. I should have timed this better. I'm covered in sweat in a sleeveless workout shirt and gym shorts. Not exactly presentable.

Poppy stands at the threshold. Her hair is burnished copper in the golden morning light surrounding her. She steals my breath more forcefully than a punch to the gut. The light rims her body, emphasizing the surprising lushness of her petite frame. I want to trace every curve.

"You're here!" Belle cries.

Poppy smiles at my daughter, and then her gaze wanders to me. It stops in the vicinity of my exposed arms. I resist the urge to flex.

"Hi." I run a hand through my sweaty hair. Damn, I need a shower. Maybe she's not silent with admiration. Maybe it's disgust. "Sorry. I'm just finishing my workout."

She blinks and then shakes her head, snapping to attention.

She turns back to Belle. "Good morning, little one. I'm excited too. I love your hair."

"Thank you. Father did it."

Poppy looks surprised.

I shrug.

"He can do all the fancy styles. I bet he could do your hair," Belle adds.

Poppy blushes. "Oh. Um. I think your dad has better things to do."

"Hair's my new superpower," I say. And then I want to cut out my tongue. A year ago, my superpower was kicking ass without breaking a sweat—on a movie set, of course. Now, I'm bragging about mastering children's hairstyles. Becoming a dad has turned me into someone I hardly recognize.

I grab the easels and large bag she's barely balancing.

"Where do you want to set these up?" I ask.

She steps into the entryway and looks beyond it, at the large living room that leads into an open-plan kitchen. "Maybe by the windows? It's so beautiful," she says, admiring the lake view. "I've always wondered what it was like in here. I saw it once when I was a kid in an open house. I knew the last owners renovated it, but I hadn't realized they'd made so many changes." Her eyes scan the rooms, seeming to miss no detail. "It seems more modern and…emptier than I remember."

I look around, seeing it through her eyes for the first time. She's not wrong. The walls are bare. So are all the surfaces. It's pristine, but there's an abandoned feel to the house. Any personal touches are Belle's. A doll on the counter. Coloring book on the table.

"It's just temporary. We're only here for a few months until we wrap just before Christmas. This will do for now."

"Hmmm." She doesn't look convinced. Her attention moves to setting up the easels.

"I thought we could do a still life with watercolors today," she addresses Belle. "And since you are new to Snowflake Harbor, we can paint a snowflake."

"Of course," I mutter.

She looks at me. "What?"

"Snowflakes in October?"

She rolls her eyes. "It's the name of the town. We have snowflake themes all year round."

"Exactly my point."

"Do I need to put you in a time-out? You may be easy on the eyes, but you can't get away with dissing my choice of art project. So begone."

"Begone?" At least she noticed my biceps.

"Scram. I could have brought a pumpkin and been more seasonally correct. But I can tell Belle is a snowflake girl. She digs *Frozen*."

Poppy has me there. My daughter is obsessed with the movie.

"I love snowflakes," Belle says. "But I'm not very good at drawing them."

"That's why I'm here. This is going to be the best snowflake painting in the history of Snowflake Harbor." She flashes an impish smile at me, her dimple on full alert.

I shuffle, needing to escape her force field. Everything about the scene is too inviting. The two of them in my living room, looking fresh-faced and bright on a Sunday morning.

"Okay. Well, I guess I'll just begone, then." My mouth kicks up in a small smile against my will.

"Unless you'd like a lesson as well?"

"I'll pass," I say, though the idea of Poppy up close and personal giving me other lessons is way too appealing. "I need to shower. When I'm done, I'll be in the library working, if you need anything. There." I point to a room next to my gym.

"Father starts shooting his movie tomorrow. That's when the nanny arrives." Belle glowers.

Guilt churns in my belly. Belle is upset at having yet another caregiver watching her, in what I understand is a long line of them. But we need a live-in nanny. Once production officially starts tomorrow, I'll have little to no control over my schedule, with long hours, late nights, and early morning calls.

"I'm sure your nanny will be nice," Poppy says. "Imagine all the fun you'll have."

"I guess." Belle pauses. "I wish *you* could be my nanny. Father, why can't she be my nanny?"

I freeze, imagining us having dinner at the large wooden kitchen table. Poppy's laughter. Poppy wearing just my T-shirt making breakfast. Why the nanny would wear my shirt is not explained in my vivid daydream.

"If I were your nanny, silly, I wouldn't be your art teacher."

"You could be both. Please, Father. This new nanny could be mean. What if she hates me?"

I kneel to my daughter and take her small hand.

"I've already hired someone, and she's on her way to us. It wouldn't be fair to fire her now. But I promise you, we won't keep anyone who is mean. I'm sure she'll love you." The word *love* feels thick on my tongue.

"If you say so," she says dully.

"Come here, Belle. If you don't watch me mix the paint, you'll miss the best part."

"But isn't painting the picture the best part?"

"I'll tell you a secret." Poppy bends down to my daughter. "They're all the best part," she says in a loud whisper.

Belle giggles, and the sounds of their mingled laughter carry through me.

Poppy looks up as I hover, unsure of what to do. "We're

fine. Go shower," she says with a raised eyebrow and a slight flush.

I nod. A feeling I don't recognize washes over me. It might be peace. Perhaps contentment. It's similar to what I felt in the elevator when they were singing together.

Poppy's presence fills this empty house. I suddenly want nothing more than to stand here watching them paint in this patch of sunlight.

Which is why I turn and walk away.

Poppy

Five days later, I'm prepping for my workshop at Miracle on Main Street. I have a group of ten kids signed up for my painting and craft session, but my heart's not in it.

I had to say goodbye to kindergartners today. Their regular teacher's maternity leave ended, and she returned to the classroom. My heart is full from the hugs and handmade gifts they gave me, but it was still difficult to leave them.

Sadie pokes her head into the room. "How was your last day?" she asks.

I try to smile. "Hard. It always is. So I got treats to cheer me up. You're lucky I like to share." I hand her a small paper bag.

"Pumpkin spice muffins. You know they're my drug of choice." Sadie gives me a big hug. "For the muffin. And because I know today was a tough one."

Tears pool in my eyes. I hug her back. "Don't make me cry. The kids and parents will be here in fifteen minutes."

When we break apart, I wipe at my eyes and give a watery

laugh. "Sorry, I'm a hopeless crier. Sad commercials. Cute animal videos. Greeting cards. Hugs."

She smiles at me. "I know. And I also know how attached you get to your students."

I put paint on each palette. "Yes, and also, while I was still substituting, I didn't have to make any decisions about the future. Now, I need to decide whether I'm going to take the fourth-grade job in January. Maybe I should have looked harder for an art position, even if it meant moving."

"Or you can call the real estate agent about the building next door, maybe talk to the bank."

I pull out sponges and line them up.

"I'm still thinking about it," I say. "You look great, by the way. I love your outfit. Do you have a hot date tonight?" Sadie is wearing a short blue-and-black plaid skirt and a black sweater with a white Peter Pan collar. Her blue curls matches the blue of the skirt. She looks adorable.

She blushes. "I do. With Lonely Book Boy."

I gasp. "No way! Tell me everything. How did this happen?" Sadie always stops at the bookshop down the block after she closes up on Friday nights. She picks out a book to read over the weekend. And she often runs into someone we call Lonely Book Boy, who also is there on a Friday night. In a town where we know pretty much everyone, coming across a mysterious guy is a surprise.

"Last week, I got up the nerve to talk to him. I asked for his number."

"This is amazing."

She tilts her head. "I think I might really like him. He's funny and cute. We both like *Star Wars* and *Dr. Who*. I've had far worse potential for a first date."

"Well, you look gorgeous. He won't be able to resist you."

I walk around to the tables and put the paint palettes, sponges, and paper at each table.

"I'll let you get finished before the heathens descend," Sadie says, walking swiftly toward the door. Kids wielding paintbrushes strikes fear in her heart.

"Hi! You can go in," I hear Sadie say a few seconds later from the hallway. I look at my watch. Someone is early. Hopefully, it's one of the better-behaved children I can put to work.

"Poppy!" Belle bounces into the room, looking cute in a pink dress and tights. Ronan must be off his hairstyling game. Her high ponytail is bunched up and crooked. I wouldn't think twice about the style on any other child, but I know that doing her hair is their thing, even if Ronan would rather eat nails than have that widely circulated.

"Hi, cutie! What's up?" I ask. We have a lesson scheduled again at her house for Sunday, so I hadn't thought I'd see her back here again. Ronan wanted to avoid causing a scene.

"I can join your lesson today. If you have room for me."

"Oh, where's your dad?" I look around, my heart racing at the thought of seeing him again.

A tall woman about my age with long blond hair and perfect features strolls in after Belle.

"He's shooting. Tiffany is with me." Belle imbues all her disdain into that sentence. Tiffany doesn't look like any nanny I've ever seen—in leather pants and stilettos, typing into her phone. I'd introduce myself, but she hasn't bothered to look up.

"Oh. Great." I clear my throat as disappointment settles in my stomach. "Is Tiffany your—"

"My new nanny," Belle confirms. "The movie started shooting this week. So it's just me and Tiffany now."

Belle looks like she could use a hug, which I doubt she'll get from her nanny.

I squeeze Belle's hand. "Why don't you help me set up while your nanny registers you with Sadie if she hasn't already. I mean, if that's okay with her."

The woman rolls her eyes and shrugs. Without speaking to me or Belle, she turns around to leave, still typing into her phone.

"Okay, bye! We'll be done in an hour!" I call to her as she walks out the door. She doesn't even turn around.

I breathe a sigh of relief when she's gone. So does Belle, I notice.

We both stare after her. "How does she walk in those shoes?" I ask in wonder.

"She's just like the others," Belle says.

"What do you mean?"

"She's only nice to me when Father's around. She wants him to like her. But when it's just us…" She looks down at her hands.

Something twists in my gut. I try to give people the benefit of the doubt. But I hate the idea of someone like Tiffany caring for this little girl, who needs a warm presence. I'm also not ecstatic about her living with Ronan. But maybe that's just because it sounds like my dream scenario, and I'm a little jealous.

"I wish Mrs. Cranwell were still here. She was my babysitter and really nice. She always smelled like cookies. But she didn't want to leave California. Father says to give Tiffany a chance."

"Well, let's focus on having fun now," I suggest.

Soon, Belle's helping me get the rest of the supplies ready and greeting the kids who filter in with a shy smile. I seat her up at the front so I can give her and her pumpkin painting extra attention.

This is always my favorite part of the day. I liked teaching art at the school, but there were so many parameters, and I hated grading and report cards. This—helping children find the joy in art—is what I love, having complete freedom over the projects we do without worrying about assessments or sticking to a particular curriculum.

My mind has been mulling over the studio. I have so many ideas for the gallery space and classes. In addition to art lessons, I could arrange wine-and-paint nights for adults, do private events, and so much more.

But all that would take money. Sadie is encouraging me to go for it, but she's never had to pay a mortgage. She inherited her parents' thriving general store when they retired. Sadie has changed a lot about the shop, given it her own special twist, but she never had to start from scratch.

I know the building next door won't be around much longer, though. The town, with its quaint Main Street, Victorian mansions, and charming waterfront, is a popular place, even more so now that it's famous for our Dickens festival. The building won't be free long. But even if I can get the bank to agree to a mortgage, it will take several more months of spending next to nothing, of taking every substitute teaching job I can, to save the amount I've calculated I'd need just for the business costs.

I could take the full time teaching job and put my dream on hold, but I have this bone-deep fear that if I do, I'll never open the studio. Before I'd lost my job and my fiancé, it had just been a fun dream, not anything I believed I could ever have.

My parents drilled into me to always be practical. Derek was the same. He had a five-year plan, a ten-year plan, and a twenty-year plan. He'd made it clear that we'd both teach and have secure, stable jobs. He scoffed at my dream of opening a studio someday.

It should have been no surprise, then, that he dumped me soon after I lost my job. He replaced me quick enough with another teacher from our school, though secretly, I think the joke's on him because I doubt Monique will stay in our small town for long. I've known the beautiful French teacher for a few years, and she's never made it a secret that she thinks she's made for bigger things.

And maybe I am too.

With my life in shambles, I have a blank slate. The rare chance to reimagine what I could do just for myself, to figure out what the little girl who loved to paint wants to do with her life.

I'll worry about that later, though. Until then, I just need to focus on helping this awesome group of kids and their awesome pumpkin paintings. I have opportunities and choices, more than many people have, and I'm grateful for that.

When we wrap up, the kids line up to wash their hands in the small sink at the back of the room. They sing our clean-up song as parents filter in.

Belle makes her way to her seat, admiring her art.

"I love the colors you've used," I say.

She looks up at me, her face glowing with pleasure.

Tiffany strides in, and the moms watch her with ill-disguised envy. She grimaces at the paint-covered table.

"See what I made," Belle says when she spots Tiffany, holding up her painting.

"It's not bad," Tiffany says. "Though I told Ronan that taking language lessons would help you more. The children I was a nanny for in New York City spoke three languages by your age." She frowns. "Are you ready? I have to pick up our dinner order before we head home. Even though your dad will be late, I want to make sure he has something nice waiting for him."

"He won't be home to put me to bed?" Belle asks, twisting her hands on her painting and making the paper bunch at the edge.

Tiffany's focus has returned to her phone. She looks up. "Pardon?"

"Never mind," Belle mumbles.

"Belle asked if her father would be home in time to put her to bed," I say, gritting my teeth at the oblivious nanny. Ronan Masters is toppling off the pedestal I'd put him on. This woman may look good in stilettos, but she'll crush the sensitive girl's spirit. It's obvious Belle desperately misses her father. Shooting a movie is bound to be stressful, but he's rich and powerful. Surely he can arrange for a better fit to care for his child.

She looks at me with narrowed eyes. "Who are you again? Oh yes, the art teacher."

She glances at Belle and says in a sugary-sweet voice, "You know that your father is a busy man. He doesn't have time to put you to bed. That's why I'm here." She shoots me a calculating look. "That's why I'm in charge. Now, enough dawdling. We have to go."

Belle follows her out of the room with sluggish steps. At the door, she waves goodbye to me.

I wave back, a lump in my throat. I know it's not my business. But, I decide, my jaw firming, if Ronan Masters is home on Sunday at the art class, he's going to get my opinion of the new nanny. I hate confrontation and avoid it at all costs. Unless one of my students' happiness or welfare is on the line.

CHAPTER 8

71 DAYS TO CHRISTMAS

Poppy

I ARRIVE AT THE LAKE HOUSE FOR BELLE'S ART LESSON ON Sunday at 10:00 a.m. Just like last week, I balance my art supplies and canvases. As I walk up the stairs, Tiffany barrels out the front door, wrestling with two large pieces of designer luggage.

Her face enraged, she glares as she passes me on the stairs, almost knocking me over. "Good luck with the brat. And don't think I can't see through your sweet girl-next-door act. You want *him* too. But if he didn't go for me, he sure as hell won't go for someone like you, with all that frizzy red hair and freckles."

She storms down the rest of the stairs in mile-high boots, her obviously expensive luggage banging behind her in a way that makes me wince. I watch, shocked, as she fights to get her bags into the trunk of a black car I'd parked next to, slides into the driver's seat, and reverses down the long driveway, almost running into the mailbox.

As her car's tires screech in the distance, I debate whether I should go in and what I'll find if I do.

I doubt it will be the idyllic scene of last week, with Ronan greeting me at the door, post-workout gleaming, and Belle's sunny smile.

Squaring my shoulders, I decide they might need the distraction after whatever that was. On the bright side, I no longer need to break the news to Ronan that his nanny's not Mary Poppins. Clearly, he realized that on his own.

"Hello!" I call a little hesitantly and rap on the door. On my fourth knock, it swings open.

"I told you to get the hell—" Ronan's frown is fierce, but his breath whooshes out when he sees it's me.

"Poppy." He runs a hand through his long hair. I've never seen him look frazzled before. He's always calm, watchful, self-contained. Now, I can feel the anger rolling off him.

"Hi!" I chirp, dropping all my equipment on the porch. What does it say about me that my first instinct is to take this man in my arms—if they can even fit around him—and comfort him? "Is everything okay?"

"Poppy!" Belle peeks her head out the door. In contrast to Ronan, she's elated.

"It's my favorite artist," I say.

Belle is blissfully unconcerned with any drama that just transpired. I'm relieved that whatever happened hasn't affected her. But it makes me that much more curious.

"Did you see? Tiffany left." Her smile is radiant.

"Yes, we…er…ran into each other on her way out."

"Father scolded her for not being nice enough to me. And she got mad. And then he overheard her say that she took sneaky pictures of him and was going to sell them to a tabloid."

"W-what?"

Ronan's jaw hardens. "It seems we're without a nanny." He bends over and picks up the equipment I'd dropped. "Come in."

"I-I'm so sorry." I follow him into the house, feeling awkward as he sets up my easels in the same area I placed them last week, in the patch of diffuse sunlight overlooking the lake.

"Can I do something?" I ask.

He shakes his head. "You can get started on the lesson. I need to make some calls. I'm an hour late to set, but I've got to figure this out."

As he walks to the library, he barks into his phone, "Emma, I need you to tell Jordan that I'm going to be late. Then call the agency and explain to them what happened. That she was trying to sell our story and photos to the tabloids. No, I don't want them to send a new nanny. The last one was shit, even before this went down. Find another agency. Just do whatever it takes. I have night shoots coming up, and I need someone here for Belle. It would be too disruptive to take her with me. I need to know she's safe. And happy."

He closes the door to the library, and his voice disappears.

I shake my head, my focus shifting as I realize Belle is patiently watching me. "So, Belle. I thought we'd paint a wreath today. This one has pretty fall colors, but we could paint a Christmas one if you'd rather, just to bug your dad." I grin.

"You can do it."

"Do what?" I ask, taking out both wreaths from my bag so

she can decide. I secretly hope she chooses the Christmas wreath. It's such fun to irritate Ronan, and it seems like he could use the diversion.

"You can be my new nanny."

I laugh. "I'm a teacher. Not a nanny."

"But at the lesson, you told us that it was your last day teaching kindergarten at the school and that's why you were a little sad."

"It's true I'm not working there anymore. But your father wants to hire someone experienced with being a nanny."

"Like Tiffany?"

"Um..." I say, setting out the paintbrushes. "I'm sure he'll find someone better."

"I don't want anyone else. I want you," Belle insists, her chin stubborn.

"Please, Father?" She begs, looking behind me.

I turn to find that Ronan has emerged from the library. His eyes and face are impassive as always. But even impassive, he's larger-than-life. His body is too big. His face too handsome. His hair too long and too golden. He's a Viking portrait come to life, as if he were built straight from CGI.

"Can I talk to you outside?" Ronan asks, all stern politeness. He wears it well.

"Sure." I follow him to the covered porch that looks off to a small gazebo, wooden dock, and the shimmering lake beyond. The sky is the cloudless blue of a brisk fall day.

I'd taken off my coat, and now I shiver. He removes his plaid flannel overshirt and puts it over my shoulders. It falls to mid-thigh.

"No. Now you'll be cold."

"Keep it."

I'm about to protest again, but he silences me with a look.

"Thank you," I acknowledge, resisting the urge to bury

my nose in the flannel. I'm not sure what cologne he wears, but damn, it's good, all nature and masculinity, like pine and sandalwood and something that's uniquely him. The soft shirt is still warm from his body heat, which adds another layer of intimacy, as if I'm enveloped in him. Is this what it would be like to wake in the morning, after a long night of sex, and put on his shirt?

I don't need the flannel to keep me warm anymore. My hot blush could power the warmth of a small city.

"Can I help with anything? I don't know any hit men, but I have a few large cousins who are what you might call underemployed. I bet they could catch your runaway nanny for a small fee."

He blows out a breath that might have been the start of a laugh then looks out at the horizon before his gaze lands back on me.

"I hate to ask, but can you watch Belle?"

My breath skips. Belle asked me to be their new nanny. Had he overheard? Is that what he's asking?

"Just for today," he clarifies. Disappointment settles through me. Which is silly. Like I told Belle, I'm not a nanny. Even though I'm now without that substitute teaching job, I have a full schedule. But watching her for a day, that I can do.

"I know it's a huge favor," he says, studying me. "I'm sure you're busy. I wouldn't ask, but I'm shooting until late tonight, so I don't want to take her to set with me again. Plus, she loves you. And she doesn't love many people."

"Of course," I rush out. "Don't give it another thought. I'm happy to."

"I'll pay you." He names a figure that makes my eyes widen. He's already been more than generous for the art lessons. This number is something else entirely.

It's tempting. But I don't feel right taking his money.

"No," I say firmly. "I don't need payment for this. I'm not a babysitter. This is a favor, not a job."

He gives a small smile, and damn if it doesn't make my breath catch. "In my experience, a person has to pay for everything."

"Well, maybe you aren't hanging out with the right people," I challenge.

The way he watches me, like I'm a puzzle he's trying to figure out, makes my stomach flutter. He shoots me a long, intense look, and I stare right back at him because I can. The view is extremely pleasing.

He breaks eye contact. "I don't have time to argue now. But we'll revisit this later."

I may be a people pleaser, but not about this. I can wrangle a classroom of five-year-olds into submission, so he's no match for me, even with all those pretty muscles. However, I don't argue because I know he's late and stressed, and it would add to his worry now. When we walk back into the house, Belle stares at us expectantly.

"Well? Are you going to be my new nanny?"

"I'm going to watch you for today," I clarify.

"Yes!" She jumps up with a fist in the air. "We're going to have so much fun!"

Ronan's phone rings again. He answers with a short, "Yes?" He listens for a minute, then growls. "I'm on my way."

When he's off the phone, he's all business. "The fridge and pantry are stocked. I have no idea when I'll be back. This is for any activities or food." He pulls out a stack of crisp hundred-dollar bills and sets them on the kitchen counter. There has to be at least one thousand dollars there.

"Take the Range Rover. The car is in the garage. It has a booster seat in it. Here are the keys. You have my number, but if you need anything and can't reach me, call this," he says, handing me two keys and a piece of paper with a phone number and name scrawled on it.

"Emma," I say, reading the name on the paper. That's the girl he was on the phone with. "Your assistant?" I hope she isn't a girlfriend.

He nods. "Sort of. Emma, my costar's assistant, has been helping out since Belle came to live with me. She'll make arrangements for a locksmith to change all the locks. I don't want Tiffany returning."

He leans down to Belle. "Be good for Poppy."

She grins. "Poppy doesn't need me to be good. She just needs me to be me. She says I'm perfect that way."

"She's right, as always." His words give me a warm glow in my belly. He sets his hand on her head, ruffling her soft hair and messing up the intricate double braids. It's been so chaotic since I arrived, I failed to appreciate the hairstyle.

"Are those braids your work or Tiffany's?" I ask.

Belle snorts. "Not Tiffany's. She said it was a ponytail or nothing. So Father did them. We looked up a new video. Tomorrow, we're going to try a sock bun."

"What in heaven is a sock bun?" I change my mind. "You know what? I don't even want to know."

"That's smart. That way, you can be surprised when you see it," Belle sasses, flipping her bright blond braids.

I try to hold back a laugh and fail. "You're such a softy," I say to Ronan. Even with his hectic shooting schedule and crazy morning, he still did his daughter's hair because she wanted a fancy style.

It isn't until he opens the door to the outside, a gust of cold air blowing in, that I realize I forgot to give him back his flannel. He grabs a gray coat from the rack next to the door and shrugs it on over his T-shirt.

"Wait, your shirt," I say.

Silhouetted in the doorway, he appears larger than life. "Keep it. It looks good on you." And with that mini heart-bomb, he's gone.

We wave as we watch his car, a black BMW, back out of the drive with less speed and far more control than Tiffany. I know he could have shown off his stunt-driving skills. I'm sure he has them after years of being on movie sets.

But he doesn't. He's probably concerned about safety. And small animals. I like that. I like him. Far too much.

When the car is out of sight, quiet descends on the house.

I grin. "Right. Let's have some fun."

CHAPTER 9

71 DAYS TO CHRISTMAS (STILL)

Poppy

"Tell me one more story."

Belle looks at me so sweetly that my heart turns over. I sit on the edge of her bed, marveling at how tiny she looks in it. It's a bed fit for a princess—four posters painted white, with pink flourishes and a pink canopy.

"I've already told you three," I say as sternly as I can.

"Pleeease."

"You know, this is quite a bed you have here," I say, changing the subject.

"I hate it," she confides in me.

"But why? It's beautiful."

"It's so pink."

"I thought you loved pink." I recall her saying that the night we first met.

"Not anymore."

"Since when?"

"Since Tiffany said it was for babies. I'm a big girl. I like blue now. Do you think I could paint my room blue?"

I think for a minute. "You probably can't paint your room since this is just your temporary house. But if you really want to, I bet we could add some blue pillows and decorations."

"Really?"

"I don't see why not. We can talk to your dad about it. But from one artsy girl to another, understand that the color 'blue' is way too vague. There are a million shades. For example, do you like turquoise blue? Or periwinkle? Sky blue? Indigo? Cornflower?"

"I know cornflower. That's the name of one of my crayons."

"It is. One of my favorites. So which will it be?"

"The blue of Miss Sadie's hair," Belle says with a happy sigh.

"Royal blue it is."

"What are you girls talking about?" a deep voice asks behind me.

"Ahh!" I startle, losing my precarious seat at the edge of the high bed and going crashing to the floor.

I look up to see Ronan peering down at me, a ghost of a smile playing on his lips. Of course it's Ronan and not some serial killer breaking into the house. It just surprised me because I hadn't expected him home for hours.

I feel like an idiot lying in a heap in front of my number one crush. So much for looking cool. I haven't even reapplied any lip gloss or brushed my hair.

"Are you okay, Poppy? You look funny lying like that!" Belle giggles.

"Thanks?" I stand up, ignoring Ronan's outstretched hand.

"Sorry for sneaking up on you. Are you hurt?"

"Just damaged my dignity. Though it *is* a long way to fall. What's with the giant bed?"

He rubs his strong jaw, which is covered in stubble now. It's a darn good look.

"I hired a decorator. When she found out Belle's name, she did a princess theme." He looks so proud of the pink explosion, which kind of reminds me of the prom gown I wore the night we got stuck in the elevator.

"It *is* exceptionally princess-y," I say with a grin. "You're back earlier than I thought you'd be."

"The director changed the schedule." I feel there's more to the story, but he doesn't elaborate. He turns to Belle. "How was your day?"

"We painted pictures, and then Poppy took me to the store, and we bought all the ingredients to make cookies, and she made me spaghetti for dinner. It was almost the best day *ever*." Belle says it all in one breath.

"Almost? Why almost?" he asks with that lopsided ghost-of-a-smile. I'm taking the Ronan Masters course of body language and coming to realize that his ghost smile is the equivalent of most people's full-out grin.

"It can't be the best day ever without you," Belle says with such perfect, reasonable assurance.

I admit it. My eyes get misty. I turn to see if Ronan's eyes are misting up as well or if he's made of stone, but he's looking down, so I can't tell.

He clears his throat.

"There's spaghetti and salad downstairs if you're still hungry," I say. "And, of course, cookies for dessert."

When he finally looks up, his face is back to stoic, but do I detect a little shimmer in those baby blues? He swallows. "I already ate on set. But I might take a cookie. Just don't tell my trainer."

"You don't look like you need to refrain from cookies." I say it with far too much admiration. I try not to be creepy, but I can't help it.

"I'm always in training. I have to eat protein every few hours. Usually, it's plain chicken breasts."

"Seriously?" I ask, appalled and amazed at the same time.

"He does!" Belle says. "They're gross."

"A nutritionist delivers my meals and snacks."

"Is that what's in all those containers in the fridge?"

He nods.

"God, that must suck."

"I'm used to it, though sometimes I'd kill for something sweet."

I know I'm not the sweet he's referring to, but the way he says it and the way he looks at me make me break out in a full-body blush.

"It must take a lot of discipline to look so…fit." My mind is supplying far more vivid descriptions. Insanely hot. Lickable.

"You'll love Poppy's cookies," Belle interjects.

Ronan makes a coughing sound.

"Poppy? Why are you so red?" Belle asks.

Kill me now. "Oh? Am I? It's a little warm in here. But now, it's time to turn out the lights." I glance at Ronan. "I mean, sorry, unless you want to read her a story. If so, I can go now."

"One more story!" Belle cries but then ruins the effect with a big yawn.

Ronan shakes his head. "Much as I hate to admit it," he says dryly, "Poppy's right. It's time for lights-out."

"What?" I cup my hand around my ear. "Did I hear you say I'm right?"

He raises an eyebrow. The small smile playing on his lips makes me feel triumphant. "Didn't I tell you earlier that you're always right?"

He turns back to his daughter. "Good night, Belle," he says, reaching down and smoothing the covers.

"Night, Poppy. Night, Daddy," Belle murmurs, eyes closing.

Ronan freezes. He stares at the almost-sleeping girl for a long moment and then, hesitantly, leans down and brushes her forehead with a whisper of a kiss.

We walk out of her room into the dimly lit hallway, where I notice his expression.

"Hey, is everything okay?" I put my hand on his biceps. *Focus, Poppy.*

He nods. "It's nothing. Just—"

"It's just what?" I encourage, with a little pat on his tree trunk of an arm.

He avoids my eyes. "She called me Daddy."

"For the first time," I say, understanding now. I realize Belle usually calls him Father but never Daddy.

He nods and swallows hard.

I love seeing this man, larger-than-life on a movie screen, felled by such a sweet, simple thing. "She thinks you hung the moon, you know."

"She does?" He looks so cautiously hopeful.

"She does. I pinkie swear. Belle talks about you nonstop. We had to make snickerdoodles tonight because she said they're your favorites, even though she loves chocolate chip cookies best."

"Well, I haven't seen her smile as big as she did tonight. You make her happy," he says.

"Well, I'm pretty fond of her as well."

He shuffles his enormous feet. "I've got something to ask you."

And just for a moment. For a brief, confusing, elating moment. I think, maybe. Just possibly. In some dream world. He might ask me on a date. Or ask to kiss me.

I hold my breath, waiting, heart beating on overload.

"Are you interested in...?"

"Yes!"

His light blue eyes go wide. In the low light of the hall, they're almost the color of the cornflower-blue crayon Belle and I were talking about earlier.

"You don't even know what I was going to ask you."

"Oh, sorry." I wave. "Please go on."

"Would you be interested in being Belle's new nanny? I know it's a huge ask. But I'd be a crap father if I didn't try. She lights up when she's around you." He looks away, his jaw ticking. "She deserves to be happy. This is temporary. We only have two months more of shooting, and then we leave just before Christmas."

My mind whirls. He wants me. As a nanny. I'd be living with Ronan Masters and his daughter. The whole thing just doesn't compute.

"I'm not a nanny," I remind him and myself, just as I had reminded Belle earlier.

"You're a teacher, though. I'd pay you generously."

He names a figure that's almost a year's teaching salary.

When I don't answer right away because I'm in shock at the bananas amount he just offered, he says, "I'll double it."

"No!" I'm appalled he'd think I'm making a play for more, when what he's offered is more than I could ever imagine.

He frowns. "I get it. I just had to ask. For Belle's sake."

"No. I mean, no isn't my answer. I just... I don't need

more money. Your first offer was incredible. But I've never done something like this."

"You'll do it?"

I look down and press my lips together. I've got a million things going on in the two months leading up to the holidays. Favors for family and friends I've promised, committees I'm organizing. I still need to figure out what to do in the new year for work. But this is Ronan. This strong and stoic man is asking me for a favor, when I can tell he doesn't ask people for help very often. And I think of that little girl upstairs, someone who is desperate for a friend right now.

It isn't my schedule that keeps me from shouting, "Yes!" And it's certainly not the money. It's the fear that living with Belle and Ronan could decimate my heart. I'd have to steel myself against their charm because it would be so easy to fall for them both, even more than I already have.

But they need me. And the one thing I can't resist, my one instinct that I heed over everything—over self-protection, over caution, over being smart—is to help when needed. It's my downfall and drug of choice.

And with his generous offer, I might be able to make my dream of an art studio come true. It could help finance my first year if I'm frugal. If I can get that mortgage. If I can gather the courage.

"I'll do it," I say.

This isn't one of his movies. He doesn't whip me into his arms and twirl me around. He doesn't whoop and fist-pump the air. He doesn't kiss me silly.

Instead, he gives me that wisp of a smile. It's so slight and so subtle that I might have imagined it. But the here-then-gone brush of joy across his face makes my knees turn to jelly.

I'm in so much trouble.

CHAPTER 10

70 DAYS TO CHRISTMAS

Poppy

I SHOW UP TO THE LAKE HOUSE AT 8:00 A.M. THE NEXT morning with two suitcases in the car and carrying two coffees and a bag of cinnamon muffins.

Okay, it's closer to 7:30 a.m. I arrive a little early in the hopes he'll answer the door shirtless again.

I'm almost successful. He appears to be mid-workout. Sadly, he's wearing a shirt, but—bright side—it's a loose tank-top style that doesn't hide his impressive physique. Sweat streams off big, glistening muscles. His hair is brushed back from his face in a ponytail.

There are benefits to being an early bird.

"Good morning! Isn't it a beautiful day?" I thrust a coffee cup and the bag of muffins at him. "I got you a maple latte. It's the coffee shop's new flavor for fall. You can thank me later. And the muffins are fresh this morning from my favorite bakery. You've never had a cinnamon muffin until you've tasted this."

He takes a sip, then winces.

"This isn't coffee. This is dessert." He holds it as if it's a ticking time bomb.

"Don't glare at me like I'm kicking puppies. You said you like sweets. I'm offering you a cup of autumnal goodness, one of life's perfect pleasures. Only a monster wouldn't love it."

I'm tempting him on purpose. After hearing about his sad nutrition regimen, I've decided it's my life's goal to corrupt him. Seduce him to the dark side of sugar and carbs. I'd like to seduce him to other things as well, but we all have to start somewhere.

"Come on." I smile, waving a muffin in front of his face. It's gooey with cinnamon glaze. "You know you want a bite."

Ronan's eyes flare, and I'm caught in his burning polar gaze. My breath catches and heat pools low. In my panties.

"You gotta live a little, Mr. Strong and Silent," I say, breathless now.

His strong jaw clenches. "Where are your bags?" He ignores my muffin, darn him.

"In the car. I'll grab them." I could use a cooling down, and it feels downright wintery out there today.

"No, I got it." He brushes past me and steps out the door. My body goes tingly in the places we touch.

"You're wearing shorts and a tank top. You'll freeze," I protest.

He doesn't deign to answer, just jogs down the stairs of the porch in that casually athletic way he moves, strolls up to my car, opens the trunk, and pulls out my oversized suitcases as if they're tiny handbags.

"You should lock the doors," he admonishes.

I laugh. "This is Snowflake Harbor. I don't think I've locked a door in…ever." I follow him back inside, admiring how his forearms pop and the effortless way he manages my heavy bags.

"What did you pack in here? Boulders?" He leads the way up the stairs to the second floor. I follow closely behind.

"A girl needs shoe options. And art supplies."

We walk down the hallway past Belle's room.

"This is yours," he says, opening the door to a bright room with expansive views of the lake beyond.

I wonder if he's in the room next to mine. I'll save that thought for tonight, when I'm alone. I'll imagine him in bed, naked, on the other side of the wall. My imagination tells me that he sleeps in the buff because my imagination is nice that way.

"Thank you for carrying my bags. It was very manly of you."

He tips his chin.

"Where's Belle?" She hasn't made an appearance yet, which is unusual for her.

"She's getting dressed. She's thinking about what shade of blue to wear."

"Well, color is an important consideration. I was obsessed with yellow at her age."

"Big surprise." Sarcasm drips from his words.

"What? Why do you say that?"

"I don't know. It's…a happy color."

"Exactly!" I slap his arm in enthusiasm, feeling a jolt of electricity at the contact. "That's why I love it! Alas, it wasn't a good look for me, so that love affair was short-lived."

"I doubt that." His gaze traces over me, and I shiver in response.

"With this red hair? It's a struggle."

"It's not just red. It's more...cinnamon," he says after a pause. "Shot through with caramel."

I start to giggle. "You're describing the muffin I brought you," I gasp out.

He shakes his head, a smile peeping out. It's enough to brighten my day. My month. My year.

"You're impossible." But he says it like a compliment.

I turn away and look around the bedroom to gather my composure because the reluctant affection in his gaze has my thoughts scattered.

"Sorry, no yellow in here." Ronan gestures to the room.

There *is* a distinct lack of yellow—or any other color, for that matter. It's white on beige, beige on white, and the odd shade of cream thrown in. It is, however, light and airy, with a huge picture window and nothing else competing for the magnificent view of the lake. I can imagine waking up in a room like this, having a cup of coffee in the cozy—white, of course—chair in front of the window, and sketching the way the light falls on the water. I imagine inspiration comes easily for an artist with a view like this.

"Will it do for a few months?"

"I think I'll manage in this hovel." I grin. I'll save my opinion on the absence of color and personality for another day.

When I turn back to Ronan, I realize that the room is smaller than I first thought, or, more likely, that he's bigger. His presence sucks up all the space, and I become acutely conscious of the bed.

"Poppy, you're here! You're really my new nanny!"

Belle rushes to me for a hug.

I kneel to her level. "I'm glad. It's going to be fun, little one."

"I like these." She touches my dangly green earrings. I changed about ten times this morning, trying to figure out what a nanny-to-the-stars should wear, especially when I have a crush on that star. It had to be comfortable and casual enough to suit my actual job but still look cute for Ronan. I settled on my favorite jeans and long-sleeved cream top. The fabric is soft, and the sleeves are romantic and flowy.

"Thank you. They're good-luck earrings."

"They are?"

I nod. "They were a gift from my sister at my first-ever gallery show."

"What's a gallery show?"

"It's when an artist frames and puts up their work for other people to look at and maybe buy."

"Oh! I'd never want one."

"Why not?"

"I wouldn't want people to see my pictures. I'd be too embarrassed."

"You should never be embarrassed about anything you create. I used to feel the same way and still do sometimes, but it's also fun and exciting."

"Did people buy your art?"

"Some of it."

"Have you had another show?"

"No. That was in college. There hasn't been time for painting or shows lately."

Ronan's gaze feels like a brand on me.

I stand up. "Now, Little Miss Magic, let's go and get your hair done. Something tells me you've decided on your style for the day."

"But can you really do braids? As good as Daddy?"

I smirk at Ronan.

He raises one manly brow.

"Maybe," I say.

Ronan tilts his head. "You think?"

"You haven't seen my skills," I brag. "I have a twin sister. I had a partner to practice with every morning. Let's show your dad what we girls can do!" I high-five Belle, and she takes my hand to lead me to her room. Ronan follows us into the hallway, and before we cross the threshold, I turn to peek back at him.

He stands by the stairs, still in his loose shirt and workout shorts, still gorgeous. But the look on his face is like nothing I've seen before.

There's humor and affection and something deeper.

Something that makes me wonder how I'll keep from throwing myself at him during these next few months.

IT SEEMS ALL MY WORRY ABOUT FALLING FOR THE SEXIEST Man Alive is for nothing.

You can't fall for someone you never see, sexy or otherwise. Ronan has barely been home since I moved in over two weeks ago.

Every morning, I wake up a bundle of nerves about seeing him. I spend thirty minutes on makeup, only to wash it off again because I'm hopeless at anything besides mascara and a slick of gloss. Then I practice calmly and casually making morning small talk.

I can't get over the idea that I might get to see Ronan Masters at breakfast. So, every morning, I show up in the kitchen, and…nothing.

On the first morning, he left me a note saying he had an early 5:00 a.m. call. He left detailed instructions on bedtimes, routines, and emergency information. He even listed a local doctor, the number for the hospital, and Belle's blood type. I'm impressed by his organized thoroughness.

But then I remember his stringent workout and nutrition routine posted on the fridge and how his personal items are never out of order in the house. Beneath his quiet exterior, I suspect he's a control freak, which I find hot, in a master-of-his-domain sort of way.

For almost two weeks, the trend of disappearing dad continues.

He's up before I am in the morning and home after I go to bed. We communicate via notes on the kitchen table.

I doodle on mine.

He doesn't.

He leaves spending money for incidentals.

I leave baked goods.

Belle leaves sweet notes and paintings we create together, telling him about all the things we do with our days. She tells him about how we're baking our way through the *101 Holiday Cookie Recipes* we found at a used book sale. About how Mr. Nguyen and Mrs. Peel from the senior center pretend to hate each other, but we think they are secretly in love. And about how much she likes being the star student when I take her to my art classes.

He writes her back with his own attempts at drawing that make us laugh and make my ovaries quiver, just a little.

He calls Belle every night to say good night.

And we text throughout the day. I share anecdotes and photos of us at home and around town. He shares updates from the set.

Despite the communication, Belle misses him more and more each day. In my mind, he's gone from Hottest Dad Ever to Dissapearing Dad. Belle tries to keep up happy appearances, but I see the look in her eyes when it's just me reading her a bedtime story. She had a meltdown last night when we couldn't find her stuffed puppy Biscuit, and I know it's not just her puppy she's upset about.

I remind myself that it's not my business. He knew his shooting schedule would be intense, which is why he hired me. But I admit to myself, it's not just Belle who wishes he were here.

Luckily, keeping busy distracts me. So when Belle's asleep, I try to catch up on my painting. And baking. Which is why, at 11:00 p.m. on a Friday night, I find myself perching on a step stool to reach the muffin pans for my next midnight baking session. Tonight, I'm making banana nut muffins.

I reach for the top shelf above the stove. Strong arms come around me.

"Eeeep!"

Large hands grip my waist, and I'm plucked from the stool and set on the floor as if I weigh no more than a toddler. Which is definitely not the case.

"Ronan!" I breathe.

My heart races in surprise that he appeared in the kitchen just as I was thinking of him, as if I conjured him up from one of my many daydreams.

Long blond hair falls around his razor slice of a jaw. His eyes are softened by faint lines of fatigue bracketing them. And the set of his shoulders, rounded slightly, is so unlike his usual stance. There's a bone-deep weariness to him. A Nordic warrior returned from a long battle, needing the arms of a good woman to welcome, soothe, and make him believe in home. I volunteer as tribute!

"You're going to kill yourself on that stool." His low growl skates across my nerve endings. Equal parts soft and steel, it turns my stomach to quivering jelly.

"You're home!" I exclaim. Okay, it's closer to a squeal. It's squeal-adjacent. I force myself to be too-cool-for-school, as the elementary kids say.

"The muffin tins won't get down from the cupboard by themselves. It's not my fault this house was designed for giants like you," I say tartly. But I can't hold back my wide smile.

I'm just the nanny.

He shakes his head and grabs a tin from the cupboard. No stool needed. "This one?"

"That's a pie tin."

He tries again.

I shake my head and bite my lip to hold in a giggle. "Cake pan."

He grunts and pulls out something else from the cupboard.

This time, I can't hold back. "Cookie sheet." I gasp, laughing. "Try the one with the holes for the muffins."

He gives me a flat stare and reaches back in. Finally, he comes out with the right one.

"Why didn't you tell me that in the first place?"

"First, who doesn't know what a muffin tin looks like? And second, I was having too much fun."

He rewards my sass with one of his half smiles. I love the subtlety of his expressions. Learning them is like mastering a foreign language—an ancient, valuable code to crack, which holds indescribable riches.

Just. The. Nanny.

"It's a little late for this, isn't it?" He makes a valid point.

"I'm making muffins to take to the senior center. Belle and I are going in the morning. But I also wanted to finish a batch for you. I found a website with recipes for disgusting baked goods that are right up your alley. These beauties are made with flaxseed, gluten-free flour, honey instead of sugar, and extra protein." I make a face.

"You're baking for me?"

"Of course. Trust me, Belle and I aren't gonna touch that batch. Our muffins are vastly superior, made the way God intended them to be, with real flour, butter, and sugar."

He ignores my tirade against his nutrition obsession and swallows. "Thanks."

"You know," I say as neutrally as I can manage, "Belle really missed you this week."

He rubs his neck. "I hate this schedule, but we've had more technical issues. I only have a few hours to sleep and then have to be back on set at six a.m. But I'm hoping to be home in time for dinner tomorrow."

I tamp down the happiness that I'll get to see him. That Belle will get to see him, I correct. "Good. That's really good."

He picks up the Christmas mug on the counter.

"I hope you don't mind that we've gotten festive," I say. "I know it's very early and you aren't staying here for Christmas, but Belle wanted to surprise you with some holiday decorations. So I brought a few boxes of decor that I had in storage at my parents' house. It must be Snowflake Harbor rubbing off on her."

I've tried to be restrained since I know this home is temporary. But Belle was so excited.

He gazes at the mantel, with its eclectic collection of pumpkins and snow globes. And then he looks pointedly at the twinkle lights that now decorate the edges of the large kitchen windows.

"Everyone loves twinkle lights," I said defensively.

He gives a short laugh. "I'm just not used to it. It's nice for Belle. Thank you."

My posture relaxes. I hoped he wouldn't go full Grinch

on me, but I couldn't be sure. I overstepped, I know. If he'd been home this week, I would've asked if it was okay to decorate.

"Belle's already wondering if you'll be getting a Christmas tree this year," I say. In for a penny, in for a pound.

"It doesn't make sense," he says with a frown. "We won't be spending Christmas here."

I nod, not surprised by his answer.

"I'm sorry I've been gone so much."

"I love being with your daughter. We've been having a blast together."

"Still, you deserve a day off."

My heart plummets. Of course. When he's back, he's not going to play family with the nanny. He'll want one-on-one time with Belle. I need to remember my place.

"You're paying me more than enough to make up for the time," I say, reminding myself that we're not a family. This is a business arrangement.

He turns toward the stairs. "I have lines to memorize. And then I have to get a few hours of rest."

The house feels empty when he leaves.

Just. The. Nanny.

CHAPTER 11

57 DAYS TO CHRISTMAS

Ronan

"I'M OUT OF HERE," I SAY, GRABBING MY BACKPACK AND hoisting it over my shoulder.

"Leaving early?" my costar Sebastian teases, blowing on a hot cup of coffee, probably his tenth one of the day. I've had more than my share of coffee today as well. For warmth. It's freezing, spitting rain, and we've been shooting at a lakeside location all day.

"I've been on set since five-thirty a.m.," I grumble. "Where was your sorry ass this morning?"

He shrugs. "I had a late night last night. I can't help if the girls didn't want to leave."

"You better be careful, Blake," I warn.

Sebastian Blake, the son of Hollywood royalty, was once a child star, but he burned a lot of bridges when he turned eighteen and—in the time-honored tradition of child stars—went wild on sex, drugs, and drinking. He eventually cleaned up his act and landed his role in *The Wanderers,* which rebuilt his teetering career and polished his bright star. In the last few years, however, that shine has begun to tarnish again.

"Careful is boring," he says lightly. "What about you, Masters? Getting any with the ladies? You've been quiet lately."

"He's always quiet, Sebastian. Leave Ronan alone," my other costar, Chase James, defends me with a roll of his eyes.

"No, not his usual grumpy shit. This is different. I think he's got a woman."

I snort. "You don't know what the hell you're talking about. When would I have time for a woman?"

Sebastian shoots me his trademark careless grin. "Deny it all you want, but last time you brought Belle to set, she couldn't stop talking about some chick named Poppy. Is she your local piece? Are you fucking her?"

I lean forward, grab him by the shirt, and say softly, "Don't. Talk. About. Poppy."

Though Sebastian isn't a small guy, he isn't as big as my six-foot-four. He works out, but he doesn't train like I do, and he hasn't studied martial arts for the last twenty years. We both know I could kick his ass if I was so inclined.

"Okay, okay. I'm just joking around."

"Joking or not, she's off the table." I let him go.

He smooths his shirt. "This was five hundred dollars. You stretched it out."

"You're the dumbass who spent five hundred on a shirt," Chase snorts.

"Like you don't buy expensive shit. Besides, I didn't spend a dime of my money on it. I haven't bought clothes since we started this franchise. Designers just send it to me, and Emma decides what I should keep," Sebastian says.

"How has Emma been working out for you?" Chase asks, changing the subject.

"She's good," I say.

Emma is great. But it's been weird. I'm used to being independent. But now I need an assistant, nanny, babysitters, a tutor, and a maid.

Having people in my business is uncomfortable. Growing up the way I did, with a mom who had mental health and dependency issues, reinforced my private nature. I hid how we lived when my mom was in a bad phase and self-medicating with pills and alcohol. When she was struggling, I made dinner with whatever I could find in the house and forged my school permission forms. I didn't confide in friends, and I never invited them to my house. I got used to keeping people at a distance, and over the years, it became second nature.

Until Belle. And Poppy. *Temporarily,* I remind myself.

Now, I don't just have employees to assist me like Emma. I have people waiting for me, expecting me at home. It complicates things, this eagerness to leave work, the disappointment when shooting runs so long that I'm not able to greet Belle or Poppy in the morning and I'm not there to say good night.

The longer the franchise continues, the harder it is to sync up everyone's schedules, which means we're trying to squeeze a six-month shoot into less than three months. For the first time in my life, I have other people to consider, and the guilt of falling short with Belle is crushing me. So tonight, I'm determined to arrive before her bedtime.

I say goodbye to my costars and drive home in the dark as fast as I can and still be safe. Over the years, I've learned a lot from the stunt drivers on my films. But unlike many of the stuntmen I know, I don't live for the powerful rush of adrenaline. Stunt work was just a job. One I'm good at because of my size, fight skills, and methodical nature. It was just dumb luck that it put me on a path that led to money and fame.

When I pull into the long driveway, a sense of peace washes over me as the rolling lawn spreads out and gives way to tall trees and the lake beyond. Many of the trees have lost their leaves, but there's beauty in their stark shapes against the moonlit glow of the water. The house glows as well, and I see the light in the kitchen is still on.

I look at the clock on the dash and breathe a sigh of relief. Six-fifty p.m. I've done it. Every night, I wanted to make it home before Belle's bedtime, but every night, I failed. I even missed Halloween. Belle had dressed up as Elsa from *Frozen* in a costume that Poppy's mother made her. Poppy sent me photos.

Tonight, though, it's still early. They might even be eating dinner.

I try to tamp down the eagerness and open the door. I walk into a scene that's foreign to me, except on television or in my daydreams as a kid.

There's the smell of something delicious cooking on the stove and the warmth of a fire, music coming from the house's old radio, and Poppy and Belle in the kitchen laughing. When my footfalls alert them to another presence, they turn, startled.

"Daddy!" Belle runs toward me and hugs my leg surprisingly tight for such a wisp of a girl. "You're home."

Emotion clogs my throat. When has anyone been this excited to see me? The enormity of my situation slams into me with far more weight than a forty-pound girl. Fatherhood was thrust on me, but I still don't know what the hell I'm doing. It's a constant round of being off-balance and unsure of myself. But here she is, happy that I'm home, even as guilt eats at me for my absence since we started filming.

When we first arrived in Snowflake Harbor, I didn't have a regular babysitter or nanny, so we became even closer than we'd been in LA. Belle got used to coming to set with me every day during pre-production. It feels wrong now not to see her every day. How quickly she's become an integral part of my world, which makes this even more dangerous.

What will happen when her mom comes back for her? How can I give her up again? If I fight for custody, there's no guarantee I'll win. The odds aren't in my favor since I've been absent from her life for so long. But if I did win, I'm not sure what kind of life I could offer her. I have no clue how to be a regular father. I never had one. Plus, I'm rarely in one place for long. Belle needs a situation that's more stable than I have to offer. It's her shit luck that Claire, her mother, isn't any better. It seems that Belle spent more time with her nannies than with her mom.

I shut the door firmly on that dark train of thought. I can't change the past or know the future, so I need to live in the present. I know the value of having single-minded focus on the here and now, and it's saved me more times than I can count. If I had a religion, it would be that.

I give Belle a half-hug, half-shoulder pat, feeling awkward with her affection. She tilts her head up and smiles, and the weight of fatherhood gets both heavier and lighter at the same time. Yes, this responsibility is the hardest burden I've ever had to carry. But it's not a load I'll ever put down. I can't. Being a father is now an intrinsic part of me. *She's* part of me.

Blinking, I look up to see Poppy watching us. Her

cinnamon curls are falling out of her ponytail in wild strands. Freckles blend with the pink of her cheeks. Her hazel eyes are soft.

"You're home early," Poppy observes. She sounds breathless, and I wonder what she's like after a night of sex, after I've pleasured her for hours. I go hard at the thought, remembering the kiss we shared the night of the wedding.

She's off-limits now. That much was certain the second I made her my daughter's nanny. If I remind myself often enough, I might finally remember it.

"We're making pizzas. Do you want one? Or is that not on your nutrition plan?"

It isn't. I'd have to do an extra workout to make up for it. But fuck it. "Do you have enough?"

"Here, Daddy." My daughter holds out a red rolling pin. "Poppy says we have to roll out our own dough."

I make a mess of rolling a ball of sticky dough on the parchment paper Poppy passes to me.

They laugh at my misshapen pizza pie, and I pretend to be offended. It feels almost like we're a family. I have to remember this is all just temporary.

Pizza sauce and grated cheese are in bowls, as well as cut-up vegetables and pepperoni. Poppy loads her pie with every topping. Belle makes hers with sauce and cheese. I spread on a little sauce and fill mine with veggies. I'll have to eat one of my nutritionist-approved meals before I go to bed, but I don't have another shirtless scene until next week, so I'll take this small treat.

Poppy eyes up my pizza. "That's a little sad."

I shrug. "Maybe. But I only have to be really disciplined when I'm training for a role or filming."

The ripped body Hollywood expects isn't possible without extreme measures. Even for someone as large as I am, it takes intense training, discipline, and even dehydration to have the proper muscle definition the audience wants to see.

"And how often is that?"

"Almost always," I admit. "But my delivery meals are pretty good."

She raises an eyebrow.

"Well, maybe not good, but they're passable," I amend.

"What about when you wrap the movie? You said you'll be done by Christmas."

Belle hops up and down. "That means on Christmas you can eat all the cookies you want!"

I laugh at her excitement.

Poppy slides the pizzas into the oven on a large slab that looks like a pizza stone. Another thing I don't recall us having.

"Where'd we get that?" I ask.

"I brought some of my kitchen items. I put them in storage when I moved into my parents' place. I hope that's okay," she says with an uncertain smile. "This kitchen only had the basics, and I love to cook."

"I gave you money. You could have bought whatever you needed instead of bringing your things from home," I point out.

"I know. But you're only here a short time. It would be a waste when I have it all sitting in boxes in my parents' basement."

"So were you staying with your parents because Derek broke up with you—and you were the one who had to move?"

"Yes."

I need a few hours with my boxing gloves and a bag.

My feelings must show on my face because she says, "But

it worked out for the best. That townhome was never my style anyway. He chose it."

"Can I set the timer again?" Belle interrupts my darkening train of thought.

"Sure," Poppy says. "Do you know how to set it for twenty minutes? I'll lift you up."

My daughter glances at me with a giggle. "Daddy's better at lifting me than you."

"Your wish is my command," I say, feeling one thousand feet tall that Belle prefers me even to Poppy, whom she adores.

I lift her, and she turns the dial.

"Now it's time to take a bath," Poppy tells Belle as I set her down. "And we'll have to wash your hair tonight. When you're done, the pizzas should be ready."

"Do I have toooo? You always make me wash my hair. But Daddy only has me wash it once a week."

Poppy looks at me, startled.

I rub my jaw, feeling like a teen busted for not doing my homework. "Ah, yeah, sometimes we forget that step."

"Yes, you have to take a bath *and* wash your hair. It was hard to brush it this morning. Washing and conditioning will help."

"I see you had trouble with the hair today," I tease. It's a lie. Belle's hair is immaculate, with braids circling in a crown around her head, secured by glittery pins. I'm not sure I could do as well, even with all the other dads on YouTube helping me out. But I won't tell her that. I'm enjoying this too much.

When was the last time I teased a girl? With my intimidating size and reserved nature, few people feel comfortable enough around me to joke and laugh. But with Poppy, it's easy. Fun.

"Is this a competition?" She asks.

"Maybe."

"Belle, who do you like doing your hair better? Your father, with his big, clumsy paws? Or me? Who gave you the triple twist braid bun? Hmmm?"

"I object. That's leading the witness." The little cheater. I'm competitive, even in the art and science of hairstyling.

Belle bites her lip in serious thought, then grins shyly. "Both," she proclaims, pleased with herself.

"Very well played," Poppy says with a laugh. "Now, go to your room, and I'll be up in a few minutes to help you with your bath."

I watch my girl run up the stairs and marvel at the change in her. Like me, she's lighter, happier.

I turn my attention back to Poppy and can't help noticing that she looks good in formfitting denim that's faded and frayed. Her T-shirt proclaims that "Artists Do It Better." I want to find out if it's true. Her feet are bare, with toes painted a surprising red, making me wonder if maybe she has other surprises hidden beneath her casual clothes.

She gazes at me expectantly, and my mind draws a blank. My brain waves are still focused on what type of underwear she prefers. I immediately decide on white cotton, with delicate flowers, soft and pretty yet practical. But maybe, just maybe, her racy nails echo in her choice of lingerie. Skimpy, delicate red lace. It's a conundrum I'd love to unravel.

I rub my jaw, trying to banish the sexy images that keep popping back up like the whack-a-mole game I once played at a local fair.

"Are you sure you don't mind getting Belle ready for bed while we wait for the pizzas? I need to look over the revised script for tomorrow. Then you can take the night off, and I'll put her to bed. You deserve some time to yourself. I haven't been around much."

"Oh—of course. You must want some time alone with Belle," Poppy says, but her smile seems forced.

"No. I don't mean—Not unless—" And that's when I realize that this is different. She is different. With the other nannies, as soon as I got home, I couldn't wait for them to retire to their room. I hated if they lingered after dinner, wanting to talk or flirt. It's usually awkward having a stranger in my space. I can't relax or breathe easily, and Belle normally prefers it to be just us.

But this is Poppy. I want her to have dinner with us. I want her to laugh and smile as we put Belle to bed together. I want to walk back downstairs and listen to her talk as the fire roars in the hearth and the wind blows outside. Peace and companionship. Friendship and heat. It's something I've never known, never knew I even desired.

Now, I see how many empty spaces there are in my life. Spaces that Poppy and Belle are filling.

"When we were in California, we started playing cards at night," I say. "Would you want to play a game tonight with us?"

"Sure, like Go Fish?"

"I've been teaching her poker," I explain. And then realize how that sounds.

"You've been teaching a seven-year-old poker?" She tries to look disapproving, but she's fighting a smile.

"She's really good. She's like a card-sharp savant."

"I'm good at poker, as well. My dad taught me to play, and he's merciless," Poppy boasts. "Winner gets to choose the book for story time."

"It's a *deal*," I say with a straight face at my terrible joke.

"Ronan Masters, your fan club will be so disappointed.

First, you can't rescue us from an elevator, and now, instead of sarcastic wisecracks, you're telling dad jokes."

But she doesn't look disappointed.

She looks at me in a way that turns me inside out. And that scares the hell out of me. Makes me think that it's safer to walk out the door with Belle and not stop until we're back in California.

Poppy

I'm eating dinner with Ronan Masters. I'm playing poker with Ronan Masters. I'm living with Ronan Masters. That refrain has been playing in my head all night, throughout our simple, sweet night of pizza, poker, and bedtime rituals.

I try to chill myself out, but I catch myself watching him, marveling at how large he is, at the icy blue of his eyes and the slash of dimple in his right cheek on the rare occasion he laughs. I recall him laughing a lot tonight. He's different—relaxed, open.

After putting Belle to bed, I'm my typical awkward self. Ronan and I chat outside her door. Our whispers make it seem more intimate than it is. He asks if I'm going downstairs. For a moment, I hope he's asking because he wants me to keep him company. But I can't tell from his wary expression, and even though I'd give up triple chocolate chunk ice cream for a night in his company, he probably wants the house to himself.

I'm an employee. He has to share his house with a stranger. Of course he wants to chill rather than make small talk. I imagine he spends a significant part of each day fending off admirers. The poor guy doesn't need one more in his home.

So instead of spending the rest of the night sipping wine in front of a romantic fire with him as I'd like, I sit in my new room, *dreaming* about doing just that.

To keep myself from rushing back downstairs, I call Sadie.

"I've been thinking about you. Was he home tonight?" No "Hello" and "How are you" for Sadie. She believes in getting straight to the point.

I've talked to my friend every night since I arrived here, and every night I've had to disappoint her and say that Ronan came home after I was in bed.

"We ate dinner together, then we played a game and put Belle to sleep. He's so freaking hot and quietly funny and nice, and I have a full-blown crush. This is bad," I say, flopping into the bed. I whisper-squeal all this into the phone because I'd be mortified if Ronan overheard me.

"I knew it. I knew he would be like that." Sadie sighs. "Is he like he was in that movie about the spies? You know the one, where he mostly grunts, but you can tell by the tone of his grunts and the way he stares longingly at the heroine and how he's all gruff and protective that he's secretly sweet and sensitive underneath all those muscles?"

"Um, sort of?" I fib. Because she nailed it. That's exactly what he's like. But I'm mindful that I need to walk the line between sharing with Sadie and protecting Ronan's privacy.

"Poppy O'Brien, stop being vague."

"Okay, okay!" It only takes two seconds to break me. I guess it's not so bad for her to know he's perfect. "Yes. God, yes. That's exactly what he's like. *Exactly.*"

I close my eyes. "But I'm just the nanny, and not even a

real one. I'm temporary. I need to keep a professional distance."

Sadie laughs.

"What?" I say, offended.

"Poppy, you're many things. Sweet and loyal. A do-gooder. And you have puppy-like enthusiasm for the things you love. But you are not good at keeping a professional distance. You treat every person you meet as if they were your long-lost best friend, or you adopt them and try to solve all their problems."

"That's not true." Well, maybe it is a little. "You think I'm like a puppy? I'm not sure how I feel about that." I think for a minute. "What kind?"

"A golden retriever," she says right away. She's clearly considered this before.

"Huh." I can't be mad. They are super cute, and I do have reddish-gold hair. "Thank you. I think." I pause. "Well, you'd be a—" I shake my head even though she can't see me. "You'd be a cat, not a dog."

"I don't like cats," she snorts. "*You* don't even like cats."

"I do, just not as much as dogs. You're like a cat because you're independent and you don't take shit from anyone. Plus, I'm not one hundred percent sure that you actually like people, despite being in the retail business."

"That's exactly why I dislike people." She exhales a heavy breath into the phone. "Fine. Maybe I am more like a cat. But don't change the subject."

The silence lengthens until I break it with a soft, "Sadie?"

"Hm?"

"Am I going to get super hurt when this is all over?"

"Probably. But what's the alternative? You wouldn't be you if you didn't jump in and try to help, Poppy. Besides, you'd be the stupidest girl in the world to pass up this experience."

"Even if it ends with no man ever living up to Ronan Masters and me being by myself forever and dying alone?"

"Stop being so dramatic. We can live together when we're old and alone. I'm a cat lady, remember?"

"True," I agree. And with that life plan sorted, I change the subject.

"So what did I miss on Main Street today?"

CHAPTER 12

42 DAYS TO CHRISTMAS

Ronan

I HOBBLE UP THE STAIRS, FEELING LIKE A ONE-HUNDRED-YEAR-old man. I spent my day and night waiting for hours for my scenes, punctuated by brief bursts of activity and pain.

Though I started as a stuntman, the more famous of an actor I've become, the more producers have discouraged me from doing my own stunts, citing it as too much of an insurance liability. But I still insist. It's my thing.

The fans love it, and it adds authenticity to the scenes. I think of Poppy giving me shit about being an action hero who failed to save the day in the elevator. I smile, and then I wince because it even hurts to smile.

Today was one of those days I wish I hadn't insisted on doing the stunts when I signed on to film this. There wasn't anything too risky. The director, producers, and insurance company would never allow that. But I've got bruises and sore muscles from being slammed against a wall a hundred times. And worse, it doubled the hours I had to be on set.

It's been a month since Poppy arrived, and with each day, it gets harder to keep my distance. I've had to stop myself from calling her a dozen times today. I wanted to hear her say hello in her cheerful way and find out how her day is going with Belle.

But I didn't. I even slowed down on texting, keeping our messages strictly confined to Belle. I'm worried about how much I crave her company.

I miss Belle, and that's troubling enough since I don't know how long I'll have her. But I miss Poppy as well. And that isn't something I'm prepared to handle. There's been too much change in my life as it is.

I open the door to the lake house, frowning that it isn't locked. Anyone could break in. I need to remind Poppy to use the extra locks I installed.

I walk into the quiet dark of the house, and my mood plummets. I'd known the time, known I would be too late to see Belle's shy smiles and hear her chatter about the day. To have dinner like we've had a handful of times. But tonight, she'll be asleep by now. The most I can do is to check in and risk waking her.

All day, I'd hoped I'd be done by late afternoon. Everything was smooth until the end, when there'd been last-minute rewrites.

My bag falls with a soft thud. I grab a glass and get ice from the ice maker. I turn at a sound, and every sense that had been tired a minute before goes on high alert.

"Hey," I say, attempting a cool composure. My eyes aren't sure where to look first. At long, pale, bare legs or red hair that curls wildly around her shoulders. She clutches a pale-pink robe that ends mid-thigh.

I avoid the dangerous areas and look into her eyes, then remember too late that those are a danger as well. They look more green than gold tonight. Ice from the ice maker overfills my glass.

"Oh, shit." I bend to retrieve the small cubes scattered across the floor. I reach to get a piece that's rolled under the bar and touch Poppy's hand as she also reaches for it.

I look up to find her staring at me.

"Welcome home," she says and drops the ice we both reached for into my palm before hopping up.

I stand with less dexterity, every bruise and muscle protesting, and try not to wince.

"Are you okay?" Her brow is knitted in concern.

"Fine," I grit out.

"Do you want dinner?" she asks. "It's just chicken, pasta, and broccoli, but I saved some for you. I also made whole-grain pasta." She makes a face as if it offends her.

"Thanks," I say, touched. "I appreciate it. But I ate on set. We were waiting forever for the rewrites to come through."

She tilts her head. "Frustrating day?"

I roll my tight shoulders, trying to relax. I have nothing to complain about. I have a place to sleep. A job I mostly like, even if it can be a pain in my ass, literally. And I have a healthy daughter, even if I'm terrified of being her dad.

"It's all good."

"Belle missed you," she says with a frown.

"Yeah?" She wants to say more, I can tell. I wait.

"I tried to keep her up as long as possible, but sleep won out."

"Don't do that. She needs her rest." An emotion cuts through me, sharp and destructive as a blade.

"She wanted to stay up. I'm only sad she couldn't quite manage it tonight."

I clench my jaw and look away.

She lays a warm hand on my sleeve. It burns me through the thick fabric. "I told her you had to work. She was just disappointed," she says softly, reassuringly, but also with gravity.

I know firsthand just how damaging it is when someone is not enough. When a person gets let down, over and over. Especially someone as needy and impressionable as a child. That's my family legacy. And now here I am, repeating the cycle. I need to balance my responsibilities to my job, one I have an ironclad contract to complete, with the needs of this little girl whose life is now in my hands.

I know something needs to change. I can't cut out all the hours on set, and I can't quit, but maybe I can shorten the days by having my stunt double take on more of the work. I vow to talk to the director about it.

I don't say any of that to Poppy, though. It's my problem to manage.

"Do you want a drink?" I ask, wishing I could have something stronger than water tonight. Sitting by myself is the last thing I want right now, which is odd. I prefer silence to voices. Except I crave her company.

It's as if Belle carved open my heart, and in the crack she made, Poppy wandered through.

Her gaze meets mine, then slips away. At first, I think she's going to refuse and I'm more disappointed than I should be. But then she lets out a breath and nods.

"Okay. Yes, thank you," she says.

"Great." I feel like I won the lottery. "What do you want?" The house has a long mahogany bar with a row of cabinets and a large wine fridge. "I'm not even sure what we have. Emma had the house stocked when we moved in."

"Oh, you have enough alcohol to keep a college fraternity happy for a very long time," Poppy says. "I've already dipped into the white wine. I hope you don't mind. You said everything was fair game."

"Of course." I open the large wine fridge to investigate. "What the hell?"

"I told you." She laughs. Bottle after bottle of wine and champagne fill the fridge. "I guess someone thinks that Hollywood stars need to be set for a party at any moment. And you don't even drink." Poppy's eyes twinkle up at me.

"I do occasionally," I say, distracted. "Just not during training." I open a cabinet, looking for a wineglass.

"Here." Poppy moves behind the bar.

Her arm brushes mine as she leans down, and an electric current runs through me. I try not to let my gaze linger like a creeper where her robe parts. I can see the soft material of her nightshirt clinging to her petite curves and valleys.

She opens a different cabinet and pulls out a glass. "The red wine is over here if you feel like going wild." She stands, and her cheeks turn pink. Is she as affected as I am by that brief touch?

"When I do drink, it's hard and clear, like vodka."

"More yummy wine for me, then. You make me want to corrupt you," she says innocently.

I can't help but wonder if she's talking about more than just the alcohol. My mind turns to all the ways she could corrupt me, with her coppery curls, full lips, and ever-changing eyes.

I pour her a generous glass of white wine. Then, after a moment's deliberation, pour myself a vodka from the row of liquors lining the bar.

She smiles. "You're walking on the wild side tonight. But I can't believe you drink that stuff straight."

"Not with just any vodka. But this is smooth. Try it." I hold out the glass, wanting her lips to be where I'd just had mine.

She sniffs and then wrinkles her nose.

I think she's going to refuse, but my breath catches as she licks her lips. She takes a sip.

When she's done, she steps back, and I feel the loss. She breathes out shakily. A hand goes up to the loose V-neck of her nightshirt.

"It's better than I imagined," she says.

She grabs her glass and I follow her into the living room, trying, and failing, not to notice the way her waist curves in and her ass curves out, the way her wild hair tumbles over her shoulders.

The room's wooden walls take on a warm tone with the glow of the fire. And so does her hair. With the fire going, it's hot in here, almost over-warm. But maybe that's just me.

She stands awkwardly, as if waiting to see where I'll sit, but I don't move. Our choices are leather club chairs next to the fire or a long cream sofa in a velvety soft material. I've had fantasies about taking her in both spaces.

But I can't. I'm not in a place where I want a relationship, I remind myself. And I don't need more complications. So getting involved with the nanny would only lead to heartbreak. If it were just my heart on the line, it would be one thing. But it's Belle's heart that's at risk, if her favorite new nanny left us because I messed up and couldn't keep my dick in my pants.

Which is why I shouldn't be doing this.

Poppy sinks into a leather chair, and I take the one opposite her. At least it's not the sofa, I think.

When we're settled, I stare at the fire. So I don't stare at her smooth bare legs.

"What are you and Belle doing for Thanksgiving?" She finally breaks the silence.

She must read the answer on my face because she says, "Oh, Ronan," like she's chastising a small child. "But what about Belle? She'll be sad to miss it."

Great. I rarely celebrate the holiday. I get invitations, but making small talk with acquaintances over an interminable meal isn't my idea of fun. But then again, I'm annoyed by most holidays. All the expectations and the inevitable disappointments. The biggest expectation is that a person has a family. Which I don't. At least, I didn't until now.

"Belle's been living abroad. I doubt she's even heard of Thanksgiving."

"She's seen all the signs and decorations around town. She wants to try turkey and pumpkin pie."

"Shit." The last thing I want to do is to disappoint Belle. Now, I have no choice but to figure out how to give her a traditional Thanksgiving experience like Norman *Fucking* Rockwell.

"Maybe..." Poppy smiles.

"Maybe what...?" I repeat warily.

"Maybe you two can come with me!" She claps her hands like Belle might. "To my family's for Thanksgiving. It will be fun!"

"No—we'll be fine."

"Psh. Are you kidding? My family would be in heaven to have you there. Especially my mom. She could brag about you to her Zumba class. And Belle will be in heaven. The adults will spoil her rotten, and she'll have my neighbor's daughters to play with. Plus, we'll have all the turkey and pumpkin pie she could ever want."

I scrub my hand over my face. "We can't. That would be too big of an imposition." I leave the rest unsaid. That she's an employee. It isn't her place to invite us, and it isn't our place to accept. It would break down barriers, ones I desperately require. Ones that are already fraying and on the verge of collapse.

Plus, I hate pity invites. It's easier just to be on my own than play the outsider for the day.

But Poppy's expression tells me she's not about to take no for an answer. *Hell.*

She crosses her arms. "What are you going to do instead?"

"Belle and I can hang out together. I've barely seen her this week. It will be good to have the whole day with her. If she wants pie and turkey, I can order some in."

With a mighty frown, Poppy leans forward until our knees almost touch. I hadn't realized how close our chairs were positioned together. Her eyes glow in the dim light, and the fire burnishes her hair into a red-gold halo. "Thanksgiving isn't just about turkey and pie, as heavenly as they are. It's about family." Her gaze slides away. "And friends."

"Is that what we are? Friends?" I ask, my voice rough.

"I wouldn't enjoy Thanksgiving if I thought of you two here by yourselves." she ignores my question.

She lifts her head, and it's all there in her eyes. Her sweet determination. Her stubborn kindness. Hell, maybe this is a pity invite. But being a father means setting aside my discomfort and pride to give Belle what she deserves. And yes, there's a part of me that wants to spend the day with Poppy. She radiates sunshine, and Belle's not the only one who basks in that light.

"You won't give me a choice, will you?" I hedge, though the battle's already won.

At that, she peers at me with a small smile. "What do you

mean? You're Ronan Masters, action star and heartthrob. I'm just a nobody who works for you. How could I make you do anything?"

"Bullshit." The word is nothing but a forceful breath, but I can tell by the flare of her eyes that she hears it.

Since the night we first met, she's become the center of my thoughts, enthralling me as much as she enthralled my daughter.

Her dissecting gaze splits me open, as if she can read my thoughts, discern my secrets. Even I don't know all that lurks beneath my calm. Maybe I don't want to know.

We're leaning so close that we're almost touching. Her gaze turns to the scarred skin on the back of my hand.

"What's this from?" She rubs the line of my scar with her fingers.

"One of my first jobs doing more than just fight scenes. I hesitated jumping off a building, and I got caught in the cross fire of explosives. I never made that mistake again." I say it casually to mask that I'd like to throw her on the couch and show her every last scar.

Her hand touches my forearm. "And this one?"

That brush of skin feels so damn good, I struggle to understand what she's asking.

"Knife. I was young and stupid and spent time in underground fight clubs."

Poppy's hand smooths my marred skin, as if she can wipe away the memories with her touch.

She leans and strokes the scar that bisects my eyebrow. Interviewers always ask me about it. Fans debate whether it's from a bar brawl, a stunt gone wrong, a car accident. But no one gets it right, and I've never talked about it.

"Lost a fight with a glass table when I was eight sleepwalking."

I grit my teeth against the horrifying urge to tell her more. That my mom was passed out one night, from her usual cocktail of prescription medicine and alcohol, and I couldn't wake her. That head wounds bleed like crazy. That I spent the night trying to stop the blood, praying to God, petrified I was going to die. The cut never healed right because it never got stitched up.

"Ronan," she says softly. Just my name. But it's everything.

I've never wanted to unburden myself to anyone before. But even though I keep the words in, it's like she hears beyond my silence; she sees me and all I hold back. I close my eyes. There's a string tightening between us, and I can't stop the pull of her. Just a few more inches and our mouths will touch. I close my eyes and give in.

The fireplace gives a loud crackle, breaking our connection. My eyes pop open at the sound. Poppy's eyes are wide. I can see every green and gold swirl.

"Poppy. Shit. I can't—" I don't finish the sentence because what can I say?

I can't, even as I want to. I can't kiss you, fuck you, be with you, even as I'm dying to with every inhale and exhale.

"Oh, um." She jerks back and stands in one unsteady move. I jump up to balance her, my hands landing on the soft curve of her hips, almost encircling her. She lets out a gasp. I want to sink my fingers into that yielding flesh. Want to urge her closer, bury my face against her stomach and go lower.

I force my hands to drop away.

She takes a step back, then another. "It's late. I better get to sleep," she mumbles. "I'm sorry for pressuring you about Thanksgiving. I know you have other offers and better things to do. And I'm sorry for being nosy. I'm—"

"We'll go."

"What?"

"I said we'll go to Thanksgiving." I look at the hearth, at the strong, silent wood that blisters and burns and turns to ashes from the touch of a flame.

"Belle will enjoy it," I add. Am I justifying the decision to her or to me?

"I'm glad," she says. I think she's going to say more, but she doesn't. "Good night, Ronan."

"Good night." My eyes follow her departing figure as she makes her way up the stairs. When she disappears from sight, I turn back to the fire, wondering how long I can keep denying the heat between us.

CHAPTER 13

31 DAYS TO CHRISTMAS

Ronan

It's not that I've never experienced Thanksgiving before. I've sat through my share of turkey and pie. But I prefer to pretend that Thanksgiving is just another day. I wish I could do so again this year, I decide, as I walk into Poppy's parents' loud, hot, crowded house.

Why is their house so small? And how does one person have so many cousins? I stoop to avoid a ceiling fan as Poppy introduces me to a litany of relatives.

The truth is, I'm not good with people, especially large groups of them.

Belle, however, is glowing. If she smiles any harder, she might crack open, pure joy pouring out. Poppy's mother has already welcomed her with a big hug and introduced her to a crowd of kids.

I'm relieved. Earlier this morning, Belle had a tantrum while getting ready. I think she was nervous, but once we arrived, those nerves disappeared.

A smooth hand slips into mine and squeezes. Poppy looks up at me in encouragement, as if she can feel my unease, as if she is silently bolstering me. It works. I stop thinking about everyone else. My entire focus narrows into the electric space of our clasped hands, our eyes connecting, the heat of her body next to mine in the small hallway.

"Sorry," she whispers. I lean down until her lips come closer to my ear. "My family is a little overwhelming. We won't give you a quiz on their names, I promise. Though you probably met most of them at the wedding—or at least, they remember you." Her hazel eyes twinkle. Her dress is the dark yellow of fall leaves. It dips into a deep V that pulls my gaze.

"Poppy!" Her mom bounds back into the hallway with a playful slap to her daughter's arm. "Why are you keeping this big hunk of a man to yourself? You, my girl, are needed to sort out your aunts' mashed-potato debate. And Ronan needs to relax."

I follow Poppy's mom. Or, more accurately, Poppy's mom drags me into the heart of the living room, where I'm pushed down into a sofa that engulfs even me. My legs, though, stick out so far that they attract a group of young children who decide that I'm some sort of human jump rope, or perhaps a limbo stick. They jump over my legs on one side, then crawl under them from the other, giggling the entire time.

One small child crawls up my leg and launches herself onto the couch next to me. She reaches up and tugs at my sleeve. I look at her.

"Hello," she says. She has Poppy's red hair and freckles. The genes in this family are strong.

"Hey."

"You're really big."

"I know," I reply, not sure what else to say about that.

It seems to satisfy her. She scampers off.

I turn to watch Poppy. She's in the corner of the living room, presiding over an argument between two older women, whose hands are flying in passionate gestures. She sees me and grins, then follows the women into another room.

"They're going into the kitchen," a husky voice says next to me. It's Poppy's father, who I recognize from the wedding. I didn't meet him that night, but she pointed him out. Poppy favors her mom, with her red hair, deep dimple, and vivacious smile. But her bright hazel eyes are just like her dad's.

"Her aunts argue over the mashed potatoes every year. One insists they're too lumpy, and the other gets mad and says they shouldn't be whipped any more. Then they both complain that we don't own a potato ricer, whatever that is. Every year, we get lumpy, glue-like potatoes, but we never buy the damn potato ricer." His grin is mischievous, like a little boy's. "We take bets each year about who will win."

"What do they need Poppy for?"

"What everyone needs her for. To keep the peace and make people happy."

"And who keeps Poppy happy?" I can't help asking.

"She's always happy," her dad says, his bushy eyebrows forming one line.

I think about his answer. Is she? Poppy gives that impression. But in my experience, people aren't that simple. At her sister's wedding, she drained glass after glass of champagne to cope as the man she thought she'd spend her life with danced with another woman. That he was there at the invitation of her family was a betrayal. Did her parents think she couldn't be hurt just because she hid it so well?

"She wasn't jumping for joy when you invited her ex to her sister's wedding. You didn't invite him today, did you? No disrespect, but if he comes and makes her upset, I'm throwing him out. Just thought I should warn you." I have no authority to say that. I'm not her family. I'm not her anything, except for her employer. But that doesn't matter. I stand by my words.

Her dad's eyes widen. I turn back to the kids, who are now playing some version of hopscotch across my feet.

"No. We didn't—We just thought—" He takes a quick breath. "He won't be here."

"Good," I grunt.

Her father shifts back into the couch. "I agree it wasn't the best decision to invite him to the wedding. We thought they might get back together if they were at a romantic event. They'd been with each other for so long. We all assumed that the breakup was temporary."

"He's an ass. Poppy deserves better."

"Y-yes. He's out of the picture."

"Good," I say with satisfaction, folding my arms over my chest and watching for Poppy to reappear from the kitchen, as if I can make her show by sheer will.

"So." Poppy's father clears his throat. "You're leaving in a few weeks?"

"We leave on December 23, so you'll get your daughter back for the holidays."

His shoulders relax. "That's good. That will give her a little time off before the next school session starts. There's a fourth-grade position opening at the elementary school. Being a full-time art teacher was never viable in this small town," he continues. "We tried to tell her that in college, but she insisted on doing a dual major and keeping art."

"It's what she loves."

His eyes glint. "That may be true, but it's not practical. The arts are disappearing at most schools. Luckily, there's always a need for classroom teachers. She's a little confused now, after losing her job and then what happened with Derek. It was a double blow." He sighs. "What she needs is a steady position and to find a nice fellow here in Snowflake Harbor, and she'll be right back on track."

I feel my temper rising at the thought of Poppy being pushed into something other than her chosen field. And at the thought of Poppy with another man. I take a deep breath and unclench my fists.

It's not my business. Despite my protective feelings toward her, I know Poppy loves her family and has a good relationship with them. Getting into an argument with her dad over her career goals is not the way to start off the afternoon. I'd already pushed the limit with my comments on her ex.

I channel my patience, willing my resting tough-guy face to relax.

"Poppy says you collect *Star Battle* action figures." She told me earlier that her dad was obsessed with the classic sci-fi franchise.

He smiles widely, and I'm reminded of Poppy's grin, which dissipates some of my annoyance toward him for wanting her to hook up with another hometown boy.

"I've been collecting them since the eighties. Have you seen all the movies?"

I nod. "I shot a movie with the director. He liked to talk about his early days filming *Star Battle*."

Her dad's eyes get a fan-guy gleam, and he peppers me with questions for the next twenty minutes. He's a stronger interviewer than any journalist I've met.

"George!" Poppy's mom calls to her husband from across the room. "Come and help me with the turkey."

He sighs. "It was nice chatting with you, but duty calls. The turkey and my wife wait for no man."

I watch his departing figure. He kisses his wife on the forehead, and she gives him a small hug in return. I wonder what it's like to be part of a loving couple, a well-adjusted family. I've rarely seen examples of that in my life, certainly not in my own family. My father left my mom when I was just a baby. And Hollywood couples tend to be the opposite of well adjusted.

"Now you've done it." I turn to find Poppy grinning down at me. I didn't see her leave the kitchen. It must have been while I was distracted by the *Star Battle* inquisition. I want to grab her to me and count her freckles.

I frown, struggling to recall what she's just said. "I've done what?"

She sinks next to me on the couch, the side of her body warming mine. "You'll never be free of my dad's clutches now that you've talked *Star Battle* together. But I just came to tell you we'll be eating in about fifteen minutes."

I look around. "Have you seen Belle?"

"She's outside playing with the neighbor's kids."

"And did you settle the great mashed-potato debate?"

She laughs. "You heard about that, huh?"

"I hear you're the mashed-potato whisperer." I smirk.

"I know my way around a spud."

"I bet you say that to all the boys."

"I say that to none of the boys." Her wide smile dims. "My big family is probably a point in my disfavor when it comes to dating." She shrugs. "But I want a guy who will want me, overly involved family and all."

"Have you started dating again? Your dad wants you to

get back out there," I say, my lips pressing together in a flat line.

It shouldn't matter because I'm leaving for good in a few weeks, and it's not like I'll have a reason to visit again. The thought doesn't make me relax, though. It just makes my gut churn harder.

She groans. "My parents are relentless, trying to fix me up. I've given in once or twice," she admits.

"And?" The need to toss her over my shoulder, claim her as mine, and ransack cities in her honor rises up.

She shrugs. "It was underwhelming. It doesn't help that I'm in a small town. I've known most of the single guys my age since we were kids. They're more like brothers than romantic prospects."

Everything in me exhales.

She looks down, then peeks up at me shyly. Flirtatiously, even. "But there might be someone new to town who *is* interesting."

I want her to mean me. So fucking bad. Because if she doesn't, it means she's interested in someone else, which I sure as hell don't want.

But if she does mean me, it's even worse. Because it will be that much harder to stay away from her.

It's a dilemma. *She's* a dilemma. One I don't know what the hell to do about.

CHAPTER 14

31 DAYS TO CHRISTMAS (STILL)

Poppy

"AND THEN MARYANN DARED ME TO STUFF *FOUR* COOKIES INTO my mouth—the ones with the powdered sugar—and I did!" Belle chatters happily, sitting up in bed, rosy from a bath, her wet hair plaited in a loose braid, and wearing her embroidered pajama bottoms that came from France. I know because I checked the label. We paired her fancy bottoms with the "Gobble Gobble" Thanksgiving T-shirt that my grandma gave all the kids.

"Four, huh? That's very impressive." I smile at her, and my gaze seeks out Ronan. My stomach free-falls like I'm on a roller coaster at the soft way he smiles down at his daughter. Belle asked for both of us to put her to bed tonight, and I certainly didn't object.

"Ha! That's nothing," Ronan says with a boastful grin. "I could do ten."

"Liar. Only if they were high-protein, low-sugar, whole-grain cookies. Then maybe," I tease him.

He makes a face at me and tickles Belle.

"Daddy!" She giggles.

He swallows, his eyes suspiciously bright. I know how much it means to him when she calls him that.

Ronan leans down and kisses Belle on the forehead, then tucks the sheets around her, adjusting her stuffed dog, Biscuit.

"Good night, Belle."

"Good night, Daddy," she repeats.

As I lean down for my turn to kiss her, my shoulder brushes Ronan's. Heat tingles along the path as our limbs intersect.

"Good night, pumpkin. And I can call you that because you've finally tasted pumpkin pie," I say.

Belle makes a face before her trained politeness kicks in and her expression smooths out. "It wasn't my favorite," she says diplomatically. One of her nannies must have been rock solid in teaching manners because all the seven-year-olds I know would have cried "ick" if they didn't like something.

"I agree with you, kid," Ronan says. "There's a reason people only make it once a year. It's one time too many."

I bump Ronan with my shoulder. "Hey, don't knock it. I love pumpkin pie."

Belle giggles again, not looking at all tired. I fear this will be one of those nights with a dozen curtain calls. Requests for water. For a snack. For anything and everything to delay sleep.

"Good night, pie monster. See you in the morning." I walk to the door and flip the light switch, bathing the room in darkness except for the soft glow from the night-light on her desk.

I turn to see Ronan give a last kiss to his daughter's forehead. I step into the hallway, and he pulls the door, leaving it open a crack.

It feels far too intimate, the two of us standing together in the dark.

"Thanks for the day," Ronan says. "Belle obviously loved it."

"Of course. I hope it was okay. I know my family is a little much." I'm whispering so as not to disturb Belle.

There were multiple times tonight that felt surreal, having him at my parents' home surrounded by my relatives.

I was worried in the beginning. He'd seemed uncomfortable, especially when he was talking to my dad, who, with his many opinions, can come on strong. But, gradually, as the day wore on, Ronan relaxed. He laughed at jokes and gave as good as he got with my large, loving family. He even played tag with all the kids, who were delirious with delight when they caught their favorite action hero, tackling him to the ground in cheers and fits of laughter. And Ronan didn't go running into the night when the men wanted to take turns arm-wrestling him. He took it easy, not demolishing them at the first count of go.

Now that he's been in my parent's house, I feel closer to him. My family means everything to me. And by inviting him into that space, I invited him further into my heart. If it had been a test, he would have passed. Spectacularly. And that scares me.

He tilts his chin down. Our eyes meet.

The space gets narrower. Time and distance shrink until it's just us. His eyes, the blue of glaciers, pull me in until I'm drowning in a clear lake of feelings. Across, I can see forever. Below, there's no bottom.

I weave closer, and he leans down, our coming together inevitable.

Heat flashes in his eyes, those glaciers melting, and my breath catches. Closer, infinitesimally closer.

And I think he might—I think we will—I close my eyes because thinking a complete sentence is no longer possible. I can only feel.

And then—

Nothing. Again.

My eyes pop open, and though he's only moved back a few inches, he's no longer in my force field.

My fuzzy mind can't compute what happened, both in the slow almost coming together and the abrupt breaking apart.

It's as if I stumbled upon shelter after wandering through a frozen wasteland. The glowing house. The heat from a fire. Every bounty I could ever want right there to take. And then, just as I'm at the threshold, the door slams shut in my face. I wonder if I imagined it all.

He clears his throat, looking away. "Excuse me. I have to study some lines for tomorrow."

"You have to work tomorrow? It's not a holiday?" I ask, disappointed. But he's shooting a movie, not on vacation. It's why I'm here, getting paid a ridiculous amount to be a nanny to his daughter.

He shakes his head. "I'm sorry, I thought Emma sent you my updated schedule. We're behind and need to catch up so we don't have to return after Christmas." He doesn't meet my eyes. "At least it's not another four a.m. call, but it's a complicated action sequence, so it might run late. Is that okay?"

"It's fine. Thanks for letting me know." The space

between us feels uneasy now, the connection we'd had all day gone.

He nods.

"I'm going to—" I point to the door to my room. I hadn't planned on retiring so early. It's only 8:30 p.m., and I'm not the least bit tired, but I feel in the way now, an interloper intruding on his space.

"Well, good night," I say.

"Night."

I feel his eyes on me my entire walk down the long hall to my room at the end. I will myself not to look back.

I shut my own door, softly but firmly.

CHAPTER 15

24 DAYS TO CHRISTMAS

Poppy

I THOUGHT AFTER THE ALMOST-KISS, THINGS WOULD HAVE been awkward, but I worried for nothing.

Because once again, Ronan becomes an absentee parent, a thief in the night.

Every day that Ronan misses being with Belle, she gets a little sadder. Every day that he isn't there to say good morning and he isn't there to kiss her good night, a little more of her sparkle leaves. I've tried my best to distract her. We have fun together. But I can only do so much. She wants her dad.

So, this morning, I'm elated when he calls to let me know that he only has a half day on set today, and that he plans to be home early. When I tell Belle the good news, she can't contain her excitement.

We keep occupied by doing the writing lessons her tutor in Los Angeles put together and then going to the park, but Belle keeps an eye on the clock and asks every hour what time her father will be home. I tell her all I know is sometime this afternoon.

At 1:00 p.m., we clean up the lunch dishes and settle in to work on her math homework. Then we do a short art project involving reindeer. I smile when we dust glitter across Santa's sleigh, thinking about how Ronan pretends to dislike glitter glue. I see through him.

At 3:00 p.m., while Belle watches a show, I take a shower, blow-dry my hair in an attempt to smooth the frizzy curls, and put on my favorite sweater and jeans. I try to squash the butterflies taking up residence in my stomach.

It's entirely likely that he'll come home and tell me to take the rest of the day off. I should be happy if he does. There's plenty I need to do. I have responsibilities that have nothing to do with my nanny job. I need to prep for my next art workshop. I'm only teaching two a week now, one at Sadie's shop and one at the Kids Creativity Center, and Belle participates in both.

I also promised Sadie I would call the Realtor about the building for sale on Main Street. I'm still not convinced it's viable, but she's right that it won't hurt to look into it.

But as much as I need a day off to get things done, I don't want one. I'd rather spend time with Ronan and Belle, which is dangerous to my heart.

At 4:00 p.m., Belle asks me again when her dad will be home. I suggest a game of War to distract her. War lasts approximately one billion years, so it will keep us busy until he arrives.

But at 5:00 p.m., as it gets darker out, I tell her he must be delayed.

I'd texted him earlier and I keep checking my phone for a response. But there's nothing.

At 6:00 p.m., we make dinner. She creates place cards for each of us, carefully decorating the cards and writing our names. I even help her light the candles.

At 7:00 p.m., I give up waiting for him. We eat dinner by candlelight, with me asking Belle cheerful questions. Her happy chat has dwindled to nothing, and she answers me in one-word answers.

He seemed so certain that he'd be home early. Objectively, I know it isn't his fault he has to work. Even I, someone who knows nothing about how movies are made, realize that their schedules are inherently chaotic. But he'd said he'd be home, and he knows how much Belle has missed him.

That's when I do what I know to be a bad idea. But I can't help myself. I check social media to see if his fan sites have any information on filming today. I started this habit last week, sitting in my room alone at night. I feel guilty every time I look. It's like I'm spying on him, which I kind of am. But *The Wanderers'* fans are up on every detail of the stars' lives and the movie's production schedule. Normally, there is little news about Ronan. His fandom is remarkably drama-free, just like the star. But today, when I type in his name, photo after photo appears of him with a beautiful brunette wrapped around his large body. The photos, the fans say, are from today.

I read, and my heart sinks as I recognize the woman. She's a famous model. If you believe the superfans, she and Ronan are dating. Some fans hate her, some love her, most call her his friend-with-benefits.

The cast and crew are celebrating someone's birthday with shots of Patrón. And the model-girlfriend-friend either has a small part in the movie or is on set visiting Ronan, depending on who you believe. The one thing everyone on *The Wanderers'* social media agrees is that Ronan is definitely getting some action, in bed or in his trailer.

I slam my phone down and decide, for my mental health, I won't waste a moment more searching for information on Ronan Masters or worrying about what he's doing. I don't know him at all, no matter what I tricked myself into believing. And this is a good reminder. Belle is what's important, and I need to do damage control. Taking her mind off the fact that both her mother and apparently her father are douche canoes.

At 8:00 p.m., Belle is fresh from her bath and cozy in her pajamas as we read her favorite book, *Anti-Princess*. Reading *Anti-Princess* in her very princess room is somewhat ironic.

A door slams, followed by heavy footsteps on the stairs.

Belle sits up, listening.

"Sounds like your dad is home," I say in as bright a voice as I can muster, shutting the book with a loud snap. Nothing good will come of me showing my irritation.

Belle frowns and sinks back down in her bed. "Please keep reading."

"Your dad can finish the story."

She burrows farther under the covers and pets her stuffed puppy. "He's too busy, just like my mother. She always said she was too busy to read to me, too. She said that's why we have a nanny."

I squelch the urge to stalk downstairs and hit Ronan over the head with the *Anti-Princess* book. I'd also like to say a few choice words to Belle's mom, as well.

"That's not true, Belle. Your dad loves spending time with you."

"I don't want him to read me a story. I don't need him."

It's all the more heartbreaking because she doesn't say it angrily. She says it with simple resignation.

Belle deserves better than this. I thought Ronan was better, but clearly, I was wrong. I've given him the benefit of the doubt this whole time, trying to tell him how much his daughter misses him in a gentle way, assuming he was trying his best. But perhaps I've done them both a disservice.

The door creaks, and I turn to see Ronan standing silently in the doorway. His crystal eyes are opaque, his mouth in a tense line. At his expression, I realize he's heard what his daughter just said.

Our eyes clash, and then as quietly as he arrived, he shuts the door with a soft click. "Wait," I say, but it's too late. He's gone.

"I've been waiting all day," Belle says in a wavering voice. "I just want you to finish the story."

"But your dad—" And I realize she hasn't seen him and doesn't know he was in her room.

"He has more important things to do," she says matter-of-factly.

Anger flows through me. Did Ronan have me fooled? I thought he was a genuinely good guy. The way he braided his daughter's hair. The way he carried Belle and looked at her with such softness that first night we met. He hadn't seemed like the typical Hollywood playboy. When we spoke, he expressed regret and frustration about his busy schedule, and I believed him. But the man I thought he was is not the same man who would disappoint his little girl in order to party with a model.

And instead of making things right, he retreats when confronted with the consequences of his actions.

I finish the story, trying my best to make Belle happy again, but nothing works, not silly voices, tickles, or jokes. I almost wish she would cry or complain, but she doesn't. The resigned sadness tells me she's used to feeling like this, passed off to the hired help when the people who should love her are too busy. When I'm done with the story, I reach over and turn out her light.

"Stay with me?" she asks.

I nod, even though she can't see me in the dim light. I lie down on top of the covers, stroking her hair.

"What's wrong with me?" Belle asks into the silent night.

"What do you mean? There is absolutely nothing wrong with you," I say, turning toward her.

"Then why doesn't my mom want me? Why doesn't my dad?"

And that's when my heart breaks into a thousand pieces.

"You're perfect, just as you are." I sigh. "I'm sure your mom loves you, and so does your dad, even if you two haven't had much time together. But sometimes…sometimes it's the adults who aren't perfect. And they make mistakes." I'm unsure how to explain the complexity that is life and love.

"Like when my mom left me with my dad because her boyfriend doesn't want a daughter?" she says.

I don't know how to answer that.

"No one thinks I'm listening because I'm small. But I always am. It's the only way I learn anything important."

"I believe it, honey. But you shouldn't have to do that. You shouldn't have to learn things that way."

She shrugs, a slight movement I feel more than see.

"Your dad loves you," I tell her. I know he does. Even with his questionable decision-making, I've seen it on his face. "And you know what? I do too." I squeeze her shoulders.

I can feel her big, serious eyes on me. "I love you, Poppy," she says solemnly. "But you're my nanny, which means you'll leave soon. My nannies never stay long."

"It doesn't matter how long we've known each other. You're in here." I press her hand to my heart. "And once you're in my heart, you're part of me and part of my whole family. I'm an O'Brien, so you're one of us now. You can't escape an O'Brien that easily."

"Really?" Her voice is full of something I recognize. Something that sounds like hope. Tremulous, but it's there.

"Really," I say. "Once you've had Thanksgiving with us, you're stuck for life. You can call me, write me, or visit me anytime you're allowed."

"I want that to be true."

I smile. "You'll see."

"Promise?"

"Promise."

And maybe what I said is reckless. She's right; I'm just the nanny with little power or control over her situation, so I shouldn't be making promises. But I vow to do whatever it takes to make sure that Belle knows what it feels like to be loved and important while I'm here and for as long as I'm able to after they leave.

Once Belle's breathing turns even and I know she's fallen asleep, I tiptoe down the stairs. I was tempted to turn right and go straight to my room, but I need to keep my promise to Belle. Which means I need to have a conversation with Mr. Masters. My stomach flips with nerves at the idea of a confrontation. But this is too important to back away from.

My footsteps falter at the bottom of the staircase as I hear a noise from the kitchen. It occurs to me for the first time that Ronan might not be alone. He could have brought his model home. This is his house, after all. The urge to run and hide in my room is almost overwhelming. But Belle's tear-stained face makes me square my shoulders and forge on.

I pad into the kitchen on bare feet, pulling at the sleeves of the sweater I put on earlier. So many hours, so many emotions ago. Then, I'd felt almost giddy with the crush I'd formed on Ronan. Now, I regret being that naïve girl.

I want to believe there's a logical explanation. That he'd been working. But I saw all the party photos of him doing shots with his coworkers, and I saw him with that model. In one series of pictures, she was even sitting on his lap. He said he would be home early to spend time with Belle, and he hadn't even called to say he would be late. I can't explain that away.

When I see him, he's alone. There's no model. He's looking out the window at the falling snow, holding a glass. He could be a man in a whiskey commercial, with his beautiful profile, brooding at the window, drink in hand. But then the differences emerge. He's not drinking whiskey like some sophisticated playboy; he's drinking a glass of water, looking defeated.

All my anger holds and falters on a pinpoint, and when he turns and looks at me with eyes that are red-rimmed with fatigue and what looks like pain, my anger shifts, turning and gentling in my heart.

I'm still upset for that little girl upstairs, but I can't pretend that he's the Hollywood party boy I'd built in my mind tonight. I can't pretend he doesn't care about Belle. Maybe he made a mistake, but everything he's shown me up to this point says he's trying his best, even if his best isn't always good enough.

All the things I've been dying to say to him since I saw those pictures online stick in my throat.

"Hey," I say. Quiet and unsure now.

He runs his hand through his wild, long hair. "Hey." His eyes slide away.

"She didn't mean what she said upstairs. What you heard." I wish I could leave it at this. The part of me that hates confrontation, that always wants to be nice and kind and never make people uncomfortable, cringes.

But I need to say this for Belle, even if my emotions are tempered.

"She's upset because she was looking forward to you coming home early. We made a special dinner. She even decorated a sign. She's been missing you a lot, and with her background with her mom, she struggles to trust because she's afraid to be disappointed."

"Fuck," he says and lets out a breath. "But I didn't—I never promised her—"

"You told me you were going to be home early. I took you at your word and told her you'd be home."

"*Dammit.*" He doesn't yell. He doesn't even raise his voice, but there's simmering emotion in those soft-spoken words. "I'd planned on it. But the schedule got shot to hell today. That happens." His eyes narrow. "Which is why I never told Belle I would be home early. And I never told *you* to tell her."

I feel his frustration coming off him in waves. In the time I've known him, I've never seen him anything but calm. His reserve keeps his emotions behind an icy barrier, away from the world. But that reserve is cracking.

I sift through the words of our conversation. "But you never told me *not* to tell Belle. And you didn't look like you were suffering in the pictures of you partying it up with your *friend*."

His stormy eyes narrow. "What are you talking about?"

"I saw it online. The model was sitting on your lap while you were doing shots."

He takes a half step forward. "What were you doing looking me up online?"

Some of the heat leaves me, and guilt and embarrassment surge up. "I was trying to find out why you were delayed. You didn't answer my texts, and I didn't know what to tell Belle."

"She's not my *friend,* as you call her. She has a part in the movie. I didn't get your texts. My phone has been having trouble getting a signal lately. I'm sorry if you couldn't get through to me. But I gave you backup numbers. You could have called them and talked to me directly."

Silence echoes around us as he looks down, and I can almost hear him counting to ten. He finally lifts his head, his gaze meets mine, and I feel chilled all over. "I don't like drama." His tone is as icy as his eyes. "You didn't need to stalk social media in an attempt at playing gotcha. What's happening here?"

"Nothing's happening," I say, defensive now. "But the news said you wrapped early and there was a party. It looked like you were having a *really* good time."

"Some people finished early and let off steam." His normally quiet voice goes hard. "I didn't. It's Francesca's birthday, so there was a cake and shots. Francesca is sleeping with Sebastian, not me. I don't know what pictures you saw, but she likes attention and she likes to flirt, especially when she's been drinking. I shut her down and left the second I finished my last scene."

My anger dissipates, and I'm left deflated. My anger was for Belle. But I can't lie to myself. A part of it was also fueled by jealousy.

Because I like him, darn it.

The big jerk.

I stare at him, trying to make sense of my conflicting emotions.

Frustration is evident in his weary-looking eyes.

"Maybe I should have taken her up on her offer," he says softly. "I haven't had a single damn day or night to myself in months. So if I want to stay out all night and get laid, I can." He stares down at me with barely contained tension.

And just like that, my anger is back in full force.

I advance on him. "No. You. Can't." With each word, I poke him in the chest. "You have a little girl upstairs who is devastated because she's been waiting for you all day. I know you're working insane hours. And I'm sorry if I told her you'd be home when maybe I shouldn't have. I know you're burned-out and exhausted. I get it. But you have to do better if you don't want to damage Belle any more than what her mom has already done."

I lean even closer until I feel the heat of him. "Beneath all her cuteness and her spunk, she's sad and lonely and vulnerable. She needs you. What she doesn't need is to feel like an afterthought. She's already been dumped by one parent. She might not continue to be the same loving little girl if her heart gets broken again, and this time by her father. It might not be your fault, but life isn't fair, and it's up to you to fix this. A movie or some hookup is not more important than your daughter's heart, so you are just going to have to figure it out."

Ronan is frozen. Is he angry, in pain, or just annoyed that the temporary nanny overstepped her bounds?

I can't regret what I've said, even if I wish I'd had more tact. But I stand by the truth of my words because I'm trying to protect Belle. And though Ronan doesn't realize it, I'm trying to protect him as well. Because, despite everything, I know he wants to be a good father, and in the long run, it will shatter him if he fails his daughter.

I've seen too many students who've turned into a shell of themselves because of family issues. I patch up the kids as best as I can, offering them a comforting space, somewhere they feel seen, valued, and loved. Somewhere their pain can get an outlet in the art therapy I call lessons. I'll always dedicate my everything to help them overcome their losses and make sure their scars don't define their future in devastating ways.

I know from experience. I'm not sure who I would be if my seventh-grade art teacher hadn't helped me after my dad had a heart attack. She's long since retired, but I vowed to be that light for other children. I'll be that for Belle.

Even though Belle is so much younger than I was, I see the familiar pattern in her. Rarely sharing her feelings, pretending she doesn't need anyone—there's deep hurt just below the surface that she's determined to mask.

That pattern is also Ronan's, I realize. He's got his own mask of chilly indifference back on.

My hand falls from his chest. After that first flash of anger left, my anxious mind is already bent on doing what I always do. I want to soothe and smooth things over.

I'm still jittery from the former flash of adrenaline as I reach into my teacher's bag of tricks. The positive reinforcement. The compliment sandwich. The clear expectations. They work when I command a classroom full of students. They work on defensive parents when their child won't follow the rules. Will they work on a movie star? That remains to be seen.

Ronan hasn't responded to my speech; he just watches me.

I clear my throat. "That was a good talk." I nod as if the matter is settled. "I'm sure you'd like to know how to make this up to Belle. Getting her a Christmas tree would be a fabulous start. Belle told me she's never decorated a tree before. You're a loving father, so I know you'll do what makes her happy. I'm sure you can find the time to get a tree together and decorate it. Even if you won't be here for Christmas, it will mean a lot to her. It's such a nice thing for you to do," I praise.

Ronan watches me warily, poised, a prizefighter ready for another round.

Set clear expectations. "I have complete faith that you will find the time to do this for Belle."

I nod as if it's settled, turn, and make my way up the stairs, and it might be my imagination, but I feel his confused gaze following me the whole way up.

CHAPTER 16

22 DAYS TO CHRISTMAS

Ronan

"SO WHAT YOU'RE SAYING IS YOU NEED TO LEAVE EARLY because you're in trouble with the nanny?" Sebastian cracks up. He turns to Chase. "Chase, did you hear this? The toughest dude on the planet is in deep shit with the nanny, and so we're all rearranging our schedules."

"I'm not in trouble with the nanny," I growl.

Okay. Maybe I am, but I don't need to share that level of detail with them. I talked to the director weeks ago about needing to spend more time with Belle and asking him to reduce my hours on set. We talked about me doing fewer stunts. Unfortunately, my requests had gotten stalled somewhere. Today, I'd had a more *urgent* discussion with production, and this time, actual changes have been fast-tracked.

"And we're not rearranging everyone's schedules. I'm just not doing as many stunts. And I'm not putting up with production wasting my time waiting on everyone else when they show up late and screw around." I stare pointedly at Sebastian.

"Admit it. You have a hot nanny. You've been all over your phone with the same moony smile Chase gets when he talks to Olivia."

I glare at Sebastian.

"Sebastian," Chase says lazily. "Do you remember when you asked me to warn you when you were pushing things too far?"

"Yeah."

"You're pushing things too far. A little more and you're gonna get punched by Ronan, and I wouldn't blame him for it."

"You're always on his side," Sebastian grumbles.

"Just trying to help, man."

"So?" Sebastian asks. "What did Abrahms and production say about your requests?"

"That they're going to make it work."

"Abrahms is a dad too," Chase says. "I'm sure he gets it."

Francesca struts over and leans down, her arms coming around me. I do a side step, trying to disentangle myself. I don't mind Francesca, but she's gone too far in her flirting with me lately. My guess is it's to make Sebastian jealous. But I can't risk another picture of us getting out on social media.

I recall Poppy's anger the other day. She was a warrior for Belle, fierce and protective. I was defensive; I admit it. Disappointing Belle like that broke me in ways I still can't fully process. All my fears about not measuring up, not being able to be the father she needs, came true. And I shut down.

But the more I think about it, the more grateful I am for

Poppy confronting me. She did it because she cares about Belle. Enough to make me upset and jeopardize her well-paying job. No other nanny would have done it. Most of them are more concerned about buttering me up than taking care of my daughter.

I can admit that Poppy is right.

I need to do better. I'm used to work being my life. I thought, by hiring a nanny Belle liked, I satisfied my duty to her and she would be fine while I put in long days filming. But as great as Poppy is, she's no substitute for a father.

Belle is my first responsibility, for as long, or as little, as I have her. I can't let fear of getting too attached and having her ripped away keep me from doing what's right. Nothing else matters as much.

I can't drop the movie, but I *can* try everything to make the schedule better. Working was my life. But now, I am a dad, and I have other responsibilities beyond my career.

"So where are you headed?" Francesca asks. "Want to come out with me? Have some fun."

"I can't. I have plans."

"Maybe I can join."

I look over at Sebastian. He doesn't seem annoyed that his sometime hookup is hitting on me.

"No. I—we're going to a Christmas tree farm."

"A Christmas tree farm?" Francesca asks blankly.

"Like where you cut down your own tree?" Sebastian makes a swinging motion with his hands.

"Something like that."

"Dude. And who will you be with when you're cutting down this tree?"

"With Belle." I give Sebastian my mean stare. The one that makes my movie enemies quake.

No surprise, Sebastian doesn't even blink. I need to get

less obnoxious costars. "And the hot nanny? Will she be there?"

"Pushing it," Chase warns him again.

I can't hear his answer because I'm already out the door, eating up the pavement with my long strides. It's still light out, a bright blue sky and crisp wintery day. It feels as fresh as a new a beginning. As if anything's possible.

Poppy

I'M IN THE CAR ON THE WAY TO THE CHRISTMAS TREE FARM with Ronan and Belle.

Though I'm just an employee doing a job, it feels like we're a proper family. With Ronan here, I could have this time off. But I wanted to come. And I suspect that maybe Ronan wants me here as well because he didn't tell Belle no when she suggested I join them.

When Ronan came home early from set, he changed into jeans and a dark gray shirt, a long navy-blue coat, and a dark gray beanie. I thought maybe he would dress lumberjack-hot for the Christmas tree farm. Instead he looks like a sexy assassin in a winter-themed Bond movie. His icy eyes and half-day scruff complete the look.

I was worried there would be awkwardness after our fight or that he just wouldn't show. But he was home promptly at 2:00 p.m., when he'd messaged me he would be.

As I predicted, Belle brightened at the prospect of picking out a Christmas tree with her father.

Every year, the farm sets up rides, with Newfoundlands pulling a jaunty red sled. They have a barn with handmade gifts, the most delicious pies and treats, artisan-made ornaments, and hot chocolate.

I know Belle's sadness didn't just disappear, but kids are resilient, and I hope we can use today to help Ronan build back trust with his daughter.

"Are we there yet?" Belle asks, her head pressing to the glass of the car window.

"Almost. Turn here," I instruct Ronan. We pull up to a long driveway that ends with a big red barn. Cut trees are off to one side. Children dart between the booths, and a little stall sells cocoa and cider.

I smile. I've been coming to this farm ever since I can remember, and it's always magical.

"It's like a Christmas movie!" Belle gasps. "Look at those dogs! They're so big! And a sled!"

"The owners breed Newfoundlands. They have them pull a sled for the children."

"Can we take all take a ride?"

"Sure," Ronan says, but he looks dubiously at the sled and the dogs.

"Well, you can have a ride, Belle." I laugh. "I'm not sure they're equipped to take adults, especially not your dad."

We decide to do a tour of the Christmas barn first and end the day picking out and chopping down a tree before it gets dark.

In the barn, Belle runs from one handmade ornament display to the next.

"Can we get them all?" she asks.

I grin. "That's a lot of ornaments. But you know, in my family, we have a tradition. We choose an extra-special ornament to add to the tree each year. It's important to pick it carefully. Maybe you could do that."

"Is it too late to start? I've never had a Christmas tradition before," Belle says. "Or my own ornament. Mother says that's what decorators are for."

Ronan looks down at his daughter and says softly, "It's never too late to start a tradition. Why don't you pick out seven special ornaments?" His voice is hesitant. "One for each year we missed."

I get a lump in my throat when I think about how much time they've missed out on.

"Thank you, Daddy!" Belle throws her arms around his legs.

Initially, he looks taken aback at her enthusiasm, but then he rests his hand on top of her head and a smile of such tenderness unfurls that I have to look away for fear of getting more teary.

Belle picks up a hand-blown snowflake. It's beautiful. And expensive. She has good taste. I grab an empty basket and hold it out to her. "Here, put your favorites in here."

"Rudolph, definitely. And this cute little carved bear with the Christmas story. And this star, isn't it pretty? It looks like fairies made it," she chatters happily.

We end up buying a basketful of ornaments, decor, and all sorts of baked goods, and then make our way back outside into the cool winter air. Belle signs up to make a Christmas craft at the booth run by a local artist I know.

We stand at the edge of the Christmas trees watching her decorate a delicate snowflake, giggling at the antics of the boy next to her.

My eyes lock with Ronan's. He leans into me, and his stubble skirts my cheek. At first, I think he's going to kiss me, and my breath locks. But he just whispers, "Thank you."

"For what?" I ask.

"For giving us this." He gestures around at the magic fairyland that surrounds us. "For pushing me to make changes. I'm really sorry for being such an ass the other night. You were right. About everything. I hope you can forgive me." He runs a hand through his long hair. "Work is all I know. I don't have a blueprint on how to create a good home for Belle. It was just me and my mom growing up, and she had a lot of issues. So, being part of a family is something new to me. But you cared enough to call me out when I was fucking up."

He turns away and blows out a slow breath. "Being a father is also new." He shifts his gaze back to me. "Perhaps Belle has mentioned that we haven't…been in each other's lives for long."

"She said some things to make me wonder. I-I wasn't sure. I thought maybe you didn't have the chance to visit her often."

He shakes his head. "I should have talked to you about this earlier. It might have helped you understand Belle better. But I'm wary of trusting people. I know you're not like Tiffany. But I have to be careful, for Belle's sake."

"It's okay. You don't have to tell me."

"I know I don't have to tell you. But I want to. I trust you. The truth is, I didn't even know I had a daughter until recently. Belle's mother lied—about a lot of things. So Belle and I only learned about each other six months ago. And then her mom left on a trip with her boyfriend and left Belle with me out of nowhere. I'm glad to have this time with her. But I'm trying not to hurt her more than she's already been hurt by this whole situation. I spoke to my director and producer again, and they're changing some things so I can spend more time at home."

His eyes roam my face.

"Spend more time with Belle," he repeats, "and maybe y—"

"Poppy! It's good to see you!"

No. No. No. We can't be interrupted. Not when Ronan is finally opening up to me. Life's not fair.

I drag my gaze from Ronan and look at the interloper, only to see my old friend, Conner. I've known him since middle school. He's a recently divorced single dad with a daughter about Belle's age. The two girls met during my art lessons and hit it off, so I've arranged a few playdates for them.

"Poppy and Belle! Great to see you two." He leans over and gives me a lingering kiss on the cheek and a warm hug. Maybe the hug is a little more than warm. He's always been a flirty guy. He's tall and handsome. As a successful real estate agent, he's considered a catch now that he's single again. But his touch does nothing for me, not compared to Ronan's.

"Oh hey, Conner," I say distractedly, taking a quick step back. He would be a pile of ash now if Ronan's eyes could shoot lasers like they did in the sci-fi flick he made a few years back. That movie also showcased to the world just how good he looks in spandex.

I wish Conner would leave, but he stands there staring at me, so I sigh and turn my attention to him. Maybe if I introduce him to Ronan and his laser-like eyes, he'll go.

"Conner, Ronan. Ronan, Conner."

My boss crosses his arms over his chest.

"Play nice, Ronan. This is your neighbor, and his daughter Sasha is friends with Belle. They had a playdate the other day. I texted you about it."

"Hmm, right." His mood seems to lighten at that. He

shoots Conner a less suspicious glance. "So, neighbor, does that mean you're married?"

Wow. Subtle. Could he be…jealous? I can't help but be thrilled by that idea.

Conner looks justifiably taken aback. "No. At least, not anymore. Divorced," he says. "Last year."

Ronan's friendlier gaze slams back shut.

"And you're friends with Poppy?"

"We went to school together. She was a year younger than me. I had a crush on her." He sends a flirtatious smile my way. "But once she and Derek got together, she never gave me the time of day."

I roll my eyes. "You did not. You had half the girls in our class in love with you. And I don't think your popularity has waned since then."

"Daddy! Poppy! Look at my ornament! And look who's here!"

Belle and Sasha run up together.

I smile at Sasha. "Hi, sweetie. It's good to see you again. Belle, you know Sasha's dad."

Belle smiles shyly. "Hello again. It's nice to see you."

"Daddy, can we go pet the sled dogs and listen to a talk about them? The owner said they're friendly," Sasha asks her father.

We look to see a small crowd of children gathered around the oversize, wagging dogs and an older couple.

Conner nods, ruffling his daughter's hair. "It's okay with me."

"Just be careful," Ronan says. "Dogs can be unpredictable."

"Oh, Daddy," Belle says with dismissive affection.

"And there they go," Conner says. "Seven going on seventeen."

Ronan nods, and for a moment, I think there might be

solidarity between the two single dads. But then Conner's eyes slide back to me, and Ronan steps near, setting his giant hand at my waist, pulling me toward him. I lick my dry lips. The things this man can do to me without so much as a word.

Conner zeros in on Ronan's hand with a surprised expression. He clears his throat. "So, Poppy, are you joining the New Year's parade committee again this year?"

"Oh," I say. "I wish I could, but I'm helping out with the Christmas ball and auction to raise money for the Creativity Center. I don't think I have the time to do both. I'm pretty busy with my new nanny job as well."

"Come on, Poppy. You're always the most important person on the committee. Most of them are only there for the free snacks. You practically organized the parade by yourself last year. You won't let us down, will you?"

I look at my hands, torn. I don't have the time, and Conner is right about one thing. I'm usually the only one to do the work, which is annoying. But I hate to disappoint everyone.

"Um. Maybe I can look at my schedule again," I say. It might be possible if I—

"Poppy," Ronan growls.

"Yes?" His voice halts my mental juggling of my calendar.

"Do you want to organize the New Year's parade this year? Practically by yourself?"

"Not really," I admit. I can't believe that pops out of my mouth in front of Conner, but it does. There's something about Ronan's no-bullshit approach that inspires me.

"But you're so good at it." Conner looks a little shocked.

"The lady said no," Ronan snaps.

"I didn't mean to—"

"Didn't mean to what? Guilt her into volunteering even

more of her time when she's already said she can't? Do you have any idea how much she does for this town? She volunteers at the senior center. She's on a million committees. She teaches free art classes. She's helping with the charity ball. She's constantly doing favors for her family and half the town. If you respect her, you'll respect it when she says no."

"Ronan." I set a hand on his tense muscles, feeling the steel of his biceps beneath my palm.

Mixed emotions roll through me. My cheeks are pink from being the cause of a small scene. But there's also the warmth of someone understanding me, championing me in a way that no one ever has. I'm always being called to volunteer for everything. My parents sign me up for things without my permission—coworkers and friends as well. They assume I'm always available.

And I guess I always have been. With no family of my own, no kids, no husband, people consider me to be endlessly available to meet everyone else's needs. And I've been so busy that it was easy to put my own projects on the back burner. My own dreams and desires.

I square my shoulders, gaining support from Ronan's mountainous presence next to me. "Thank you, Conner. But Ronan's right. My no is firm. I just don't have the time in my schedule right now. I'll let you know if that changes."

Conner nods stiffly with a glare toward Ronan. He won't be showing up at Ronan's door to borrow a cup of sugar. I hope, though, this doesn't affect his willingness for Belle and Sasha to play.

"So," Conner says, changing the subject and filling the silence that has grown uncomfortable. "What brings you here? I can't imagine you need a Christmas tree since I understand you're done filming soon. You'll be leaving before the holidays, right?" Conner says pointedly to Ronan.

Ronan's nostrils flare. "As a matter of fact, we were just about to pick out a tree now." His smile would be considered deadly if he were in one of his movies. It's the one he gives his enemies right before he knocks them out. "And that's the thing about schedules, Conner. They can change."

I look up at Ronan, startled. Did he just imply there's a possibility they could stay later? I decide he's just being contrary to annoy Conner. Even if they do stay until Christmas, it doesn't mean he'd need or want a nanny around while he was off work.

But it doesn't stop me from wishing for my own Christmas miracle and having them a little while longer.

For Belle. Just for Belle.

Can I get on Santa's naughty list for lying—to myself?

Two hours later, we're back at home. We've unpacked the Christmas boxes I brought here from my parents' storage. And we're ready to start tree decorating.

"It looks like a holiday horror movie," Ronan says in disgust as he surveys the destruction of the living room. Every piece of furniture, every mantel, and much of the floor are covered by boxes, bags, and various Christmas decor.

"Why, thank you. That's exactly the aesthetic I was going for," I say. "And thanks for reminding me. We need to have a Christmas movie playing in the background while we decorate the tree. For vibes."

I try not to laugh at his expression. But he doesn't object, so I know he's on board with the movie idea.

I search for the television remote under a mountain of tinsel. "Aha!" I cry when I find it and click through way too many channels until I find the right one. When I find a

Christmas romance, I turn up the volume and let out a contented sigh, which is very different from Ronan's grumpy sigh.

"Now we need sustenance before the decorating starts," I say.

He shakes his head.

Mulled wine and a smaller pan of hot chocolate that I made earlier simmer on the stove. I ladle out some hot chocolate, put it in my favorite Rudolph Christmas mug, sprinkle some marshmallows over the top, add a stick of candy cane, then hand it to Belle. "Make sure it's not too hot," I warn her.

"Wine or hot chocolate?" I ask Ronan. And then I hold up a hand. "Think before answering. If you say you want a green smoothie, you'll be pulled from your bed by Christmas elves and pummeled with candy canes."

"Is that a plot from one of your holiday movies?" he asks.

"Hmm. No. But maybe I'll have to write in to suggest it."

"I'll have the wine. Less sugar."

"Smart man, saving your sugar calories for our gingerbread cookies. Belle and I made them yesterday."

"I did the cutouts," Belle says.

"Nice," he tells her, admiring the misshapen gingerbread man before taking a large bite out of its head, decapitating the poor guy.

"What do you think, Daddy?" She asks.

"Delicious," he proclaims. He takes a sip from his Christmas mug. "The mulled wine is good too. Though I'm surprised it's not eggnog."

"We can't start eggnog season too early," I explain. "We have to progress in a particular order. It starts with mulled wine, then leads into hot buttered rum, and only then are you allowed to break out the eggnog, the final few days until Christmas."

He grunts, but I notice his headless gingerbread man is almost gone and his mulled wine cup is empty. Operation Christmas Tree Decorating is going full steam ahead.

Ronan wanders over to the tree, which we put in a stand earlier. He walks around it with an expression that's somewhere between a frown and a grimace.

"Stop judging it."

"You had me chop down the ugliest, scrawniest tree on the farm."

"Shh," I say. "It can hear you. If you anger the tree, it will actively repel the ornaments. It's a fact."

"I love our tree," Belle defends. "It's cute."

"See, it's cute," I repeat.

"It reminds me of that one in the movie," Belle adds.

"See, it reminds her of a movie Christmas tree," I say with a smug smile.

"Which movie, Belle?" Ronan asks.

"The one we watched the other night. With Charlie Brown. It reminds me of his tree."

Ronan laughs and shoots me an "I told you so" look.

"No one else would have chosen it. It needed a home," I defend. It's really not *that* bad. We already turned it so you can't see the giant bald patch in the back. "Besides, I like a challenge."

"We can put extra tinsel there," Belle says, pointing to the branchless portion. "It's a great tree, Daddy."

"You're right, pumpkin," he agrees.

My knees weaken a little at hearing the term of endearment for Belle. And, okay, using pumpkin at Christmastime is not seasonally appropriate, but I forgive him for the lapse in holiday etiquette because it's so darn cute and also because he's finally admitted that our Christmas tree is great.

I take a sip of the mulled wine to hold back my full-fledged sappy grin.

I can't help it. He looks so big. And manly. And befuddled. Trying to untangle my Christmas lights with a look of intense concentration.

"I love these ornaments," Belle says. She holds up a ballerina in a tutu.

I smile. "Remember when I told you my parents bought me one new ornament every Christmas? I got that one when I was about your age."

"Just like our new tradition, isn't it, Daddy?" she says.

"It is," he replies, almost proudly.

"Can we put one of my ornaments on the tree first?" She holds up a delicate crystal one. "It's a snowflake. For Snowflake Harbor."

Ronan lifts Belle, and she puts her ornament near the top. We proclaim it perfect, and then we decorate in earnest. He pretends to be annoyed by the holiday movie on the screen, calling it cheesy, but I know he's secretly invested in the couple getting together. I can tell because when we're at the obligatory breakup scene near the end, he's so riveted that Belle has to call him three times to get his attention to put tinsel at the top of the tree.

And then, the only thing left is the tree topper, which we don't have.

"We have time to pick out the perfect angel," I tell Belle.

We analyze our handiwork. It's a little lopsided. And you can still see the tree's bald patch.

"It's beautiful," Belle says happily.

"It's perfect," I agree.

"It's not bad," Ronan allows. "But it's too sparkly."

And then it's time for Belle's bedtime. We argue the entire way up the stairs about whether it's possible for a tree to have too much sparkle.

But underneath it all, I'm arguing with myself about how it's possible for a temporary situation to feel so real.

CHAPTER 17

17 DAYS TO CHRISTMAS

Poppy

"WHAT ARE YOU DOING AT THIS HOUR?"

I startle. My paintbrush clatters to the floor of the large open kitchen and little globs of paint spray on the drop cloth.

"You scared me."

I set my palette down and turn to Ronan. At the sight of him standing in a pair of sleep pants and no shirt, my brain short-circuits. Is it hot in here? Because suddenly, I'm flushed. His muscled chest and arms are chiseled perfection, as are his eight-pack abs and the line of fair hair disappearing into his low-hung pants held up by a drawstring.

It's been a week since we decorated the Christmas tree together, and he's been a more regular fixture around the house, but I'll never get used to the sight of him, especially shirtless.

"Poppy?" he queries. I drag my gaze from his body and focus on his face, which is frowning. Just like with his half smiles, I can now decipher Ronan's many types of frowns, and this isn't a grumpy one. It's perplexed, which is an expression he often directs at me. Go figure.

"Sorry. What did you say?"

"I asked what you're doing awake and painting at two a.m."

"The Christmas ball has a charity auction, and I've been asked to donate a few paintings. Only, it's been so busy, I'm behind on finishing them. I thought I'd work on one tonight, but I lost track of time."

Ronan's frown veers away from confused and hurtles into full-fledged irritation.

"I'm sorry. I hope I didn't wake you."

"Shit, Poppy. Don't apologize. This is my fault. You haven't had enough time off, so you're working on your projects when you should be sleeping. I can find another babysitter to help out or take Belle with me to set, so you have more time."

I realize he's not irritated with me, but himself, which is sweet, but misguided.

"Ronan, you're being silly. You were clear when you hired me that the hours would be intense. You're paying me a ridiculous amount of money to be available. Plus, it's not a hardship. I love all the time I've gotten to spend with Belle." *And with you.* "I know I could have taken more time for myself, but I didn't want to."

I tilt my head, not wanting to say exactly why I don't want to be away from them, because then I'd have to reveal the giant, inconvenient crush I've developed. He shouldn't feel guilty. Not when my position of nanny is one I want to play twenty-four seven.

"Well, regardless, it's not right that you're working in the middle of the night." He glowers at me.

I shrug. "I've just overextended myself like I do every year. It's no big deal. I'm used to it."

His gaze swings from my face to my canvas. I resist the urge to step in front of the unfinished painting. I'm not shy, except about my art. I still get self-conscious when sharing this aspect of myself with others. My work feels so personal that when people view it, it's like they're viewing, and judging, a part of my soul.

"Wow," he says, his gaze keen as he steps closer.

"It's not finished," I remind him.

"Poppy, you're amazing."

A blush fires my face. I'm ridiculously pleased at his comment, though I'm sure he's just being polite. "Oil paints aren't actually my specialty. Watercolors are where my heart is at, but I dabble in everything."

"Stop being so modest. This is incredible. The details and the colors. Everything."

I tilt my head, trying to see what he sees. It's hard to assess my work because I notice my flaws and how my skills always fall short of my vision. But I can already tell the winter scene will turn out well. My inspiration is a photo of Snowflake Harbor's gazebo fronting a lake. It's a festive painting, with the gazebo decorated in red bows and everything dusted with snow, but the Christmas features are subtle enough that the painting could hang in someone's house all year round.

I give a half smile. "My last professor in college said that my work is too pretty for me to be considered true art. For him, pretty is code for boring and unimportant."

"He's an ass," Ronan rumbles. There's that frown again.

"He is." I shrug. "But he was right. Neither I nor my work will be part of the art elite," I say with a smile to show that I'm joking. Sort of. "I like painting pretty things. And I like helping kids and adults discover their own joy in expressing themselves. I was never into the posturing and egos involved in the serious art world."

Ronan unleashes a slow, devastating smile that heats my insides to a melting point. "I understand. Hollywood has its own share of egos."

The cool house feels over warm now. I gather back my thick curls and lift them to get some air on my skin. Normally, I tie my hair back to contain it. But I'd taken a shower earlier and let my hair dry naturally, so it's loose and wild.

Ronan's gaze follows my gesture, and he swallows before looking back at the painting.

"Do you sell much work?" he asks after a beat.

"No. I thought with teaching I'd have all this time in the summer to paint, but I started doing the art workshops, and between those and volunteering, there always seems to be something else to do.

"And nanny jobs."

I grin. "And nanny jobs." Though Ronan and Belle are more than a job.

"Wouldn't you have more time for painting if you opened your own studio instead of teaching? You mentioned it once."

I'm flustered by his intense regard. He remembered the offhand comment I made and asks me as if he cares about the answer. The thing about spending time with someone of few words is that when they use them, those words hold weight. He isn't making idle chitchat. He's truly interested.

That quality is just as heady and attractive as his muscles. And his muscles are damn heady, so that's saying a lot.

"I'm not sure, honestly. Starting a new business wouldn't be easy. And I'd have to do a lot of lessons and workshops to help pay for a mortgage or rent on the space. But it would be nice to have flexible hours. I paint best in the morning." I smile. "And at two a.m."

"Clearly," he says.

"I've always dreamed of having a small gallery as part of my studio for me and a few other artists to show our work.

His mouth quirks up. "I thought you didn't like the gallery world."

"Only snooty galleries. This would be a kinder, gentler one."

"Ah." His smile is barely there, but his eyes are warm. "Of course."

He takes a step closer.

I'm hyperaware of his shirtless state. And my own attire. I hadn't expected an audience at this late hour, so I put on my sleep clothes after my shower, figuring I would go straight to bed after painting. I'm wearing a long shirt that comes to mid-thigh, white, with cherries covering it. I have no bra on. The shirt has been washed so many times the fabric is soft and sheer. The matching shorts are, well, so short that the shirt hides them completely, leaving the impression that I could be wearing nothing underneath.

"Cherries," he murmurs, leaning down. His breath moves the curls at the top of my head.

"Hmm?" I'm disoriented. His chest is right there. The bad girl in me wants to reach out and feel if he's as hard and smooth as he looks.

I may moan.

"Your shirt has cherries on it."

I distract myself from the golden skin of his chest by looking up at him, at his jaw covered in thick nighttime scruff, into his ice-blue eyes. But his face is just as tempting as his body, and so, admitting defeat, I close the gap between us.

He leans down farther. The poor man. I wonder if our height difference causes neck cramps. And then everything flies out of my head as we come together.

I kiss him first, just a tentative sweep of my mouth to his. That might have been all, just an innocent peck. But, with a guttural oath, his mouth captures mine, staking a claim. He's a marauder. And I'm his willing prisoner. His tongue plunders. I moan and tiptoe higher as he sweeps me against him, lifting. He grasps my curves in his large hands to hold me up, and my legs wrap around his hips.

We go from innocent to R-rated in the span of an accelerated heartbeat. I moan, shifting to find relief against him. The friction of us is exquisite, taking me higher.

"Please," I cry between long, drugging kisses.

In answer, he turns in a swift movement and settles me against the wall until I'm riding him. His hips find a deep rhythm with only my thin underwear and the fabric of his pants separating us. I've never been hotter, more turned on.

My head falls back against the wall, and he rains kisses on my neck, alternating between the gentle press of his lips and laps of his tongue as if I'm the best thing he's ever tasted, all the while grinding against me in a way that drives me beyond thought. Beyond anything rational. I'm only needy want. Flesh and pure desire.

He sucks at a spot below my ear, bites down, then soothes my sensitive skin with his tongue until I shiver. I need to be naked, need his cock driving into me with no barriers between us.

"Ronan," I plead, desperate now.

He changes the angle slightly so that there's even more friction against my clit, and when I can't go any higher, I burst apart in a thousand shattering pieces of pleasure.

I cry out, the sound loud in the dark. I've never been loud before. But then again, I've never felt anything like this short, wild ride.

He captures my mouth with his as he presses me against him with a harsh, pained groan.

He's still rock-hard against me, still breathing deeply, but he's gentle now, bringing me down from my high in long, slow, drugging kisses. We finally break to catch deep breaths of air. And I see the moment in him, sense the moment in me, when we both come out of the fog of desire and back into our senses. He slides me down his body.

"Holy heck," I say. Shocked. "I've never...that was. Yeah. Wow."

He turns away, swearing softly and running his hand through his already messy hair. He tilts his head up and swears again, louder this time.

"Fuck, Poppy. I'm sorry. That should never have happened."

"Well, it did happen," I say. "And by the way, your response is not what a girl wants to hear after being given the best orgasm of her life. But maybe it wasn't as good for you. I mean, I don't think you...um...finished. And I don't exactly have a lot of experience in this department. You know, with hookups."

"Poppy."

"Yes?"

He rubs his neck. When he makes that motion, it causes his arm muscles to pop very attractively. Damn him.

"Shut up."

I huff a little.

"That's not very nice—"

"You're fucking incredible in this department. And in every other department there is. There's nothing I want more than to take you upstairs and fuck you long. Fuck you hard. Fuck you in every way I can. All night."

"Then what's wrong?" I ask, my brain unable to focus. I'm flushing at his hot words, at every single thing he just did, every way he looks at me. "I wanted this. You didn't take advantage of me."

"I'm your boss. You're my daughter's nanny. Belle worships you, and if you leave early because this doesn't end well, then I'd be the worst, most selfish dad in the world."

"Yeah, darn it. There's that," I say, my tingly high coming down at his sobering words. Now he gets talkative. When he's explaining all the reasons we can't be together, he's been downright chatty.

"Fine," I agree, grumpy now. "But," I add. "It was really good, right? I thought it was really good."

He grunts and looks up, as if asking the other Nordic gods for patience, which is fair because he already kind of told me what he thought of it, and here I am basically begging for more words of affirmation. It's one of my love languages.

"It doesn't matter if it was good. Or if it was the best damn thing I've ever felt. Or if I want to feel it every night over and over. I can't risk Belle," he grates out.

"I know," I admit softly. Because, darn it, I do. If he were a smooth operator who was only interested in hitting it with the nanny and didn't care that it could hurt his daughter, I wouldn't respect him as much. Darn him for being so sexy *and* so principled. It's my kryptonite.

"I know, and you're right," I repeat. "But it sucks."

I'm not sure, but I think his chin dips in agreement. I want more.

"Say it after me. It sucks," I repeat. I need him to agree. Words of affirmation and all.

He shakes his head, and that right corner of his lip that I know and love tilts up. "You're impossible."

"Be that as it may, say it."

"Fine," he grumbles. "It sucks."

"It does, right?" I say. "But we're going to be strong for Belle. We're not going to do this anymore. Not kiss. Not touch. Not anything. Because we don't want to hurt her, and you're the boss and I'm the nanny. Even though I really, really want to." I bite my lip to stop the flow of words before I drop more truth bombs.

He lets out a slow, controlled breath. Then another. And a third.

"Are you doing deep breathing exercises?"

He ignores my question. "I'm going upstairs. Before—" He doesn't elaborate. Just stares at me for another long moment, turns in one swift movement, and then strides toward the stairs.

I stare after him, long after he's gone.

I've done it. The thought steals my breath. Shit, my fear came true. I've fallen for the Sexiest Man Alive, my boss, who is completely unattainable and barely has time for his daughter. When he leaves in mere weeks, I'll have to pick all the crushed pieces of my heart off the floor.

Of all the stupid things I could have gone and done.

CHAPTER 18

14 DAYS TO CHRISTMAS

Poppy

IN RETROSPECT, I THINK RONAN WAS LYING WHEN HE SAID I didn't have a problem in the hookup department.

Otherwise, why would he, the morning after we made out for all we're worth, have banished me for two entire days and nights from the house?

Okay. In reality, there's no banishment. It's more like he gave me a mini-holiday. But it feels a little like it. The next morning, he overheard me telling Sadie how much I still had left to do to plan my parents' thirtieth wedding anniversary on Friday.

When I got off the phone, Ronan said that I'd been working too hard for him and that I should take a few days off so I could spend some time with my family. He all but packed my bags and pushed me out the door to go to my mom and dad's.

He told me to do what I needed, and that he and Belle would see me on Friday night. Because of course they were invited to my parents' party. My mother wouldn't have it any other way.

I didn't think I would miss being away from Ronan and Belle so much. Since he's been home more lately, I've grown attached to our small rituals. Belle has been soaking up all his time and attention. So have I.

When he hasn't had an early call time, we've eaten breakfast together. Well, Belle and I eat breakfast, and Ronan drinks whatever horrid concoction he mixes up for himself. He even eats dinner with us when he can. Though he tells me not to bother, that he can have his delivery meals, I try to find recipes he can eat. I replace his pasta with zucchini "noodles" and his rice with cauliflower, while Belle and I eat the real deal.

I've become addicted to that tilt of his lips when I do small things for him. And sometimes he gazes around the house after dinner, when everything is soft and quiet, when the tree is lit, the fire is set, the lights are low. When Belle is giggling and I'm laughing. And he gets this expression I can't quite name but very much want to.

But my parents' anniversary party is finally—at long last—in full swing. Every balloon has been blown up. Every banner hung. The three-tier cake is bought. The table laid. The drinks are iced and the buffet of food is set out. Kids are playing and guests are mingling.

All that's left is for Ronan and Belle to show. *God,* I hope they show.

I still feel awkward after our hot encounter, and he likely does as well. Maybe he thought time apart would cool things down. But time away has only made me miss and appreciate them both all the more.

The doorbell rings, and I sprint toward the door, almost knocking over my great-aunt Maria.

"Sorry!" I say, helping her back upright. I yank open the door.

"You." My spirits plummet.

"Aren't you going to let me in?" Derek asks.

"What are you doing here?"

"Your cousin invited me."

"Which one?" I narrow my eyes.

"Randall."

Ugh. I'm not surprised. My parents are from Snowflake Harbor, and they both are from large families. As a result, my sister and I have a lot of cousins. Some we call our good cousins, and some we call our bad cousins. Randall is one of the latter. He's always been chummy with Derek, and he's always sticking his misogynistic nose in everyone's business.

I grudgingly open the door wider, not wanting to cause a scene. Stupid small towns where you can't escape an ex. At least this party is big. Hopefully, he will get lost among the crowd and stay far away from me.

"Where's your other half?" I ask, referring to Monique. I hate myself for asking.

He frowns. "She's in New York. She had an audition for a reality show."

"And how does that fit in with your ten-year plan?" I ask sweetly, remembering my dreams and how he made it a point to "practical" them away.

"I support her in what she wants to do," he says, scratching at his ear. The hypocrite. Plus, I can tell when he's lying. The ear scratch is a dead giveaway.

"Sure you do," I drawl. It's amazing how just a few

months away can help you gain perspective—gain the perspective that you spent twelve years with the wrong person. Especially when you are now living with the right one.

Derek looks like he might say something else but then thinks better of it.

"Enjoy the crab dip," I singsong after him before he disappears into the crowded house. Ha. I love crab dip. And for twelve long years, I avoided it because Derek hated the smell so much he objected to my eating it. He wasn't allergic; he just didn't like it. Now, with him gone, I gorge on the stuff.

I even made it for Ronan last week, and he, prince among men, ate a little. Not on a cracker, of course, because carbs, but with a cucumber slice.

The doorbell rings again. I tamp down my eagerness. After the last visitor, I'm afraid to have my hope dashed again. Could this be my second-grade nemesis, perhaps? Mandy-Lynne had mean eyes, long, shiny, blond hair, and was a plague on my elementary years. Or maybe it's my art professor, the one who said I'd never be a serious artist and who smelled like stale coffee.

I open the door with trepidation.

"Poppy! We missed you!" Belle launches herself at me as I return her enthusiastic hug.

"Hey, little one. I missed you as well."

I gaze up at Ronan. *And you.* I missed those rare and devastating crystal eyes.

"Hi." I shift.

"Hey."

My gaze fall to his lips, just to gauge if one side is lifted. It's the only way I can tell if he's smiling inside. And to my everlasting joy, both sides of his mouth are up—only fractionally—but that's a full-blown smile in my book. I grin back, wide.

His lips quirk up higher. I think I even detect smile lines by his eyes.

I have to look away to catch my breath.

"Belle, it's about time you showed up. Jolene and Jacinda have been asking for you." My parents' neighbors have four daughters. All a year or two apart, all with names that start with J.

"Really?" Poppy exclaims, looking pleased with herself.

"Keep your coat on. I think they're in the backyard, probably in the tree house. Why don't you run outside and find them?"

Belle doesn't wait to be told twice. I love that she's not shy here. I've brought her to visit my parents more than a few times now.

Ronan's eyebrow shoots up. "In the yard? It's a little cold, isn't it?"

"Of course in the yard. Didn't you grow up in Wisconsin? This is nothing."

"Reading up on me?" he murmurs.

I blush and ignore his question. "With all the people in here, escaping outside is the only way to avoid heatstroke. The tree house is surprisingly well insulated. I may hang out there myself later."

He pulls off his coat, and I take it from him. "It *is* hot in here," he agrees, tugging at the collar of his indigo-blue sweater. It looks like cashmere, and I really want to run my hands over it to check.

"I'm glad you made it."

"Did you doubt me?"

I lift my shoulders.

"When I promise something to you, I'll do it," he growls.

"Noted." I give a small salute.

I turn to set his coat in the room off the entry hallway. It's an old house, and I'm not sure what the room's original purpose was, but now it's my mom's home gym, where she has her step machine, her free weights, and her Jane Fonda posters. She even has a small television for watching old workout videos, which are still on VHS.

I hang his coat off the step machine. It's precarious because there are a dozen other coats piled on it and many more on the yoga mat on the floor.

"Huh," Ronan says, checking out the Jane Fonda posters.

"I bet she could take you in an exercise contest."

"Who? Jane?" He gestures to the poster. "Or your mom?"

"Jane, of course. She's the queen of fitness. But also, my mom."

"And what kind of contest? Lifting? Arm-wrestling?" Ronan asks, folding his arms over his chest.

I grin. "Step aerobics. Or Zumba."

"What's step aerobics?"

"Well, if you have to ask, you'd definitely lose. Come on, big guy, let's get this party started." I take his hand, as if it's the most natural thing. And for me, it is. I'm a toucher. A hugger.

But when his large hand engulfs mine, electric warnings go off in my brain. It reminds me of the way his hands picked me up effortlessly. And then I'm back there in that moment, dreaming of the way his mouth and body mastered mine. I want more. I want everything.

I peek up at him and he's watching me intently.

I try to pretend it doesn't affect me, even though my breathing has gone uneven and my cheeks are pink.

Because. Belle.

And also because I don't want to be rejected again, even if it's for a good reason.

I lead him into the kitchen and drop his hand on the pretext of getting him a club soda from the fridge. I hold it out.

Personally, if I were him, I'd break down, eat and drink what I wanted, and then make really good friends with the CGI team, but I guess that's why he's an action star and I'm just an art teacher. I could never keep up that level of self-discipline and commitment.

"Thanks," he says. "But I'll have one of those." He points to a light beer. "We're nearing the end of filming. It won't hurt to have one or two."

The end of filming. When the movie's done, there will be no reason for him to stay.

I smile and we move about the party, chatting and mingling, but in my head, there's a clock that's ticking down.

CHAPTER 19

14 DAYS TO CHRISTMAS (STILL)

Poppy

"GREAT PARTY, SIS," ROSE SAYS, COMING UP TO ME WHILE I'M having a cooling break outside. I'm not just overheated from the house. I'm hot from standing next to Ronan for most of the anniversary party. He stayed near the whole time. It might be because my family can be intimidating and loud, but the delusional part of me imagines that maybe it's because he craves my company.

Because, ditto.

I'm such a goner for him.

I paste on a smile and face my sister. "Thanks. I'm glad you and Kevin were able to make it."

"You know I wouldn't miss Mom and Dad's thirtieth anniversary." She grimaces. "I'd never hear the end of it."

"True." I laugh. "It would be nothing but guilt trips from

now till the end of time." I study Rose. "How are you? Really?"

"I'm good. Great. Don't look at me that way, Poppy. I know you were surprised by the wedding."

"I wasn't against it. It's just that you never wanted to get married. And then suddenly, you plan a whirlwind wedding."

"And just when you broke up with the man you thought you'd marry. I know the timing wasn't the best."

"Hey, this isn't about me. Now that everything has calmed down, I want to make sure you're happy."

"I am, sis. I really am. I know I said I didn't want to get married, but I'd never been in love before, not with someone who loved me back and treated me well. I'd always fall for the bad boys who made me cry. But Kevin isn't like that. He brings out the best in me. And I do the same for him. It's okay to change your mind. Change is good."

She smiles gently. "For example, it's a good thing you broke up with Derek. You decided you wanted to marry him when you were both so young. And you stuck with it because you're way too loyal. Now, you know better. And Mom and Dad may not agree, but it's not a bad thing you lost your teaching position. Your whole world might be upside down, but that means you can gain a new perspective. You have a unique opportunity to make your life whatever you want it to be."

"There have definitely been a few surprises lately," I say with a wry smile.

"See, that's what I'm talking about. I never thought you'd be shacking up with a movie star." Rose laughs.

"That makes two of us." I want to say more. Rose had always been my confidante growing up, but we've grown apart in the years since she moved to New York City. And I still don't feel comfortable talking about whatever is happening between Ronan and me. He needs more than the average amount of privacy. And even if he didn't, I'm not sure I understand it myself.

"I hope you're not going to let Mom and Dad talk you into taking a job you don't want," Rose says. "I know you're scared and you don't want to disappoint them. But it's your life, not theirs."

"I'm not sure. Taking that position makes a lot of sense."

"God, Poppy. Sometimes I want to shake you until you get out of your rut. I thought since losing the dead weight of Derek and taking on this nanny job on the spur of the moment that you'd come out of your comfort zone. Sadie told me about the space on Main Street that opened up. You always dreamed of having your own art studio, even when you were a kid. There was a time you even wanted to be an artist and go to New York with me."

She tilts her head and takes a sip of wine. "What happened to that girl, Poppy?"

I take her wineglass. "How many glasses of this have you had? You always play therapist when you've had too many."

Rose stares me down with her hand held out until I give her the wine back. She has a scary stare.

"Nothing happened," I say. "I was a kid. I don't want to be a ballerina now either."

"It's more than that. You were never the same after what happened with Dad. After that, you just gave up on your dreams and fell in line with everyone else's expectations. You've been living like that ever since."

I draw in a sharp breath at her words, my stomach churning with nerves. In our family, my sister has always been the one to cause storms, and I'm the storm whisperer. She never shied away from turmoil, and my instinct is to smooth things over. I guess I'd thought it was my job to fix things after what happened with my dad. It was my job to stay home and make sure everyone was okay.

"It wasn't your fault, you know. You need to move on from it."

I wince, knowing what she's referring to. I told her about the fight one night soon after it happened.

The only time I ever rocked the boat was in seventh grade. There was an art camp I wanted to attend, but it was for the entire summer, a state away, and it was expensive. My parents said no, and I was angry. My art teacher had encouraged me to apply, and I was accepted into the competitive program. I was even offered a small scholarship, but my parents didn't budge. So I argued with my dad, which was unusual for me.

The rational part of me understands that it wasn't my fault. It was just bad timing that, in the midst of our first heated argument, my dad had a heart attack. My more volatile sister argued with my parents all the time, and nothing bad had ever happened.

But ever since I saw my dad clutch his chest and fall to the ground right after I yelled at him, I haven't been able to shake the anxiety I get whenever people have strong emotions or fight. It feels like life-and-death because at one time, that's what it was.

I've been thinking about this lately. Since I woke up to the realization that I worry more about others than myself. Since Ronan started pointing out my trouble with saying no.

My dad recovered from that day, but did I?

Rose gives me a brief hug. "I know. I'm a nosy bitch. I always have been. But you're not the only one in the family who likes to fix things. I want you to be happy, and I see you with this fresh start, and I want you to make choices that are right for *you*. Don't say anything now, but just think about it, okay?"

I close my eyes and lean into her hug. I missed my sister. My twin.

Even with the needling, even with her pushing, even when she drives me crazy, Rose has always been in my corner. She's understood me more than I've understood myself sometimes.

I shouldn't be surprised that she still remembers how much I struggled after Dad had his heart attack. But I wasn't the only one affected by it, even if we reacted differently. I retreated behind my guise of being the good, helpful daughter. And Rose went in the opposite direction. She distanced herself and grew wilder, bolder, more independent.

"I will. But only if you promise not to be such a stranger now that you're an old married woman. We miss you here."

"You can visit me in New York as well. I have a bigger place now."

"Oh good. I won't have to sleep on a mattress next to the kitchen sink?"

She grins. "One of Kevin's best traits is his beautiful, rent-controlled brownstone in Brooklyn. You know who else probably has a great house?"

I tilt my head. "Who?"

"Ronan Masters. I bet that LA pad of his is a real winner. Maybe he has a place in New York as well."

"Oh my God, Rose. I'm the nanny."

"Oh my God, Poppy." She does an excellent impression of me. "You hooked up with him!"

"No! Well, maybe," I admit in a whisper, looking around to make sure no one else can hear us.

"Shit!" she squeals and practically bruises my arm, squeezing it so hard. "You hit it with a Hollywood superstar.

Holy shit, Pops. I always suspected *I* might do something like that, but never you. I never thought you had it in you, but I'm super impressed."

"Thanks," I say drolly.

"I need details."

The screen door to the back porch opens.

"Speak of the devil," Rose says.

Ronan steps onto the porch. He stiffens when we both stare at him. Me with a wide-eyed "Caught!" look, and Rose with a cat-who-ate-the-canary grin.

His eyebrows shift upward. "I was looking for Belle."

"They're back in the tree house. And before you ask, they have blankets and hot chocolate, so I'm sure they're fine. They'll come inside soon, though, because I overheard the boys making attack plans. Honestly, I'm surprised they haven't asked you to help."

"They asked if I had any tips for a siege. Should I be worried?"

"Only for the boys." Rose cackles.

He nods. "That's what I thought."

"So, Ronan." Rose's voice goes sultry as she threads her arm through his, pushing open the door to lead him inside. "Have you had any particularly *exciting* experiences during your stay in Snowflake Harbor?"

He gives her a polite semi-smile and then stops, turning back to me. "Are you coming?" It's clear he won't move without me.

My heart expands. Though we're twins, I've always been in Rose's shadow. It wasn't her fault. But when we were younger, every guy I ever liked fell for her. She was flirty and sexy, where I was perky and nice. She was the bad girl, not afraid to take dares, whereas I was the good girl, the teacher's pet, the one who got friend-zoned.

Ronan blinks at my blinding smile. "Yes," I say, "I'm coming." He takes a step back toward me, leaving Rose standing at the threshold holding the door and watching us with speculation as Ronan clasps my hand. We walk into the house together, and we're once again embraced by the heat and chaos of my childhood home. But this time, I feel like I have someone there just for me, and it feels right.

I watch my family laughing and joking. I see Belle running around with my cousins' children. I check out Ronan trying to slip under the radar while still holding everyone's attention without even trying. And I think maybe, just maybe, change isn't always bad, just as Rose said.

If I hadn't been dumped by Derek, I'd still be living in my old house and wouldn't have taken this nanny position. If I hadn't lost my job at the school, I wouldn't have the space in my life to think about what dreams I want to pursue. And it makes me wonder what other blessings, disguised or otherwise, are out there waiting for me.

LATER THAT NIGHT, RONAN OFFERS ME A CHOICE. I CAN STAY with my parents for another night or go back home with him and Belle. He said if I wanted to stay, he wasn't due to be on set till the afternoon tomorrow, so I could return to the lake house in the morning.

"I'm not sure." I deliberate. "I'm not packed. Plus, there will be a lot to clean up. I don't want my parents to have to do it."

"I can wait while you pack," he says, his face neutral. "And you planned the whole party. Aren't there other people who can help?"

"Get out of here, Pops. We got the cleanup," Rose says.

"The big stud is right. You arranged everything by yourself. You have to let other people help."

"Stop worrying about what you should do. What do you *want* to do?" Ronan asks.

And that part is clear. I want to go home with him. Perhaps I should have enjoyed having several days off. Though, technically, "off" isn't correct. I just switched roles from nanny to party planner. But I missed being home. Not this home where I grew up. But the lake house.

It's dangerous because the lake house is only my temporary lodging. But I missed the people there. Terribly. Ronan, with his long silences and indomitable presence. Belle, who transformed from a withdrawn child to a bubbly little girl. They've both lodged themselves into my heart, and I'm holding on tight for as long as I have them.

Which is less than two weeks.

So I'm not going to miss one more night.

"I'll come home," I say. My eyes widen at my use of the word. I might think it, but I hadn't meant for it to slip out.

Something bright flares to life in Ronan's eyes.

"Good," he grunts. But I think I detect a smile before he turns away.

The next twenty minutes pass in a flurry of packing and goodbyes. When, bag in hand, I look for Ronan, I find him in the kitchen, loading the dishwasher. When I'd left to pack, the kitchen counter had been stacked with dishes, but now, it gleams. There is plenty more to do, but he took on what I would have considered my portion to clean up and did it himself, as if he understood that even though I chose to leave, the guilt of not helping would have weighed on me.

"Hey, thanks. But you didn't need to do that," I say, touched.

"I didn't do it all myself. I made your uncles help."

I burst out laughing. "My uncles? How did you drag them away from sports on the television?"

"I don't think they were happy, but they did their part."

"I wish I'd seen it. That's a once-in-a-lifetime sight."

He snorts. "It shouldn't be. They ate. They should clean up."

This man just keeps surprising me.

"Should we find Belle and go home?" I did it. I called it home again. I wasn't struck by lightning the first time, so I'm just going to keep pushing my luck.

Emotion fires the ice in his eyes.

I fiddle with my bag, and he silently takes it from me, tossing it over his shoulder as if it were a Barbie accessory. We get Belle and, together, we all go home.

CHAPTER 20

14 DAYS TO CHRISTMAS (STILL)

Ronan

THE LINES ARE BLURRING.

And I don't know what the hell to do about it anymore.

Home. She called this house home. Twice. And both times, something in me shifted. It wasn't a light shift, no slow, gentle movement. It was seismic. Tectonic plates tearing up the land, creating craters and building mountains. It was earth-shattering, world-changing.

Amazing what one small woman can do with just one little word.

It wasn't just one word, though. It was everything that led up to it. All the ways she shows she cares. It was the dinners and the ornaments, the laughter and the Christmas lights. It was the late-night talks and the silent support. And especially, it was the way she handed me my ass and fought for Belle, even when she hated every second of it.

I've known a lot of people who talk a good game. They spin bullshit into fairy tales as elaborate as they are empty.

But not Poppy. Her care is concrete, a foundation built on actions. All those details that stack up together to create something strong and secure.

Our house is full of laughter and warmth now, just like the empty parts of my soul that I hadn't even realized needed to be filled.

When I saw her a few nights ago, up so late because she gave too much to everyone around her. She didn't even have time to sleep. I wanted to give something back. I wanted her to know that she deserved to receive sometimes.

It's not much, and I wonder, as we walk into the house, if maybe I haven't gotten it wrong. Uncharacteristic nerves hit. I don't usually care what others think. I learned long ago that people-pleasing was a losing bargain. My mom cared. When she was in her good phases, she cared too much, always trying to pretend that the two of us were a nice, normal family, when under the surface, she struggled with any sense of normalcy. It meant I spent my years as a child and teen pretending. Maybe it's why I'm a good actor.

So when I grew up, I went the opposite way. I do what feels right, to hell with what anyone else thinks.

Except, I care when it comes to Belle.

And now, heaven help me, I care when it comes to Poppy.

Which is why I'm worried I overstepped, and I'm tempted to forget this whole thing. Except Belle was also part of the project, and she can't hold back the surprise.

"What's going on? Why are you smiling like that, Belle?" Poppy asks, dropping her bag by the stairs.

"We have a surprise for you!" Belle grabs Poppy's hand and runs, making her follow behind with a laugh.

"In your dad's gym?" Poppy asks.

"Ta-da!" Belle exclaims as she swings open the door. "It's not Daddy's gym any longer."

"Oh!" Poppy gasps as she enters the room.

I hang back, nervous. Praying I didn't fuck this up or make everything weird. Praying it's a good surprise.

She swings around to look at me, then swings back to the room.

"Do you like it?" Belle asks.

At first, she doesn't answer, and the knife of uncertainty twists harder in my gut.

"I love it," she exclaims, and I can breathe now in relief. She leans down to give Belle a big hug. And while they're hugging, her gaze meets mine.

"How?" she asks.

"It was Daddy's idea. He said you should have an art studio. He had lots of help. I helped pick things out too."

Poppy walks around the room, touching the canvases, the easels, the paints, and the art table.

I clear my throat against the ball of something that clogs it. "I thought you might like this room. You said before it has great light."

"It does," she says. "It's perfect. But I can't believe you did this. Why? And how? You did it all so quickly."

Her eyes are filled with tears.

"Don't cry," I moan. Shit.

"I'm not crying," she sniffs.

"Poppy's just too happy," Belle says. "That's why her tears are leaking out."

"That's right. I'm just too happy."

Belle smiles. "Guess what! Daddy also hired someone to

redo my room. No more of that baby pink. Everything's blue now. And guess what?"

"What?"

"I have bunk beds!"

"Really? That's so awesome."

"Yes. Because I want to sometimes sleep on the bottom and sometimes sleep on the top. I wanted taller bunk beds, the tallest, but Daddy made me get the shorter ones. Now, if I wanted, I could even have a sleepover, and we'd each get our own bed. Do you think Sasha would like to have a sleepover?"

Poppy smiles. "I think we can definitely ask Sasha and her daddy."

"Sure," I say, trying not to roll my eyes at the mention of Conner.

"I don't know how to thank you," Poppy says, stopping next to me. She avoids my eyes as she reaches up on tiptoe.

I lean down slightly, and she brushes a kiss on my now-bristly jaw. That brief contact is enough to light up all my nerve endings. It affects me more than any wild sex I ever had when I was young and stupid, when I landed my first big roles in Hollywood. And with those roles came groupies. I was no monk. But anonymous sex soon grew old.

Sex with Poppy would be… I get hard at the thought. If the light brush of her mouth against my skin can make me ache—body and soul—sex with her would obliterate all who came before.

I shouldn't be thinking of her this way, but ever since our kiss—hell, ever since that first night when she stepped into my elevator and into my life, she's been destroying all my carefully laid boundaries, all my meticulously built walls. And now, they lie shattered at my feet. And I don't know how long I can continue to resist what I want so damn badly.

Poppy

I STEP BACK FROM RONAN. MY LIPS ARE STILL TINGLING FROM that soft kiss I placed on his strong jaw, from the feel of his rough stubble and smooth skin. Everything about him just works for me. His long blond Viking hair. His mountainous strength and his quiet, stoic demeanor. His pale blue eyes. His slow but devastating half smile, which is all the more precious because it's not easily bestowed.

Except on me.

I shake my head in an attempt to break the spell. "Really, it's incredible. I can't believe you did this."

Ronan looks down and shuffles from one foot to the other. Is it possible this giant of a man, this Hollywood god, is embarrassed? I detect a faint pink staining his cheeks and ears, but maybe it's a trick of the room's light.

He finally meets my eyes. "It's nothing. I had help."

"It's not nothing. And what did you do with your gym? You have all that equipment that you use every day."

He shrugs. "It's no big deal. I moved it upstairs into the green guest bedroom."

I know the room he's talking about. "But that's such a small space."

A shrug again. "It's fine."

My heart fills with warmth. Ronan found me painting in the kitchen once, and he creates an entire art room for me, moving his gym, which he uses daily.

Looking again at the painting supplies laid out on the wide wooden table, I gasp when I notice one set of brushes.

"You bought me these sable-hair brushes?" I'm flabbergasted. "These are expensive. Insanely expensive." My mind reels.

He shrugs.

I run my fingers over tubes of watercolors and oil paints of every shade and pigment. I feel almost dizzy with joy from the rainbow of hues. I'm itching to get them on my palette. To get them on a canvas. Speaking of which, there are canvases of every size stacked underneath one of the floor-to-ceiling windows in this room. A large, sturdy easel sits in the middle of the space.

Just like for Belle, he seems to have bought out the art shop. Though, this time, it was a professional, high-end art store. I know how much these supplies cost because everything is of the finest quality, from the best brands. In addition to the brushes and tubes of paints, there are the finest charcoals and drawing pencils, an exquisite travel case for watercolors, and pastels that make me want to weep for their prettiness. All the things I've coveted for years but never dreamed of having because I've been working with a schoolteacher budget.

"This is way too much, Ronan. I really can't accept all this. You need to return it."

"Can't," he grunts. "It was on sale."

I snort. "Yeah, right."

Belle threads her hand in mine and tugs at me. "Poppy."

I look down at her. "Yes, little one?"

"Don't argue. When someone does something nice for you, you should just say thank you."

And I'm caught. The little minx is throwing my own words back at me. I'd said that to her a few days ago when she'd forgotten to thank a store worker.

Ronan seems to be fighting a smile. "Yes, Poppy. Don't argue. Just say thank you," he teases.

I blow out a breath so hard that some of my curls go flying. "Thank you. Again." I finally acquiesce. "It's all way, way, way too much." I can't help adding, "But thank you."

And that smile he's been fighting unfurls into a devastating full grin. It's unicorn rare. It's pink-diamond-on-a-unicorn rare. It's pink-diamond-on-a-unicorn-riding-a-blue-whale rare.

It leaves me a mess of want and longing.

And this is when I know. It doesn't matter that I'm just the nanny, that he's so far out of my league, he's on another planet—Planet Hollywood. Or that we only have a few weeks left.

I'm all in.

I'm all in for Belle, who captured my heart.

And I'm all in for Ronan.

Our time together several nights ago shattered me, but it's his sweetness beneath the stoicism that does me in. I want to hoard every moment we have.

My sister advised me to be open to change. And for this man and his daughter, I am, even if it's temporary. I know now that change can be beautiful because it brought Belle and Ronan into my life, and I wouldn't trade this time for anything, not even to be safe from the pain that will inevitably come.

CHAPTER 21

12 DAYS TO CHRISTMAS

Poppy

I've been back two days, and he hasn't tried to kiss me again. It's for the best, I tell myself. He's being responsible, a good father and employer.

But I fall asleep dreaming of his roaming hands and the way he moved against me. Oh God, the way he moved. It was the hottest experience of my life, and I'm not even embarrassed about it, because it was that good.

To heck with being responsible—I really need him to kiss me again.

Hope springs eternal and all that, so I tell myself that maybe tonight will be the night. When I got dressed for ice-skating, I put on my tightest jeans and my favorite red sweater. Though I fear the reindeer antlers I'm sporting won't help make the kissing happen.

But the first ice skate of the season requires extra accessorizing. Belle agrees.

"When will Daddy be here?" She asks for the ten millionth time, clutching onto her "skate helper" penguin as she shuffles around the outdoor rink with me. Fairy lights blink down on us, making everything just a little more magical, as twinkle lights always do.

I look at my watch. "Soon, I think."

I twirl.

"Whoa!" Belle says. "Can I learn to do that?"

"Sure. It just takes practice." I'm about to tell her I can arrange weekly lessons, but then I realize she only has two weeks left here. My heart does a dip, more dramatic than any move I could make on the ice. Maybe I can talk to Ronan about getting her lessons in LA.

"How did you learn to skate?" she asks.

"I took classes," I say as we glide slowly along the ice.

"Daddy lets me do art lessons. And buys me paints."

"That's because your daddy's great. He wants you to be happy doing things you enjoy."

"Hey! Poppy! Belle!"

I turn around to see Conner and Sasha skating toward us. "Hi! What a surprise."

Sasha and Poppy look at each other and giggle.

"Something tells me this wasn't exactly a surprise."

"Did you two girls cook this up?"

"Belle told me she was going ice-skating tonight, so I asked if Daddy could bring me," Sasha says.

"Can I skate with Sasha? Please?"

I smile. "Sure. But keep using Mr. Penguin until I'm there to hold your hand, okay?"

"I'll help Belle. I've been skating for years," Sasha assures us with a breezy confidence that belies her age.

"Have fun," Conner calls to the girls' departing backs before turning to me. "Hey, I wanted to talk to you about something."

I tense. I hope he won't ask a personal question about Ronan. It's the first thing people ask me lately. *Hi, how are you? What's Ronan Masters like? Are you really just the nanny?*

"I have the listing on 24 Main Street. The building that's next to Sadie's. She told me you were interested in it. So I thought I'd check with you."

"Oh," I say, nerves making butterflies take flight in my stomach. I'm not sure if I'm ready for this step. Having a business and a mortgage, being self-employed. But I've run the numbers, and they seem sound. I have Ronan's ridiculously generous salary to help me get started.

I straighten my reindeer antlers. I can do this. "I guess it won't hurt to check it out." Excitement builds at the thought.

"The upstairs apartment has been recently renovated. It's not huge, only a one-bedroom, but it's pristine, which is unusual for these older buildings," he encourages. "I think this could be great for you. That's a prime Main Street location, and they don't come around very often. Sadie says you want to open an art studio, so I have a vested interest in your buying it. Sasha loves your classes."

Hearing Conner talk about my dream in a serious way, as if it could be a legitimate enterprise, gives me a confidence boost.

I stand up straighter. "I've been considering it," I say, testing out the words.

"It's a great idea, Poppy. And we'll be your first customers."

I'm flush with pleasure. "When can I see it?"

Conner pulls out his phone and looks at his calendar.

"How is Thursday? At noon. I can send over the property details later today for you to look over. What's your email?"

I give him my information, and he types it in his phone. "I'm looking forward to Thursday," he says with a warm smile.

"Looking forward to what?"

I turn in surprise to find Ronan standing near us at the edge of the rink. His Henley, faded jeans, and fierce frown look damn good on him, as does his long blond hair pulled back in a man bun.

"Oh," I say, flustered. "Ah, nothing. How was your day?" I ask Ronan, changing the subject. I glance at Conner guiltily. It's not that I want to hide our appointment, but this idea still feels like a long shot, like it's too fragile to be out in the world yet.

Ronan doesn't answer me, but he continues to stare down Conner.

Conner blinks several times. "I better find the girls," he says after an awkward minute.

"Good idea," Ronan grunts, crossing his arms over his chest.

"See you soon, Poppy." Conner winks at me, as if we have a secret, before gliding away.

"Bye!" I call after him. "And thanks again!"

My mind is full of the space on Main Street. I'm going to do it. I have an appointment to see the building! Taking this step is the first toward my dream. I'm sure the anticipation shows on my face.

"So are you going out with him?" Ronan breaks into my thoughts.

"What?" I ask, confused.

"Conner. And you. Are you going on a date?"

"Why would you think that?"

"You were obviously planning to meet up when I walked over. You're smiling." Ronan frowns.

I try to turn my grin to half-mast. "I always smile."

"It's the way you're smiling. Like he just made all your wishes come true."

"Can't a girl smile without it meaning anything?"

"Poppy," he growls.

"He's just helping me with a project."

"What kind of project?"

"A none-of-your-business kind," I retort.

I reach up and massage the tense muscles of his arms. Both to relax him and because I like to feel his muscles. "I promise I'll tell you about it if it happens. I just don't want to say anything until I know for sure because I'm afraid I'll jinx it."

"But Conner knows." Ronan does not look happy about that fact. Could he be jealous? My eyes glaze as I imagine warrior Ronan fighting other men over me before stealing me for his own. I silently apologize to poor Conner. The idea is more than a little attractive to me. Just in my imagination, of course.

"Conner knows only because he has to. Otherwise, he wouldn't."

"You're not making any sense."

I shrug. "Not unusual."

I do a little twirl, both to show off my skate skills and also to distract him. "Forget about Conner, big guy. Get some skates on. If they have your size, which, come to think of it, they may not."

I flash him my brightest, sweetest, most dimply smile. It's the one I use on parents upset over their children's poor grades.

This smile has a nine out of ten return on softening hearts and soothing wounded feelings.

Ronan is no match against it. Thank you, Mom, for the dimple.

He grunts but doesn't argue and heads on his long legs toward the skate shack, moving gracefully through the crowd of people. Everyone turns to watch him walk, but it doesn't break his stride. No matter what his goal, he always advances with a single-minded focus, no faltering. It's inspiring and makes me rethink the number of ways I've let others change my own path.

"See you on the ice!" I call to him. I wave to Belle, whom I've been watching out of the corner of my eye. She waves back and skates toward me alone, looking far more comfortable on the ice.

I glide over to her, but my mind is still on the handsome, grumpy man and whether it was jealousy that made him even grumpier tonight.

Ronan

I HAVE NO RIGHT TO BE JEALOUS.

But knowing that isn't making a difference.

Normally, I'm slow to anger. Or at least I've learned to control my reactions.

I've been called a lot of things in my life. Unemotional. Cold. Intractable.

Yet here I am, burning with the fire of my Viking ancestors. When I saw Conner and Poppy with their heads together while he typed something into his phone, probably putting their meet-up on his calendar, I wanted to wipe that smarmy smile off his face.

I didn't, because I've spent the last fifteen years building my practice of control and discipline.

When I was fifteen, I used to hang out with my friends downtown. There was a small dojo studio with posters on the door. I was fixated on one. It said, *The best fighter is never angry* and *An attack is proof that we are out of control.*

I was angry back then, and my whole life felt out of control. It was the opposite of what I craved, which was calm and order. I wanted whatever that karate studio was selling. Maybe it was because I'd seen the movie *Karate Kid* on TV once. I imagined that the sensei would see me, sense great things, and take me under his wing. I wanted someone to Mr. Miyagi me until I had power and purpose. And, most of all, peace.

But that's not how it happened. My first sensei may have been a decent teacher, but I didn't find a surrogate father in him. I was just another student. However, in the practice, I found the discipline and the control I needed. I got a job to pay for lessons and trained every minute I could. I channeled my anger, frustration, and strength into the gym. On the mat. At the dojo.

Training led me to become a fight extra in a movie that was filming in my hometown and then to doing stunt work, which led to my career.

Training also gave me patience in dealing with Conner. There was a part of me who wanted to hurt him, just a little, for the overly appreciative way he looked at Poppy. For all those things I knew he was thinking when he checked out her ass in her tight jeans. For the way he watched her full lips when she smiled with that Christmas-red lipstick. For that familiar wink he gave her when he left. I know what he was thinking because I was thinking the same damn thing.

And to hell with my lifelong illusion of calm. I'm still jealous.

I want her to be mine.

Only mine.

I can't concentrate. I keep losing track of the conversation. Belle asked me if something's wrong. Poppy keeps glancing over at me nervously. And I've almost tripped over my skates. Twice.

All because I overheard them setting a time for a date, or, as Poppy claims, a non-date.

But it's something.

And that's the other thing. She's not telling me what that something is.

I hate that she's holding back from me, which makes me appreciate her normally forthright nature. Where I'm closed, she's open. Where I'm contained, she's enthusiastic. She overshares, trusts me with her stories.

I wish things were different. Because I want her to trust me with it all.

"Daddy, watch!" Poppy has hold of my daughter's hand while Belle balances with no other aids. They skate smoothly, and then Poppy lets go as Belle glides along, only slightly wobbly. When she reaches me, she holds out her hands, and I grab them, catching her.

She's beaming, her cheeks pink from the cold. "Great job." I pick her up and spin us around slowly. She squeals.

I set her down again with a firm grasp so she doesn't fall, and we skate back to the edge.

"That was so much fun! Can we do it again?"

I laugh.

Poppy skates up to us. Her cheeks are as red as Belle's. Her nose as well. It's cute.

"High five, Belle babe!" She holds up a hand, and they slap palms. "You'll be hitting the Olympics soon."

Poppy turns to me. "You've got moves on the ice, big guy. Were you a *Cutting Edge* stunt double, by chance?"

"I played a lot of hockey."

The jaunty Christmas tune switches to a slow song. A few couples skate together, hand in hand.

"Poppy," Belle says, tugging at her sleeve. "They're playing your song. You and Daddy should skate-dance."

"Oh, why is it my song?" she asks.

"The man is singing about a lady in red, and you're wearing red."

She laughs, looking down at herself with a mocking expression. "I don't think I'm like the 'Lady in Red.'"

"Why not?" I ask.

She shrugs, looking uncomfortable. "I'm just not that kind of girl."

"What kind?"

She waves her hand. "I don't know. The kind that inspires love songs. It is romantic, though, isn't it?"

"Bullshit." I hate that she doesn't see herself like I see her. My breath catches every time she smiles.

"Changing the subject now," she says, blushing. "I wanted to ask you a favor."

"Whatever. It's yours."

She laughs. "Maybe I want a million dollars."

"Okay."

She shakes her head, but now it's her who sounds breathless. "Ronan! Be serious."

"I am."

"Okaaaay. Lucky for you, my favor is a little smaller. You

know I'm helping out with the Christmas ball and auction. It's on Saturday. I wondered if you and Belle wanted to come? She'd have to stay up a little late, but it would be fun. She's helped me with some of the prep, so I think she'd love to see it all come together. It's at the Holly Hill Inn. I looked at your schedule, and you're not due to be on set that night, but maybe you have other plans and—"

"Poppy," I cut her off. "Yes. Of course we'll go."

"Oh." She straightens her antlers. "Great. Thanks!"

I fight a smile. "Nice antlers."

I turn to Belle, who is now burrowing into my jacket, her own antlers digging into my side. I sweep my daughter into my arms. "I'm going to have two frozen reindeer on my hands if we don't get you both home."

"Do you want to drive with Belle, or should I?" Poppy asks.

I realize we came in different cars. And it sounds silly, but I don't want us to drive home separately. I want to be in the car with both of them. I want to know they are safe and warm. *And mine.*

"The roads might be icy. I'll drive us and arrange for your car in the morning."

"That's unnecessary. I've been driving in this town my whole life. The roads aren't that bad tonight. I've driven in way worse."

"Please?" I say.

"Okay," she agrees.

My gaze snaps back to hers. I raise an eyebrow. "That was easier than I expected."

She grins. "You said please. That should be rewarded."

I look down at her glossy red lips and want her to tell me please as I kiss her. I want her to beg, to plead for me as I take her. All night long.

But I don't say any of that. Instead, we return our skates and gather our things. And I drive us home in silence, with Belle falling asleep in her booster and the snow falling down around us, a blanket to soften the loudness of my thoughts.

Poppy

RONAN SAYS PLEASE.

Derek never said please.

Ronan opens the car door. He thanks me whenever I do anything for him, even if it's as small as making him a smoothie or watching his daughter, which is what I'm paid to do.

He listens to me as if what I'm saying matters.

And he kisses me as if he'll never stop, as if the world could end, bombs descend, floods rampage, but our kiss will still go on.

And with each quiet *please,* each thoughtful gesture, each protective inclination, and each devastating touch, I fall a little harder.

When he was just a movie star on the screen, I'd giggle and sigh over him.

When we first met, I developed a harmless crush, infatuated with someone who was impossibly out of my league.

But that infatuation has changed, morphed, deepened. And now I have to acknowledge that my crush isn't so harmless. It has the potential to be as devastating to my heart as his kisses are to my body.

"Do I have to go to bed already?" Belle whines, interrupting my thoughts.

"Yes, little one, you do," I say, brushing out her wet hair.

I know that voice. That's the voice of an overtired, overstimulated child. Ice-skating kept her up past her bedtime.

Now she's warm and clean after her bath in a new set of pajamas that we bought last week, comfy Christmas ones, these featuring snowmen.

I tie her hair back into a loose braid to keep it from getting tangled while she sleeps, as Ronan appears in the doorway.

"Story time?" he asks, picking up one of her favorites from the bookshelf. "It's going to be a short one since it's late."

I'm grateful we're on the same page. When I first started, I established a more regular routine and timetable, and Belle thrived. I expected Ronan to upend it all when he was home, but to my surprise, he's let my schedule stand, as if he respects what I've set up.

Belle yawns. I kiss her forehead. "Night night, love bug. I'll let your daddy read this one."

"Can you stay, Poppy?"

I look at Ronan. "Stay," he repeats. "Unless you're busy."

I smile at Belle. "Too busy for story time? Never."

Ronan struggles to crawl into the bed next to Belle. It's a bunk bed, but safe for younger kids, so it's lower than normal. As a result, it's almost impossible for him to fit in it. Even bending at an awkward angle, he hits his head on the bed above.

I laugh as his long legs stick out.

"I think we need story-time seating in here," I suggest. "Maybe some beanbags."

"If you think beanbags are going to be better, you're mistaken," he grumbles.

"We could get extra-large beanbags, Daddy," Belle says.

There's no room left on the bottom bunk, so I kneel next

to Ronan. He reads the story like the actor he is, playing all the parts, even using a falsetto for the mommy mouse.

He's almost on the last page when his phone rings.

He looks at the screen, and his face darkens. Tension seems to roll off him.

"It's your mom," he says to Belle, and he answers the phone with a clipped yet civil, "Hello."

Belle frowns and hugs the book they'd been reading.

Belle's mom has called to speak with her a few times since I started working here. I'm not sure what the conversations entail, but she's usually withdrawn after.

"Your mom wants to talk to you," Ronan says, passing the phone to Belle.

"H-hello," she says.

"I'll just leave now," I whisper, not wanting to intrude. "Good night, little one." I leave as quietly and quickly as I can. The peaceful room now has a heavy energy. I shut the door and walk down the hall until all I can hear are muffled voices.

I stand in front of my room, deliberating.

I could get ready for bed and have an early evening. But I'm feeling as restless and overstimulated as Belle was earlier. When I get like this, painting helps empty my mind and bring me back to equilibrium. And I'm still not finished with my last painting for the charity auction.

So I spend the next few hours in my new art room, hoping Ronan will come downstairs to talk after putting Belle to bed, but he never does.

I know he's fighting this because I'm the nanny.

But I want him to let me in. I feel like so much more. And I decide that when I get a chance to tell him that, I will. To hell with consequences. Ronan has been inspiring me to take charge of my own path. And it's leading straight to him.

CHAPTER 22

11 DAYS TO CHRISTMAS

Poppy

SHARP CRIES WAKE ME.

I jolt out of a deep sleep and race to the door, full of fearful possibilities.

Ronan's door on the opposite end of the hallway swings open, and we reach Belle's room at the same time.

I enter just after him, relief spreading through me when I see her safe, asleep in her bed.

"Daddy!" she cries out, thrashing, her eyes half open and face sweaty.

"It's a night terror," he whispers. "The child psychologist in LA said not to wake her."

We watch over her in silence. A few minutes later, she settles down and rolls over into a more peaceful sleep.

We walk out together, my heart rate settling back to normal, and I shut the door with a soft click.

Now that the worry over Belle recedes and the tension dissipates, I notice Ronan is dressed in low-slung boxers and nothing else.

My heart speeds right back up.

His gaze rakes over my state of dress—or undress. My shirt falls to mid-thigh, and all I'm wearing underneath are my day-of-the-week bikini briefs. Today's proclaim that it's Wednesday, which was what day it was when I first fell asleep. It's past midnight, so it's technically Thursday now.

Derek was not a fan of my quirky underwear.

I'm sure Ronan is the same. Alas.

I attempt to pull the shirt down lower, but it only seems to tighten across my chest, which makes my nipples show through more. So I give up and fold my arms, casual-like.

His eyes glint as they track my movements. A shiver runs down my spine.

My own gaze wanders down his body till it reaches his boxers, where there is a considerable bulge. I try not to think of just how considerable it is.

I force my eyes back to his face. It's a challenge, given the eye candy that is Ronan Masters unclothed. But I manage it.

My scrambled mind strains for a coherent thought. "Did she get a lot of night terrors in LA?" I circle back to what drew us both out of our rooms tonight.

He gives a shaky exhale and runs a hand through his hair, tucking the long strands behind his ears. "She did the first few weeks she stayed with me. The psychologist said that they're not uncommon, but they can be worse when a child is worried or has a sudden change, like her being left in an unfamiliar place."

"It would be a lot for anyone, especially a child as sensitive as Belle."

"Night terrors can be hereditary. I got them when I was younger. I was worse, though. I used to sleepwalk," he says.

"That must have been scary for your parents."

He doesn't answer, but his shoulders tense. I realize I've never heard him mention his dad, and barely his mom.

After a minute, he says, "It was just me and my mom. She wasn't…well. She was often too out of it to notice." He holds himself stiff, as if uncomfortable with the revelation.

"Your scar. The table," I say, remembering what he said about the glass table and sleepwalking.

He nods with a frown. I want to ask more. I want to understand him better. I want to console him and patch up the places that are obviously still bleeding inside. But instinct tells me to let him share at his own pace.

"Belle won't remember this in the morning." he changes the subject.

"She hasn't had a night terror since I've been here. Do you think she had one tonight because of the phone call?" I ask.

Our eyes connect. It wasn't just Belle who was disturbed by the call.

"I'm going to get a drink. Do you want to join me?" I set my fear of rejection aside because the man needs to talk.

He looks torn. Then his expression shifts. He lets out a gusty breath. "Yeah, I need something too."

"I'm going to grab a robe, and I'll meet you downstairs."

His lip quirks. "I guess I should get some clothes on as well."

"Nah. You're good."

He barks out a laugh. "You want me like this?"

I almost moan. *Yes. Very much like this.* Except maybe without the boxers.

"The majority of the world wants you like that, Mr. Superstar. But I won't be greedy. You can put on pants."

I say it lightly, as if I'm joking, but the reality is, I'm dying for him and his magnificent face and body, for his quiet soul, for all his obvious strength, and even more for the vulnerabilities he inadvertently reveals.

"I'll see you downstairs," he says, and I feel his whisper-rough voice like a caress on my overheated skin.

He doesn't move right away. And we stay in the hallway, devouring each other with our eyes, standing close, the space getting smaller between us as we lean toward each other.

I wonder if he's going to kiss me. Instead he turns and strides down the hallway toward his room. Presumably, to put on pants. He's mean like that.

Ronan

When she said she'd make us a drink, I thought maybe she meant a glass of wine. Or a cup of tea.

But she makes us hot chocolate.

I look at the cup she hands me with bemusement. There are marshmallows. And...

"A candy cane?" I ask, holding it out of the drink.

"It adds a nice peppermint flavor."

"This is a giant cup of sugar," I say with disgust.

"Chocolate is healthy."

"A little dark chocolate. Maybe. But this is not dark chocolate."

"Say thank you and drink your cup of delicious sugar."

"Thank you," I murmur and take a sip.

She watches me. "Good, right?"

"It's good," I acknowledge.

"Do you want to know the secret ingredient?"

It pops into my head that the secret ingredient is her. She makes everything special. But I don't say shit like that. *Except with her.*

"The secret is condensed milk."

I groan. "That's worse than straight sugar."

"But it's soooooo good."

I have to admit, it is good, even if it means I'll have to double my workout tomorrow. And the sugar will keep me up half the night.

She grins up at me, her hazel eyes sparkling, more gold than green in the warm light of the kitchen.

Her smile has the strength of a fist. She steals my breath, takes my voice, knocks me sideways. The way she looked earlier, standing in the darkened hallway in just a threadbare shirt, is forever forged in my brain. I could see the outline of her curves, and I'm dying to explore each one with my hands and tongue. Her dusty pink areolas, her tight nipples, the way her waist nipped in and her hips rounded out. I can't stop wondering what she was wearing beneath that shirt, if anything. Now she's wrapped all that up in a demure robe.

Her hair falls in an artful mess of curls. She usually wears it up in a jaunty ponytail, a ribbon tied around it. The times I've fantasized about undoing that ribbon and watching her cinnamon hair tumble around her shoulders and down her back border on obsession.

I started a fire while she made the hot chocolate so we can drink it in the living room.

It would have been smarter and safer to stay in the kitchen, to sit on opposite ends of the island counter while we sip our drinks with the lights bright and a broad expanse of white marble between us.

Instead, we sit close in the dim light of the fire. There's only one place we can set our drinks down—on the coffee table fronting the sofa. It's a big couch, so there is lots of space between us. But it still feels intimate. She curls her legs up on the couch and faces me.

She takes a sip and then sets her drink down on the table.

"So, you can tell me to mind my own business. But I can't help noticing that Belle doesn't look happy when her mom calls. Is she okay?" she asks.

I don't know how to answer her.

"I just want to be able to understand a little better so I can help. Belle," she adds. She watches me as if I'm a wild animal with an injury that she has to approach warily.

"She doesn't talk about her mom much."

"It must have been confusing to be dropped off like that, when she didn't know you very well," she says gently.

"Like I said, she doesn't talk about it. She didn't have a temper tantrum or complain. The only emotion she showed in the first week was during her night terrors."

I'm speaking into my mug, but when I finally look up, Poppy has shifted closer, bridging the distance between us.

She puts a hand on mine and squeezes. "I'm sorry," she says. "It hasn't just been hard for Belle. It's been hard for you as well."

"I don't think about that." I get the words out despite the tightness in my throat. "I'm an adult. She's the one who's had a hard time."

"Always so tough," she says with a gentle, knowing smile. "Adults have hard times too. And it makes it better to admit that. To have someone to talk to."

"I don't do that."

She laughs. "I know. But maybe you should."

I just grunt.

"What will happen when you two go back to California?"

"I don't know." I take another sip of the chocolate and am surprised to see it's almost empty. And I'm not sure what it is. Whether it's the warm fire and dark room with the lights of the Christmas tree shining down on us. Maybe it's the crème de cocoa and crème de menthe Poppy added to the hot chocolate, her other secret ingredients. I suspect it's all of that, but mostly it's this girl in front of me, who is so beautiful it hurts—not simply on the outside, but on the inside as well. Whatever it is, emotions that are usually wound up tight unravel. And so do my words.

"I don't know what will happen. When she got off the phone tonight, Belle asked if she could stay with me and not go back to her mom," I say. "I can't promise her that, though. I've hired the best lawyers who are trying to work out an agreement with Claire's lawyers. But even if I fight for primary custody and win, I have three movies lined up after this one, all shooting out of the country. Belle might think she wants to live with me now, but what if I screw it all up, even if I do get that chance? I know even less about little girls than I know about being a dad." I stop as abruptly as I began and look into the fire, avoiding Poppy's eyes.

Her hand on mine is warm and tight. She strokes my palm with a finger, and it soothes me. Just that small touch.

"You love her. And that's all that matters. You'll figure out the rest."

Her words are an arrow that pierces me, hitting straight and true. *Love.* I know even less about love than I do about little girls and being a dad. But Poppy is right. I love Belle with all the fierceness in my heart. It was unexpected. Her showing up in my life. The love showing up in my heart. But now she's mine, and I'm hers.

"That scares me even more," I surprise myself by admitting.

"I know," she says and squeezes my hand. "That's what love does. It's because you care. It raises the stakes on everything."

The stakes *are* high. I can't afford to get this wrong. Which is why Belle has to be my first priority and what I need to remember when I'm thinking about Poppy's hazel eyes and cinnamon hair. When I'm counting her freckles and waiting for her dimple to show. When I'm dreaming of her soft skin and smooth legs. When I want to unravel the ribbon in her hair and sink into her body.

"What if—" I clear my throat. I don't continue. I can't. I want to ask Poppy about what happens when Claire returns to reclaim Belle and she goes back to her life in England and I only get to see her on the occasional weekends. Ask her how I'll stitch my heart back together. I haven't let myself be this vulnerable since I was a child. I learned it was best to not hope, to not want things I couldn't have. It was less painful that way. The only person I could fully trust was myself.

But now, I have a little girl to protect, which means opening up to love and pain once again. Especially since Belle is only with me temporarily. Everything that feels precious lately is temporary.

Poppy tilts her head and puts her arm on mine. "My seventh-grade art teacher helped me when I was going through a rough patch. My dad had a heart attack after we fought, and I thought it was my fault. My teacher was only with me for a year, but she made all the difference. She was wise and kind, but mostly she just cared, and it was exactly what I needed, when I needed it.

"Ronan, it's got to be the hardest thing in the world, not knowing how long you have with Belle, but this time you have together will stay with her—and you—forever, no matter what happens in the future. You're her dad. I see what a difference your love has made to her. I know you don't believe it. But you are getting this right. It's clear that Belle loves and trusts you. And the fact that you worry about messing it up just means you care."

I blow out a slow breath. "I can't get this wrong. My mom…she wasn't able to get it right." I falter as anxiety, thick and cold, flows through my veins. It's hard to get the words out. I've never spoken about this to anyone. Not teachers or principals or well-meaning friends.

I push past the fear. For the first time, I want to share my burden. "I'm not sure what was wrong with her. I've—I've done some research. We never had the money for decent doctors and she was never properly diagnosed. She was a good mom when she was able to be. She would be okay for stretches at a time, and we'd have a normal life. And then suddenly everything would get bad again. I tried to help but didn't know how. She used pills and alcohol to help her cope with her mind, to help her sleep and wake, to help her with anxiety. But they'd only make things worse, make her less able to function. Maybe it would've been different if she'd lived long enough for me to help her more. I could have paid for her to get the proper diagnosis and treatment for whatever mental health problems she had. I could have helped her live a good life. But I'll never know. She died right before I graduated from high school."

"Ronan, I'm so sorry," Poppy says. Her eyes are filled with compassion. With something that turns my insides out. "Thank you for telling me," she says simply. And then she wraps her arms around me tightly and buries her head in my chest as if she could take some of my burden, as if it's the most natural thing in the world to do. I rest my chin on her head. I'm scared to move and break this connection.

We stay like that for I don't know how long. Time stops, contracts, turns in on itself. There's just the crackle of the fire and the tick of the clock on the wall.

When she finally draws back, she pins me with her clear green gaze. "You may think you didn't help your mom. But I'm sure she was thankful every day that she had you, even if you were too young to do all you wish you could. And I'm also one thousand percent certain that you'll figure out how to give Belle all the love and care she needs. You and Belle will figure this out together," she says with gravity.

Then she gives me a smile that illuminates every shadow in the room and dark space inside me. "You're Ronan Masters. You can do anything. Except fix broken elevators."

I look down at her lips forming that grin. It's a mistake because I want her. I want to drown in her simple words of empathy and faith. I want her beauty and gentleness and understanding. And I sure as hell want that mouth.

I know all the reasons why I shouldn't have her. I'm listing them in my head when she closes the scant distance and kisses me. The heat of our connection incinerates my list of good intentions, melts away any resistance or good sense, and sets my body ablaze. I lose myself in her kiss, groaning when her mouth opens under mine and my tongue brushes hers. The kiss deepens, ignites, and I'm caught in our fire.

CHAPTER 23

11 DAYS TO CHRISTMAS (STILL)

Poppy

I KISSED HIM. I CAN'T BELIEVE I JUST WENT AHEAD AND DID IT.

I wanted to take away his worry about Belle, even if just for a little while, as if he had a wound and I needed to kiss it better. What can I say? I'm a fixer.

Plus, he was looking at me with such want.

One minute, we were staring at each other, and the next, I launched myself at him.

But it doesn't take long for him to take over the kiss. He may be a man of few words, but damn, he knows what to do with his mouth.

He groans and pulls me to him until I'm straddling his powerful body and pure sensation takes over.

He kisses me over and over, soft, slow, sensual, in a rhythm I mimic with my body. When I roll my hips, he groans and kisses me even more feverishly. He's hard and impossibly big against me.

I run my hands over his shirt, and I revel in the heat and strength beneath it. Even through the material, I can feel each defined muscle. It's as if a sculptor molded him as an example of the perfect man.

In retaliation, he runs his fingers down my neck and follows my collarbone lower until he spreads my robe and dips into the collar. He pulls my sleep shirt lower until my breast is fully exposed. And only then does Ronan drag his lips from mine.

I'm bereft at the loss of his drugging kisses, but then I feel the full heat of his eyes on me. "Fuck, you're beautiful."

He kisses my neck and presses a butterfly brush of lips to my collarbone, soft and chaste.

I melt when he takes my nipple in his mouth, nipping at me slightly. Desire, hot and wanting, shoots through me. I was wet before from just his mouth on mine, but this is so much more. My robe falls open, and I wrap my legs around him.

Our last encounter in the kitchen was an inferno that blazed fast and fierce. This is just as hot, but it's softer, sweeter, more intimate, perhaps because we've opened up more of ourselves to each other.

He sucks first one nipple, then the other. I've always felt my breasts were just average. But now, I'm rethinking that. They've got Ronan transfixed, so there must be something a little special about them.

His hand makes its way down to my underwear. I gasp, and the sound seems to fuel him. His gaze follows his hand's progression as he lifts my shirt. Only my underwear and his sleep pants are between us. I can feel him long, hard, and thick against me. I can't help it. I roll my hips restlessly.

"If you keep doing that, I'm going to lose it," he warns in a desperate whisper.

"Good."

He grasps me to still my hips and then lifts the shirt up a little more, exposing my pale stomach. I wish now I'd taken up Pilates. Or my mother's Zumba classes.

He laughs, a surprised sound. "Does your underwear say Wednesday?"

Oops. I guess it's time to find out whether Ronan prefers sexy panties.

"Um, yes?" I say.

"As in, Wednesday, tonight?"

"Mmm-hmm." I kiss his neck, trying to distract him.

"Wait, I need to get a closer look," he says. I giggle as he picks me up, then gently tosses me onto the sofa and lifts my shirt higher. His head is dangerously close to my very wet and wanting pussy. I wriggle my hips a little to assuage the heat.

He traces his finger over the word written on the thin cotton, making me moan.

"So yesterday, your underwear said—" His voice is teasing.

"Tuesday." I complete his sentence.

"And when you get up this morning, you'll put on panties that say—"

"Thursday."

He smiles, one of his rare ones. It takes over his entire face and enters his eyes. Again, it makes me think of things magic and rare—rainbows and four-leaf clovers and days when my entire class is painting in silence. And I wonder, have I found my own magic unicorn of a man who gets turned on by white cotton panties listing the day of the week?

"Do you always wear these?"

"I mean, no, not always. But if I start on Monday, I like to keep the streak going until Sunday. I'm a little superstitious about it, like it would be bad luck to just stop midweek." I'm embarrassed now. "Is that weird? That's weird, right? I'm sorry I'm a cotton brief kind of girl."

"I'm not complaining, Poppy. Though I am wondering if you have cherry panties that matches your nightshirt."

Now I smile widely. Because I do. I so do. Then it's my turn to ask my own underwear-related question.

"You're not wearing any, are you? Underwear, I mean."

His smile turns sensual. "No."

"Good," I say and reach out to run my hand over his length and dip my hand into his pants. Feeling him bare, huge, hard, against my skin sends a wave of heat through me. I want him inside me.

He moans and rests his forehead against mine. "God, Poppy, you're killing me."

He slips a hand into my panties and strokes my aching center, teasing me.

"Same," I say, desperate for him.

A cry from upstairs breaks through the quiet night.

Belle. We break apart guiltily.

"Shit," he swears. "Shit." He sits up, adjusting his pants and shirt.

A cry sounds again. Belle's night terror must be back.

I kind of want to cry too.

"I'll go." His face is a mask.

I sit up, trying to break through the fog of lust, pulling my shirt down and wrapping my robe around me. "I can help."

"No." It comes out harshly. "I've got it," he says, gentler now. "It's safer for you to go back to your room."

He leaves me like that, in the living room, body still

pulsing from his hands and lips on me. And as the fog clears, I realize he isn't coming back to continue this. Not tonight, at least. And I wonder if ever.

THE NEXT MORNING, I MEET CONNER AT THE NOW-VACANT store on Main Street. Sadie joins us.

"Oh my God, Poppy. It's perfect."

"It is," I agree. I can't say anything else because Sadie is right. And if I weren't dying for this property before, I am even more now. Because seeing it empty for the first time, I realize it has all the space I want. All the windows and high ceilings make it light and airy. There's a room I could use for classes and events, and a separate area that could be set up as a gallery space and shop. The upstairs is even better than I could imagine, having been renovated with exposed brick walls and hardwood floors.

I'm dying to scream, "I'll take it!" But I don't. A lifetime of being told to be practical echoes in my brain.

Ever since middle school, I've done everything my parents expected of me.

I know I'm an adult. But as my sister pointed out, I haven't exactly established full autonomy.

I try to think of WWRD. *What would Ronan do?* He lives his life on his own terms.

What would it be like to live like that?

I run my hand along a built-in cabinet, closing my eyes as I track the pattern of the historic building. If I listen just to myself, what is it I want?

This. I want this place and my own studio.

I open my eyes. "If I said yes to buying it, and I'm not saying I am. But what's the next step?"

"Yes!" Sadie cries, fist in the air. "Welcome to the 'hood, neighbor."

"I didn't say I'd take it. I still don't know if I can get the loan."

"You will," she says with a grin. "You'll see."

Conner smiles and outlines the items to line up and steps to take. When he talks about dollar amounts and mortgages, anxiety shoots through me. I can't help but worry about what my dad would say.

I shove that thought away. I've made decisions by group consensus all my life, first following my parents' advice and then Derek's lead and, really, anyone else who felt like weighing in.

That needs to change.

My phone rings, and Ronan's name pops up on the screen.

"Hello?" I answer. "Ronan?" My face turns pink at the thought of what we did last night.

"Hi." His rich, rough voice gives me gooseflesh, even when it's over the phone. "I wanted you to know I'm heading back to set at three p.m. this afternoon, so if you could be home by then, that would be great." Ronan had the morning off and was spending time hanging out with Belle, so I'd taken the opportunity to do some errands and meet Conner.

"Oh, okay, th—"

"Poppy. I'm sorry to interrupt, but I have to leave in five minutes," Conner says, looking at his watch.

"Just one second," I say into the phone.

I turn to the real estate agent. "That's no problem, Conner. I'll call you later today and we can talk more."

"Sure. Call me anytime. And I hope you say yes. I think this is perfect for you."

I say goodbye and then speak into the phone again. "Sorry about that. Where were we?"

"Is that Conner?"

"Yeah. I'm downtown."

"Just make sure Conner doesn't make you late." His voice is tight.

"Of course not," I say, indignant. I've never been late with him. Not once.

I count to ten in my head and remind myself that he's my boss and his generous salary could enable me to make my dream a reality.

"I have to go," he growls before hanging up.

And I'm left staring at the phone, not sure what just happened.

"Was that Ronan?" Sadie asks, looking at me with curiosity.

"Yep," I say, putting my phone back in my purse.

"What's wrong?" she asks. "Is everything okay?"

I shake my head. "I'm not really sure."

I'm not sure of much of anything right now. Is he annoyed because I'm with Conner? He may be jealous, but he doesn't seem to want me enough to take a chance on us. The only thing I'm certain of is that he keeps holding back. And all too soon, Ronan, and this chance to explore whatever it is between us, will be gone.

CHAPTER 24

9 DAYS TO CHRISTMAS

Poppy

THE LIVING ROOM LOOKS LIKE A CHRISTMAS EXPLOSION. Wrapping paper and ribbons threaten to swallow me. Death by Christmas Wrap. I could think of worse ways to go.

It's nine days until Christmas now, and I'm mostly through my gift shopping. I try to choose presents that are personal and mean something, which puts on extra pressure.

The gifts with the most potential for controversy are the potato ricers I bought both my aunts so they can bring them to our Thanksgiving festivities and hopefully settle the great potato debate that happens every year. I think they secretly like arguing, though, so I'm not sure if the gifts will be a hit.

I got my mom a *Flashdance*-inspired Zumba outfit that I know she'll love. But even better than '80s workout gear is the gift for my mom that will keep on giving—a little-known, extremely rare Jane Fonda workout video I found for her. It's one that was never released. A video from the vault, if you will. I followed up on a rumor when I was researching Jane Fonda gifts, somehow managed to track it down, and used my powers of persuasion to get a copy. A mix of compliments, bribery, and tough love.

My mother is going to adore it. So. Much.

I wrap it carefully, making sure to make the edges straight. I'm not the best wrapper, but what I lack in precision, I make up for in creativity and a plethora of ribbon.

A cornucopia of ribbon. A veritable waterfall of it.

I hold up a stuffed animal and chew on my lip, debating my wrapping strategy. Soft gifts without an obvious shape are especially hard. It's for Belle. She's obsessed with corgis. And I know she wants a real dog, but though I've tried to use those same powers of persuasion on Ronan, I haven't had much success with that particular dream gift. So I bought the cutest stuffed corgi for her, a placeholder of sorts for the pet she will eventually get.

I found rhinestone custom collars on Etsy and ordered one that reads Peppermint Patty, which is the name Belle wants for her dream dog. I bought a Christmas outfit for the stuffed puppy also, of course.

I must say, so far, I've hit all my gifts out of the park this year. Except for one.

Ronan.

What do you buy a superstar who has everything? A man who could purchase the best money can offer?

I'm making him a gift, but it doesn't seem like enough. Though, I know what I wish I could give him. Me, wrapped in just a bow, in his bed. But I worry he would return that gift unopened.

He's been avoiding me ever since our latest make-out

session. We've done a few holiday activities with Belle in our joint quest to give her the best Christmas—visiting my favorite Christmas market and even a tree-lighting ceremony last night—but he's made sure we're never alone. Which means we haven't talked about the kissing—and more—that we've done.

And then there was his annoyance that day on the phone when I was with Conner.

The door swings open, and snow blows in. Along with the snow comes Ronan, as if my thoughts have conjured him up.

My stomach tightens with nerves.

"Hi," I say, looking up at him.

He stops short when he sees me, surrounded by all the Christmas paper.

"Sorry about the mess. Just trying to get some wrapping done."

His mouth draws down, and his shoulders tense up.

"It's…festive," he says, looking around at the explosion of wrap.

I smile awkwardly. Tonight, there's no cherry nightshirt, no wild hair. I haven't changed for bed yet, so I'm in jeans and a sweater, my hair in a neat ponytail, tied up with a green ribbon. No one could fault me for being unprofessional. I'm in respectable nanny mode.

He picks up the corgi, and his face softens.

"For Belle."

I can't help my grin. "Who else?"

"Peppermint Patty, huh?"

"Just until she gets the real live Peppermint Patty."

"Not going to happen," he grumps. "A dog is permanent."

"So are little girls," I say in a soft voice.

His gaze rakes over mine.

He sets down the stuffie. "I'm sure she'll love it."

"I made spaghetti Bolognese. I spiralized some zucchini for you to have with it to make it extra not-as-tasty. Though if you want to go wild, I've got some of the real pasta and a lot of Parmesan cheese."

"I already ate on set."

"Oh. Okay."

He looks at me with a guarded expression. "I appreciate you going to the trouble."

I shrug, hating how polite we are. How strained. He's probably afraid I'll jump him if he shows me an ounce of familiarity. Because I did.

And then there's a little something else I need to clear up.

"Belle was invited to sleep over at Sasha's house tomorrow, with Sasha's mom. Belle is excited because it would be her first sleepover. But it's up to you."

He tilts his head. "You trust her, Sasha's mom?"

"Libby? Yes, she's lovely. She's a pediatrician and has lived in Snowflake Harbor all her life. But maybe you could talk with her and decide for yourself."

He nods. "I guess Belle's old enough?"

"Well, I think every parent and child are different in what they're comfortable with, but I was going to sleepovers about that age. Belle wants to go. She even made a series of poster boards today to tell you why she thinks she should be allowed. There was glitter involved." I laugh. "But I wanted to warn you, so you're not blindsided."

He gives me a slight smile. "Thanks. I guess it's fine. I'll have to talk to Sasha's mom first, though."

"That's a good idea. I'll forward you her number." I pause. Here's the awkward part. "But the thing is, the invitation is for Saturday night, which is the night of the ball."

"The ball?"

Oh great, has he's forgotten? Hurt twists in me.

"Yes, the Christmas ball that you and Belle were going to attend tomorrow night. The one auctioning some of my paintings."

He sits on the edge of the couch. He's making me nervous perched there, not saying anything, though I guess it's better than when he was standing.

I shift, removing some ribbon from around my neck. "Anyway, the sleepover is the same night as the ball. I thought Belle would like to attend, which is why I invited the two of you. But she'd rather go to the sleepover, and I'm sure you don't want to go without her, so I guess you're off the hook. Ha. Lucky you."

He crosses his arms over his chest. It's his go-to posture.

"You don't want me to go," he says flatly.

"W-what? No. I mean, yes. I mean..." I stammer. "I didn't think you'd want to go without Belle. There wouldn't be much point, would there?"

It's a half-truth. I'd asked them, not only because I thought Belle would enjoy it, but also because I wanted to go with Ronan. He's my dream date, and that hasn't changed.

But I'm not sure where we stand. Am I still only the nanny? Or more?

"I'm giving you an out. I'm sure a ball is not on your list of preferred activities. And a Christmas ball, at that. I thought—"

"No," he grinds out.

My mouth forms a surprised O.

"Do you want an out? So you can have someone else take you? Did Conner ask?"

He is seriously not happy. Is this a case where he doesn't want me, but he doesn't want anyone else to have me either? Because if so, that's bull. *Men.*

"I'm not going with anyone else. And I don't want an out," I say heatedly. "I wasn't with Conner on a date. I was with him because he's a real estate agent, and he represents a property on Main Street that I might want to buy for an art studio." I shake my head. "I don't know if I can, and I'm not sure if it's a great idea, but I wanted to look at it."

All the fight goes out of him. He smiles. One of his rare ones, the kind that touches his eyes and gives him a sexy slash of a dimple that slices his left cheek. "Why didn't you tell me? That's amazing," Ronan says. "You need to do it."

"Maybe." Our eyes connect.

"Did you take it?" he prompts.

"I'm still thinking about it."

"You shou—"

"I never wanted an out," I interrupt him. I want to talk about my studio with him, but not right now. Right now, I need to make this clear. "And certainly not because of another guy."

"Good." He stares at me with an intensity I can't read.

"I just wasn't sure you'd want to go with me," I admit. "At least, not without Belle." I look down at my hands.

"Poppy, hell. It's not that. It's never been that. I've always wanted... I'm just trying to do the right thing. But every time I look at you..." He stops. He doesn't sound like himself. He's usually so definitive. So completely and exactly sure of himself. But now, he seems the opposite of certain.

He runs a hand through his hair, then runs a hand over his artfully stubbled jaw. His look in *The Wanderers* consists of the perfect amount of wheat-gold stubble, just enough to emphasize the masculine beauty of his face and make him look like he's been carved in the form of a golden god.

"It's a little over a week to Christmas," he says.

"I know."

"Belle and I are supposed to fly back before Christmas," he says. "We leave."

"I know," I rasp.

"And you go back to your life."

"I know." My voice is as raw as my heart.

"You're Belle's nanny. I can't—"

"I kissed *you* first," I say. "I'm the one who crossed that initial line. Not you."

His lip curls up in an expression that's as rueful as it is seductive. "Do you think that makes a damn bit of difference? You didn't do anything that I wasn't dying to do to you a thousand times over."

I make a quick, shocked sound. "Did you? Think about it. Before, I mean."

"Only every day. And every night. And all the moments in between since you've come to live with us, since you burst into the elevator in that ridiculous dress with your ridiculous purse and enchanted Belle. And enchanted me." His voice is sandpaper rough.

"But I didn't. I didn't do anything special."

"You were yourself, Poppy. That's all you ever have to do to enthrall me. To make me want you more than I've ever wanted anyone."

Ronan

"Oh." There's that sound again. That quick, breathless exclamation that catches in her throat and gusts out of her lips and makes me want to discover all the sounds she'll make for me, sounds of pleasure and wildness.

I shouldn't tell her all of this. I should do what I've been trying to do since the other night and keep a professional distance. But with every passing day, that distance gets harder to maintain.

I've been so twisted up with lust and longing and, yes, jealousy. I've been jealous as hell that Conner might have taken his shot with her and won because I'd stepped back. If it had only been jealousy, though, it would have been manageable. But there was also this feeling that I had lost something infinitely precious—the chance to be with Poppy, even if it's just for a week.

We only have a week.

All the good reasons I have for staying away fade to insignificance with our shrinking timeline. I don't want to waste one more minute hiding behind the bullshit of professional distance.

We may live in opposite worlds and have opposite personalities. I may have nothing to offer her for the future. I don't do relationships, and even if I did, now would not be the time to try for a long-distance one. I already face having my heart ripped open with one loss. I don't need two.

But I need this one last week with everything in me. Every single ridiculous, Christmas-filled day. And maybe even a few extra days.

"What if we didn't leave on Christmas Eve?" I say, the words popping up and out of me unbidden. They may be spontaneous, but they feel absolutely, utterly right.

"What?"

"I have the house until the end of December, and I don't need to be back in LA until the 28th. It's only a few days more, and, I mean, you don't have to spend Christmas with us. You have your own family, which I understand. But I thought Belle would like to stay here for Christmas and maybe—"

"Yes!" Poppy shouts, and she throws herself into my arms. I catch her easily; of course I do. And I swing her around, not able to hold back the goofy smile that matches hers.

"Yeah?"

"Heck yeah," she practically yells.

"Hell yeah," I repeat.

"Does this mean…?"

"It means whatever you want it to mean."

Her smile is slow and sensual. I set her down to the floor, inching her body along mine.

"I can think of a lot of things I want it to mean." She grins.

I meet my forehead to hers. "I don't want to fight this anymore. Not when we have such a short time. But we have to keep this separate from Belle. I can't risk her getting hurt."

"She can have our days," Poppy says. "And you can have my nights."

Her words and that teasing smile get me harder, if that's even possible. "God, you can't say things like that. You don't know how much I've been fantasizing about you."

"You can tell me all about it. In detail."

"How about I show you?"

"I like that idea. Upstairs?" she asks, looking shy now.

"Eventually. But I want to indulge in one particular fantasy. It involves that rug in front of the fire."

"I like the way your imagination works."

I pull her up. She squeals and wraps her legs around me. I walk her over to the rug and sit her on it then brush aside the tendrils of hair that have escaped from her ponytail.

"I have another fantasy," I say and slowly pull the bow holding her hair. Only. "Huh. Your hair's still up," I say, disappointed.

She gives a short laugh. "It's only a ribbon. It wouldn't hold up my hair. I have a hair tie beneath it."

When she gently pushes, I fall back. She straddles me, and I forget all about the hair bow. But then she reaches up and pulls out the tie herself, and her cinnamon waves fall around her like a waterfall. Desire shoots through me at the sensuality of the gesture. At the mischief in her gaze. At this girl, with her hair ribbons and days-of-the-week underwear.

Speaking of which.

"I have another fantasy, and you better not disappoint this time."

"You have a lot of fantasies. And what might this one be?"

"It's Friday." I start to unfasten her jeans.

She cracks up. "Oh my God. My underwear? You have a weird fetish."

"Every single day, I think about it. I can't stop wondering what your damn panties say."

"It's your special day, big boy. Read them and weep." She pulls her jeans down in a little shimmy that kills me and shows off the front of her panties, with the word Friday in red script.

"Damn. Get that over here."

We wrestle, both laughing, until her jeans are completely off, and she's so effortlessly sexy, it's all I can do to stare and swear and die for her.

"I want to make you come."

Though that's not quite accurate. I'm past mere want. This is an essential need. This is obsession.

What it's not is casual, and that's the most dangerous part of this whole damn thing.

CHAPTER 25

9 DAYS TO CHRISTMAS (STILL)

Poppy

"I WANT TO MAKE YOU COME," HE GROWLS.

"Yes please," I reply with a laugh. I'm not going to argue with that.

In one smooth motion, he flips our positions, so that I'm on my back on the soft rug. The light from the fire I lit earlier flickers softly, bathing everything in gold. He's above me, holding his weight on his hands that bracket my face.

He leans down and kisses me. It's soft and teasing.

"Take off your shirt," he commands.

I sit up just enough to pull it above my head. He takes it from me and throws it across the room.

Okay, then.

I'm clad in just my thin cotton bra and underwear, and he doesn't seem to mind that my bra isn't sexy lace either.

He gives me a devastating half smile and kisses my nipples through the fabric, until the cotton is damp and I'm panting in desperation.

He watches me with a hot, intense stare.

"God, look at you." The deep rasp of his voice reverberates to my core. "You don't know how beautiful you are."

But I do now. With him. I feel it. I feel it for the first time.

"I love your freckles." He places a soft kiss on my belly. "I'm making it my mission to find and kiss every single one on your body. They're like constellations leading me to heaven." I feel his smile against my skin.

"This one." He places a soft kiss a little lower.

"And this one." He kisses farther down.

"And here." He kisses the top of my underwear. I suck in a startled breath.

I wriggle, and he peels down my Friday panties. Kisses me on my mound. And I'm glad that I shaved this morning, everywhere.

"You're bare," he says and presses his mouth lower, at the seam of my sex. I gasp.

I sit up a little and look at the top of his head. "You don't like me shaved?"

"I like you any way. But I was looking forward to finding out if your hair is cinnamon-colored everywhere."

He licks me, and I almost skyrocket off the rug. He gives me another slow, sweet lick, taking his time, savoring me. And I lie back with a moan.

"God, I love the sounds you make."

"God, I love the things you do." I sigh.

And then I can't talk anymore. Words leave me. Heck, language and any rational conscious thought leaves me. I become pure sensation. He goes down on me like he does everything, with intense concentration and the intention to do things exactly right.

I've never had my pleasure focused on to such a degree, and it's intoxicating. The way he's teasing, licking, sucking me wildly, and the satisfied sounds he makes as I go higher make it clear he's getting off on this as well.

Ronan is lord and master of oral. I lose control when he pushes two fingers into me. His rhythm in and out matches the rhythm of the long, savoring licks he gifts my clit. I grasp his hair and grind myself against him over and over until eventually I shatter into a thousand tiny pieces of a bliss so intense that even the gradual drifting down from it is better than any sex I've ever had.

I'm a puddle on a rug by the fire, absolutely disintegrated. Ronan rains soft kisses on my chest and neck, bringing me back to slow consciousness.

"You're incredible," he says. "I could get dangerously addicted."

He kisses my lips, and I taste myself on him.

"Okay," I say again. "I'm not going to argue because I've never felt anything that amazing. Ever."

"Good," he grunts.

Less than two weeks, I remind myself, *that's all we have, even if he does stay a few extra days through Christmas.*

"Daddy!" a distant cry sounds from upstairs.

We jump apart.

"Fuck," he swears.

"No," I whine. "Not now. Not tonight."

He groans, a rueful sound. And kisses me, quick and rough with pent-up passion.

"I'll get her," he says when we part.

"Are you coming back?"

He shakes his head regretfully. "I have to leave."

"What?"

"I'm only here on a break. We're shooting through the night, remember? But I'm off tomorrow, so I'm all yours then."

"And I'll be yours," I say. "Completely."

"I have to go upstairs. Stop torturing me. I can't fucking wait until tomorrow."

I give him another long, lingering kiss and then push him away before I can't give him up.

As he walks up the stairs, I realize how one-sided our interaction was. Again. He didn't get to come like I did, but he didn't complain. Instead, he made me feel like a goddess.

That type of selflessness in the bedroom isn't something I'm used to.

On Saturday, I'm going to make it up to him.

Big-time.

And, God, judging by the looks of him, it will be big.

Very, very big.

CHAPTER 26

8 DAYS TO CHRISTMAS

Poppy

BELLE AND I SPENT A BUSY MORNING HELPING TO GET THE Holly Hill Inn set up for the ball. In the late afternoon, I drop her off at her sleepover, which she's both excited and apprehensive about. As I pull back into the lake house's driveway, my stomach does a funny little flip when I see Ronan's car.

Ronan, whose mouth has been on and in my most intimate places.

I walk in the door, but he isn't downstairs. It's possible he's taking a nap since he worked through the night and must be exhausted.

I look at my watch. I don't have much time to get ready before we have to leave for the Christmas ball.

It strikes me that my emotions are not dissimilar to Belle's for her first sleepover. I guess it will probably be

Ronan's and my first sleepover as well. I feel both apprehension and excitement. I know it's stupid to fall so hard for a man who will ultimately break my heart, even if it's not his fault. But I can't regret it.

I open the door to my room, thinking about how I have less than an hour to shower, do my hair and makeup, and put on my only gown, a black dress that's flattering, even if it isn't the most festive.

That's when I see it.

A dress hanging in the window. It's Christmas red. I reach out to touch it. The material is soft and gauzy, with a classic elegance and just the right amount of sexy in the off-the-shoulder design.

"Do you like it?" a deep voice asks behind me.

I turn to Ronan, looking devastatingly handsome in dress slacks and a long-sleeved white shirt open a few buttons. If this is how he looks only partially ready for the night, I can't imagine my reaction to him in a suit. Thank God it's not a tux affair because I probably wouldn't survive.

I turn back to the dress. "It's incredible," I say. I take it from the hanger and hold it up to me. It's the perfect length.

"How did you know my size?"

A smile whispers across his face. "I know every inch of your body."

I lick my suddenly dry lips. I have to look away or I fear I'll tackle him. And then we wouldn't show for the ball. It's tempting.

I run my hand over the dress, marveling anew at the softness of the fabric, but when I see the tag, I freeze.

"Ronan!" I hiss. "This is Dior!"

"And?"

"It's Dior. I can't afford a dress like this."

"Then it's a good thing I bought it and not you."

I see another hanger with a white cape.

"The cape is Dior also!"

"It is? Huh."

On my favorite white chair, there's a box.

"Oh my God. Shoes. Louboutins."

"Emma helped with the shopping. But I picked out the dress."

I walk to the mirror, still clasping the gown to myself. I'm surprised to see that the red color doesn't clash with my hair, which can sometimes be a problem. Against my pale skin, the vibrant red makes me glow, causing my freckles to stand out in relief.

I turn back to Ronan. He looks so proud. He reminds me of Belle when she presents me with a picture she's drawn.

I'm still not used to accepting things from others, especially not something like this, but if I don't accept the dress gracefully, I'll ruin this moment. Plus, I really love it.

I have to force myself not to read too much into his generosity, though. He's kind and thoughtful. He wants to do something nice for me. And he's rich as hell, so the expense isn't a factor. For him, this is probably the equivalent of a guy giving a girl flowers.

But his sweet gesture still blows every other gift out of the water. Except his gift of the art studio. Darn him. He's ruined me for anyone else, ever.

"I love it," I say finally, my eyes wet with unshed tears, which I blink back.

He nods, looking embarrassed now. "I better get ready as well. But I have one more thing for you to wear."

He hands me another small shopping bag. I peek in it and laugh.

It's underwear. Red and just for me.

As Belle reminded me before, I teach all my kids to say

thank you. So I smile and walk toward him, then lean up on tiptoes, brushing a kiss against his jaw. "Thank you," I whisper, the dress crushed between us.

When I step back down, I notice he's blushing.

I made Ronan blush. Ronan bought me a dress. And, even more incredibly, Ronan's mouth was on my pussy and he gave me an orgasm.

I guess a dress and a new pair of red-soled shoes pale in significance compared to that.

I'm ready exactly an hour later and walk down the stairs.

He's at the bottom, waiting. He's been pacing, but when he sees me, he freezes.

I stare right back. I was right.

He looks like a *GQ* model, only hotter, in a deceptively simple but perfectly tailored black suit. I'm sure it's designer. Maybe there's a Dior theme to the night.

The silence lengthens. He still doesn't move. Doesn't blink. I force myself not to fidget nervously.

Finally, he clears his throat. "You're perfect," he says.

"Well, I'm not. But the dress is." I twirl again. I can't help it. The dress is made for twirling. And so is the cape. The shoes, I'm not so sure about. They fit perfectly, but I'm no pro at walking in stilettos.

He gives me a ghost of a smile. "Do you miss the bachelorette party dress?"

I laugh. "Is that why you bought me this? You worried I'd wear it tonight?"

"I couldn't take the chance."

"Should we call Belle before we leave?" I ask.

When he first saw me in the dress, the look he gave me was hot and admiring.

But this look, this slow smile unfurling on his mouth that

reaches his eyes, is even better. It's softer. Warmer. Admiring in a deeper way.

"Let's do it."

We call Belle together, put the phone on video so she can see my dress and my hair, so we can give her kisses and she can show us Sasha's dog, Sprinkles. Thankfully, it's not a corgi, but it's still enough to renew all of Belle's pleadings for a dog of her very own.

"Thanks for that," he says when we get off the phone.

"For what?"

"For always thinking of Belle. For being here for her."

My heart turns over, but I don't say what I'm thinking. That I'm only able to be here for Belle, only here for Ronan, for such a short time.

And then, they'll be gone, and I won't be much good for anyone, not until I can stitch my shattered heart back together.

I don't say it because the shortness of our time together makes me not want to waste a single minute being sad.

It makes tonight that much more precious.

"Let's go," I say, smiling up at him.

And we head off into the night.

I feel a little like Cinderella, only in red. And instead of a prince, I have an action star.

Ronan

When Poppy walked down the stairs looking like an angel ready to sin in that red dress, she stole my breath. And if I were any other man with a heart to lose, she would have stolen that as well.

I took a chance selecting a red dress.

But I knew it would suit her. I knew my Christmas-loving girl would want to wear red to the Christmas ball. But, mostly, I wanted her to be the Lady in Red for her special night, when she was showing her paintings. Poppy, who constantly supports everyone else, who plays backup to her bolder twin sister, needs to know that she doesn't always have to stay backstage, that she could be the starring act.

It's not really the dress that shines tonight. It's her in it. It's in her red curls that are caught in a loose bun with tendrils tumbling freely down her back. It's in her freckles dusting the purity of her cheeks, chest, and arms. It's the swirls of green and gold in her eyes. It's her dimpled smile that lights up any room. But mostly, it's the sweetness of her soul, how she cares so much for the people in her life, for her town and her community, for doing what's right.

I know all the reasons we shouldn't be starting this. She's Belle's nanny. We're only here for a short time. We're from different worlds. I'm a grumpy loner who is rarely home. And I'm now a package deal, with a daughter who could be yanked away at any second. Even if I could give a relationship a shot, Poppy deserves more than the half-life and toxic fame I can offer. There is no chance that this will be anything more than a short-lived thing, so we probably should avoid the mess before we get any further into this.

But I spent my career relying on my sense of intuition to keep me safe. I learned long ago that when I follow it, things unfold far better than when I don't. Ignoring my gut feeling has caused me more broken bones than I can count. And right now, my gut is saying that, though this is short-term, I want her with everything in me.

It's also saying that I can trust her.

I can trust this. Despite my fear from the past.

That bone-deep knowing was cemented when she suggested we call Belle before we left tonight. Poppy cares about my daughter and will do everything she can to ensure she won't be hurt, no matter what happens between the two of us.

My goal is to give Belle the best Christmas of her life. And I know it's what Poppy wants as well. That can be separate from exploring whatever this is between us.

I wrap my hand around her much smaller one and smile as we stand at the bottom of the stairs leading to the Holly Hill Inn. We're back to the place where this all began.

If I thought it was ridiculous in September, the inn's Christmas cheer is completely over-the-top now. It's a Dickens fantasy of a Victorian Christmas come to life, with the historic mansion decked out in lights, holly, and garland. An antique gleaming red sled filled with presents sits on the lawn, as if ready to take off. And the giant pine tree in the yard is covered in ornaments. Candles line the drive. It's the perfect setting for a Christmas ball.

"Nervous?" I ask.

"A little. What if my paintings don't sell? I haven't displayed any of my work since I was in college. The town thinks of me as a teacher, not an artist."

"Stop doubting yourself. You *are* an artist, and your paintings will sell."

"I hope so. And I hope not just mine. This ball and auction are so important. The Center relies on this income every year. It's the biggest fundraising event."

I squeeze her hand, knowing how much this night means to her.

"I wish I were better at this stuff," I admit.

"At what?"

I shrug. "Talking. Communicating."

She looks startled. "Why?"

"So I could explain to you how talented you are and how special your art is. So you could see what I see when I look at you. But my words aren't enough."

She sniffs and lets go of my hand to rub her eyes. "Darn it, Ronan. Don't make my mascara run. It's not waterproof." But she smiles through the glistening shine of tears in her eyes.

"And I'm not special. I'm just a normal girl. In a very fancy dress, with a superstar next to me." She laughs. "Come to think of it, maybe I am a little special, but just for tonight."

I narrow my eyes at her, about to argue, but she holds up her hand.

"Okay, enough with the compliments. Let's do this, big guy."

I take her hand back again and lead her up the steps, through the lobby, past the towering Christmas tree, and into the main glittering ballroom.

I thought it might be decorated in red and green, but instead, it's blue-and-silver. It's all candles and snowflakes, Christmas trees and silver-wrapped presents.

She falters at the entrance, when every eye in the place seems to stop, turn, and stare—and the buzz of conversation fades to silence.

I'm used to rooms full of people freezing when I enter, but I know Poppy isn't. So I let her set the pace.

She pulls her shoulders back as if gathering courage, the gesture doing delicious things to her cleavage.

Thankfully, Sadie breaks away from the crowd and launches herself at Poppy.

"You look amazing! You both do." Sadie's gaze rakes over me appreciatively before going back to Poppy. "New dress?"

she asks in such a way that makes me think Poppy already told her about the dress and where she got it.

She grins, turning one way then the other, the dress moving with her. "Oh, this old thing?" Then she turns her attention to the room. "Everything looks amazing. I mean, we planned it all and decorated it, but it's even better than I imagined."

"I know, right? And everyone seems to be having a great time. The band is awesome, and Priyanka outdid herself with the catering. The stuffed mini dosas are to die for. And so are these little phyllo pastry things."

"How's the auction going?" Poppy asks.

Sadie frowns. "It's slow right now. Maybe we should have placed the auction items in the main ballroom instead of in the side room. It seemed like the right space, but no one's going in there."

"It's early yet," I say to Poppy, who looks worried. "Give it some time."

"True," she says, though she still seems concerned.

"Do you want some champagne?" I ask, remembering the last time we were at the inn.

She grins. "I don't have the hiccups, so I don't need the cure. But can I have a glass of the Christmas cocktail?"

My mouth curves in satisfaction when I note that the worried look in her eyes has been replaced by laughter.

"I'll be right back," I murmur. I hold her hand and pull it up to my mouth, not able to stop from kissing her. I'd prefer kissing other locations, but this will do for now. "Sadie, do you want anything?"

"I'm good. Already have it," she says, holding up a cocktail glass containing a festive-looking drink with cranberries. Her eyes are wide as her gaze darts between me and Poppy, confusion evident on her face.

She may know about the dress, but she doesn't look like she knows the rest. Which means that Poppy probably didn't tell her about the other night.

Though I wouldn't fault her for sharing that with her best friend, I'm relieved. Unlike many celebrities, I'd never required nondisclosure agreements for my dates. I never cared what anyone wrote about me. As long as I believed in what I did, it didn't matter what anyone else thought.

But that was before Belle. The nannies and even the maids I've hired since have been through agencies that vet the employees and make them sign a mountain of paperwork, including NDAs. Not that it stopped Tiffany from taking photos of me and trying to sell the story.

Poppy had been hired directly by me, and I never asked her to sign one. Perhaps it hadn't been smart. But I trusted her from the start. I still do.

These types of worries are just one more reason why having a relationship is complicated for me. I live my life guarded, never sure who to trust, and I'd hate to see Poppy have to as well.

CHAPTER 27

8 DAYS TO CHRISTMAS (STILL)

Poppy

"Holy shit," Sadie says, staring after Ronan.

"He kissed your hand. He bought you the most beautiful dress I've ever seen. I mean, he bought you shoes," she squeals. "Ronan Masters bought you shoes."

"I know," I squeal back at her.

I want to tell her more. I'm dying to tell her about the night in front of the fire when he kissed me *everywhere*. But I can't betray Ronan's trust like that. He's not some guy I met on a dating app. Not that I'm swiping right, but still.

I trust Sadie completely, but who I trust is not just up to me anymore. To love Belle and Ronan is to live with a certain amount of discretion. And they are worth it.

Love.

I love Belle. That part is easy to admit. I fall for every

child I teach. Each one becomes part of me. And Belle is even more special.

But loving Ronan? That's as stupid as it is inevitable. How could I not?

I went from being dumped by my fiancé to falling for a movie star. And the worst of it is, now that I know what it's like to love Ronan, I realize just how shallow my relationship with Derek was, especially at the end.

When we broke up, my ego was bruised. My hopes for the future were damaged. But my heart wasn't truly broken. Not like it will be when Ronan and Belle leave.

"What's going on between you two?" Sadie asks, interrupting my thoughts. She sounds equal parts envious and worried.

"Just me falling for a dad and his daughter who will leave soon."

"But what if they don't? Or what if he wants you to go to Hollywood with them?"

Tingles shoot through me at the idea. I admit, in the early hours of the morning, I've asked myself just that. I've allowed myself to dream.

But it's fantasy, not reality. Christmas will end with them heading back to California. He's always been clear about that, and he's never indicated that he wants anything more.

And even if he did, how could it ever work? I belong in Snowflake Harbor. And Ronan's life is in LA and on sets around the world.

"That's not the way this works, Sadie. But maybe this being so short makes it even more precious," I say. "I spent over a decade with Derek, and it's scary how much more I care for Ronan in just these few months. I want to make the most of every day until they go."

Sadie nods. "I wouldn't expect anything less from you.

You've always loved with your whole heart. I think at times you're too loyal for your own good. But that just makes you, you."

I shift, uncomfortable with her words. "Where's your date?" I change the subject. "You said you were bringing Lonely Book Boy, right?" I ask.

She frowns. "He wasn't able to make it, after all."

"Oh, Sadie, I'm sorry."

"He's an ER doctor, and he had to cover someone's shift at the hospital."

"Lonely Book Boy is a doctor?" I ask. "Whoa."

"Score one for the nerdy boys," Sadie says. "He moved to town recently, and he's been working so many hours that he hasn't really met many people. He promised to make it up to me."

"I'll let it slide, then." I look around. "Ronan's taking a while. I hope no one is bothering him. Maybe I should've gone with him to run interference."

Sadie laughs. "I think he can manage for himself. Is that him over there? Everyone is crowded by the door."

Ronan's head peeks out over the crowd, always the tallest in the room. As he comes closer, I see he's flanked by two men and a pretty woman. At first, all my attention zeroes in on the lady with Ronan, and I'm hit by a wave of jealousy. She's got light brown hair, swept into an elegant updo, and though she's on the short side—at least compared to Ronan and the other men with them—her legs look long in her mile-high heels. Her black dress is so understatedly elegant that it makes my red Dior look garish in comparison.

"Is that...?" Sadie asks, her mouth hanging open.

I focus on the two other men, and it hits me.

"Oh. My. God. That's..."

"Chase James," Sadie gasps.

"And Sebastian Blake," I manage breathlessly.

The star power that's strolling toward us in our little ballroom at our little inn is unbelievable.

"How?"

"Ronan," I conclude, and warmth that has nothing to do with the other two stars fills me. Ronan organized this to help us, to bring attention to our ball and make it a success.

Sadie turns to me, her cheeks pink. "That's a good one you got there."

"He's not mine."

"Hmm. You sure about that?"

"Unfortunately," I whisper.

"What are the odds we both can bag movie stars tonight?" she whispers back.

Then the group is in front of us. I'm surprised they got here so quickly, with no one stopping them, but I realize the crowd is still stunned into inaction. I figure we have about two more minutes before everyone snaps out of shock and bombards us.

"Poppy and Sadie," Ronan says. "This is Chase, Sebastian, and my sometimes assistant, Emma."

The first thing I note is relief that the gorgeous woman at his side is just his personal assistant. Though I guess I'm just the nanny, and that hasn't stopped us from having intimate relations.

"The hot nanny!" Sebastian Blake cries, and he does a very thorough perusal of me that makes me feel vaguely dirty, but not necessarily in a bad way. Such is the charm of the former child star turned bad boy.

"Now I understand," Sebastian says with a wicked grin.

"Blake, be very careful," Ronan growls.

"Whoops, sorry," Sebastian says to Ronan. And makes a zipping motion with his finger.

"Oh, sure, you shut up for Ronan. Why don't you shut up when I tell you to?" Chase James grumbles.

"Dude, have you seen Ronan's right hook?" Sebastian asks.

"Good point."

While the three costars in *The Wanderers* are A-list movie stars and hot as hell, they all have different appeals.

Sebastian Blake is a pretty boy, with black hair, bright blue eyes, and chiseled good looks. He's been a Hollywood fixture for most of his life and was a breakout star in his teen years.

Chase James is the hot new "it guy" in Hollywood. His hair is a rich, distinctive auburn, worn perennially messy. His eyes are a brilliant green, and his flawless bone structure looks as if it was sculpted by a master. His face belongs on an old-time movie poster or a Greek coin, with an indefinable star quality.

But it's Ronan who draws my eye. He's larger and a few years older than his costars. While Sebastian has effortless charisma and Chase draws the eye with a mysterious magnetism, Ronan is ice and steel. The other two would get by with their wits. Ronan would get the job done with his silent, towering strength.

They're all way too much together. I don't know how any of us females are still standing.

"It's good to finally meet you, Poppy. The dress looks fabulous on you," Emma interrupts the squabbling stars.

"Ronan said you helped pick it out for me," I say to the pretty assistant. "Thank you."

She tilts her head. "It was fun. I don't get a chance to pick out women's clothes enough. Usually, it's suits, tuxes, suits, tuxes. Super boring." She gives me a once-over. "Ronan was right about the red on you. You're glowing."

I blush and sneak a glance at him. As usual, he's taking a back seat in the interaction, but the proprietary look in his eyes makes me flush even more.

"So how are you liking our little town?" Sadie asks the group, watching Chase and Sebastian with wide eyes.

"It's charming," Emma says.

Sebastian shrugs. "It's cool, but I haven't seen much of it."

"The director has us on a tight timeline for shooting this movie," Chase explains.

"You never get out even when we're not on a tight schedule," Emma teases. She speaks directly to Sadie and me. "Chase has a very avid fan base. So, everywhere he goes, he causes a scene, which means he mostly stays in his hotel room."

"When Olivia's not around," Sebastian adds. "Where is she, anyway? I thought she'd visit you on set by now."

I remember reading something about Chase James being in a relationship. The media and fans made a big deal about him falling for a girl who worked in a bookshop, someone who wasn't famous. Maybe that means there's hope for us ordinary girls.

"She's in the middle of a book deadline. My girlfriend's a writer. She writes mysteries," he explains with a proud smile.

"Well, we're surprised to see you all here, though we're also very grateful," Sadie says. I could be wrong, but she seems a little glum now that Chase has just confirmed he's off the market.

"When Ronan asked us to come, we had to do it. He never asks for favors," Sebastian says. "But checking out Hot Nanny, I can see why he did."

I blush a fiery red. Again. Now I'm sure I will match my dress. Sometimes being a redhead with pale skin sucks.

"Blake." Ronan gives him a warning look. "Call her 'hot

nanny' one more time, and you'll regret it." He says it almost lazily, but with an intent that is unmistakable.

"So you don't think she's hot?" Sebastian teases. "'Cause I think she's pretty hot."

Ronan lunges for Sebastian, but I step in with a hand to Ronan's arm. I don't want him to get in a fight with his friend, especially not because of me.

"Hey," I say. "He's just teasing. Plus, it's a nice change to be called hot. It's flattering."

"But you are hot," Sebastian says. "Why wouldn't dudes call you that?"

I smile. "Thank you. But it's a small town, and I've known everyone here forever. People don't see me that way. If anything, I get called cute. There's not much sexy about being an elementary school teacher."

"Whoa. You're a teacher too. That's—"

"Hot," Chase James finishes, with a teasing smile.

I can't help but laugh. I like these guys. They're good for my ego. I slant a look at Ronan. While he still looks a little annoyed, he doesn't seem like he's about to use his fists anytime soon, so that's good.

"Well, whatever the reason you're here, we appreciate it," I say. "This night is important to our community."

"The Kid's Creativity Center is a wonderful initiative," Emma says. "I did some research on it."

Chase looks at me, his green eyes intense. "I'd like to learn more about your program. Maybe I can help."

Whoa. Chase James wants to help our little center? "That would be amazing. I'm happy to tell you all you need to know."

"I hate to break this up," Sadie cuts us off in a hurried voice, "but half the party is heading our way."

"Good. That's the plan," Ronan says. I'm surprised to see

that he looks pleased, rather than alarmed, at the crowd forming to meet the stars. "Let's head into the auction room."

"I'll ask a waiter to bring us some drinks," Emma says as Ronan herds the rest of us into the smaller room off to the side of the ballroom.

As we walk in, I feel a little queasy at seeing my pictures hanging in the makeshift gallery. Items for auction surround us, including paintings, drawings, and photographs from other artists.

Ronan steps up to my art work, and we're soon inundated by party guests wanting to be introduced to the stars in our midst. I watch as every time someone tries to talk to Ronan, he brings their attention to one of the auction items first, especially my paintings, complimenting them proudly and bringing up the good cause. Chase and Sebastian do the same.

The guests place their bids with enthusiasm, each trying to one-up the other. The auction is going to be a far greater success than ever expected, and I know it's because of Ronan. Time flies as I'm helping people, answering questions, and greeting friends and neighbors.

I've become quite popular since my nanny gig to the stars. And now, with the addition of Sebastian and Chase, everyone is clamoring to find out how I got them to attend tonight.

And the simple answer is, I'm not sure. And the not-as-simple answer is Ronan. Ronan made it happen. I'm too much of a coward to give a name to the hope in my heart. So I tell myself once again that he's just a great guy, one who helps his friends.

Is that what I am to him? Are we friends with benefits?

My mom walks over to me, beaming. "Darling! Everything is fabulous! We're so proud of you." She gives me a big hug.

"Well done, Poppy girl," my dad says. "You organized everything beautifully."

I swallow. "Thanks, guys." No matter how much I want to be like Ronan and cut back on my people-pleasing, I can't help but bask in the glow of my parents' approval.

"Are these your paintings?" my mom asks, moving closer to my winter landscapes.

I nod with a nervous swallow. I take a sip of my Christmas cocktail.

"They're gorgeous. Darling, look at what Poppy painted." My mom calls my dad over.

He peers quickly at my paintings. "Very pretty," he says. "It's a nice little hobby you have here."

"Thanks." That proud glow dims, and my shoulders slump. I know my dad means well, but I'm not sure if he'll ever understand me or realize that being an artist isn't just a little hobby—it's an intrinsic part of me.

I frown, mulling over that sobering thought as my parents move on to bid on a special dinner at one of their favorite restaurants, when Ronan breaks away from the crowd and walks toward me.

"Are you okay?" he asks, looking so debonair with his large body all wrapped up in a black suit.

When he places a hand on my waist, almost spanning the width of it, I lean into his side, not able to hold back my elemental response.

He leans down, and his lips brush my ear. I make a sound that's a cross between a mewl and a moan.

"Dance with me," he says in a rough voice.

"Okay."

With his hand still on my back, he leads me to the dance

floor. It's been so busy that I haven't danced all night, and I realize that the evening will soon come to a close.

The beginning chords of a song I try to place start up. It's familiar, nagging at me. They've been playing Christmas music for most of the night, but this isn't a holiday song.

I tilt my head, and then it comes to me.

"'Lady in Red,'" Ronan murmurs, confirming my guess.

"That's it," I say as he takes me in his arms.

"I love this song." I'm mesmerized by being held so close to him.

"I know," he says. "I requested it."

I back away just enough to look up at him and catch my breath at his expression.

"The dress..."

He gives a ghost of a smile as his fingers brush my low neckline, branding my skin. "You said you weren't the type of girl who could inspire a song like that. I wanted to show you that you're wrong, my lady in red."

Leave it to him to make me topple even further into love. So far down, there's no hope of escape. It's going to take a lifetime to get over him.

THE REST OF THE CHRISTMAS BALL IS BOTH FUN AND ACUTE torture. I danced a few more songs with Ronan, wrapped in his arms, only forfeiting the floor when the slow songs end. I'm desperately aware that when we leave here, we will head home. Together. Alone. To a house where we will have no interruptions.

I want it badly. But worries crowd my mind. Most of them are silly insecurities. Will I be enough for a man who has had his share of models and starlets? Will all this fade on his part once we've had sex? I know it won't on mine, but he's a million times more experienced than me.

Once we leave the inn tonight, everything changes irrevocably.

So I keep finding things to do while Ronan stays at my side, until Sadie tries to chase us out.

By then, Emma had already dragged Sebastian out of the place, pulling him away from his groupies, who consisted of my mom and her Zumba ladies. He was an equal opportunity flirt, not discriminating by age, which endeared him to me more than I expected, even with his bad-boy reputation.

I did notice that Emma kept a strict eye on Sebastian's drinks and kept plying him with club soda in between the bourbon he got from the cash bar. A local winery supplied wine for the evening, but he preferred something harder.

I'm not sure when Chase left. He snuck out not long after he got there, after he bid on a number of items. Before he left, though, Chase talked to me more about the kids center. It was clear that he's no stranger to charities—and, specifically, charities like ours for disadvantaged youth. He took my email and said he'd follow up.

Chase James might be emailing me, and I'm not even giddy about it, except that it might help the center.

That's how hung up on Ronan I am. He's the only one who makes my stomach tie up in knots with just a look.

"Seriously, leave now," Sadie insists again. "We got this."

"But there's so much left to do."

"You two are driving me crazy. Nobody wants to see you make adoring eyes at each other all night. I'm too emotional that Lonely Book Boy didn't make it. You need to leave right now, because if I were on a date with a superstar, I can tell you for damn sure that I wouldn't be hanging out here. I would be doing far better things with my time and body, if you catch my drift."

"But we're not—It's not—"

"Just. Leave," Sadie repeats, putting her hands on her ample hips that are rocking in her gold dress.

I hold up my hand. "Okay, okay. We're skedaddling."

Ronan rubs his hand over his chin. "You did not just say skedaddle."

"Of course I did. It's a good word."

He barks out a laugh but disguises it as a cough.

My smile widens. "It's a great word. It made you laugh," I say.

"Bye. Have a fun night, you two," Sadie says, waggling her fingers at us.

I blow her a kiss, and Ronan puts a hand on the small of my back as we make our way into the chilly night.

"Oh," I say as we step out into the cold. I wrap my white cape tighter around me. "It's snowing."

Tiny snowflakes drift down on us. I lift my head, feeling the soft wetness on my face. I laugh in bliss, smiling up at Ronan.

He watches me, his eyebrows drawn.

"What are you thinking?" I ask when he continues to stare at me.

He gives me a slow, sexy smile, one that makes desire pool in my center and heat bloom, even in the snow.

"Let's go home, and I'll show you what I'm thinking," he says.

Home. The word brings me joy, and the word brings me sorrow.

It's only our home for a little over a week more. Only that short time left to decorate Christmas cookies with Belle. To wrap the last of the gifts. To make Ronan smile and laugh and to learn to decipher all his moods. Only that short time left to feel like I have a home and family of my own.

And that's the part that's so dangerous. It's not my home. And it's not my family. I'm deceiving myself to think of these people as mine. I'm just a girl who is in between lives. And I'm pretending that this role I've stepped into is real.

But it's not.

It is real. A stubborn, rebellious part of me insists, though.

It *is* real. It's temporary. But it's real.

And deep in my heart, I believe it, despite it all. My love for Ronan is real, my love for Belle is real, for the things they do for me and the way they make me feel. And I'm going to hold onto every bit of it for as long as I can.

CHAPTER 28

8 DAYS TO CHRISTMAS (STILL)

Ronan

TONIGHT.

We're going to make love tonight.

Make love. I've never said—or thought—those words before now. I'm not a manwhore like Sebastian, but I've fucked. Many, many times. That's what sex has always been for me.

Now, it's all different. Because Poppy is different. And I'm different. With her.

I've imagined *making love,* having sex, fucking Poppy a thousand times in the last few months. And I've thought about this moment all night. The moment I would get her alone.

I imagined us barely making it past the front door before

I unzip her dress and watch it pool around her in a puddle of Christmas red.

How she'd step out of it, in just her heels, wearing the panties I bought for her today. Underwear custom embroidered with only one word. *Saturday.*

That was one scenario I imagined for the night.

Or, I pictured us making out in the car, like we were kids in high school, because we were too impatient to wait.

Or perhaps I'd carry her to the bedroom, kicking the door open and laying her spread out on the bed. A feast for me to devour.

But it's not like any of that.

When we pull up to the house in the car, I curse the historic home's lack of a covered garage.

The snow falls in earnest now, and the pathway to the door is covered in icy snow. Poppy's new heels aren't up to the job, so after a few minutes of her slipping, I sweep her into my arms and carry her up the steps.

After her initial yelp of surprise, she clings to my collar and buries her head in my chest. "You smell good," she murmurs throatily.

Lust slams into me, and I can't wait to get her into the house so I can take her against the door.

But when I insert the key, turn the handle, and the door swings open, I cross the threshold with her in my arms, and everything changes.

We enter the dark house in silence, in something approaching reverence. It feels almost like a wedding night. Her in my arms, the anticipation of making love for the first time.

It should freak me out. But it doesn't. It's just right.

And the only thing that feels wrong is that this isn't the

first night in a lifetime. I'll have to give her up in a week. But I push aside this thought.

I want to worship at the altar of her. I want to remember everything about the way she looked tonight when she stood in the snow, face up to the sky, catching snowflakes.

She's magic.

And I'm not sure if I'll ever be able to get enough.

She's glitter glue and glow sticks.

She's hot chocolate with marshmallows and Charlie Brown Christmas trees.

She's kind and thoughtful and so full of joy, she glows.

I want to drink her in and learn all her soft sighs and the secrets of her body. I want to make her orgasm over and over until the only name she knows is mine, the only man she remembers is me.

And then I want to take her all over again.

I kiss her at the threshold and walk her up the stairs of our temporary home. I take her into my bedroom, flip on a lamp so I can see her, set her down, and then I do what I imagined.

I slip the red dress off her shoulder, one side at a time, until it pools into a red puddle at her feet. And she does what I imagined, stepping out of her dress, still in those high, fuck-me shoes, and I smile, looking at that slip of red lace with the black embroidery.

"I bet you're feeling rather proud of yourself at this moment." She gives a throaty laugh.

"I don't know what you're talking about," I say with pretend innocence.

"*Saturday*. Where'd you get day-of-the-week underwear?"

"They're custom."

She half laughs, half groans. "Emma ordered them for you, didn't she? She must think you're crazy."

I shrug. "I don't really care what Emma thinks."

"Does this mean you don't like my cotton panties?"

"It means I fucking love any and all of them. And I like you out of your panties even more."

At my words, she starts to take them off slowly, and I want to watch her seductive show, but my patience runs out.

"Let me," I say and grasp the lace. In one smooth motion, I tear the delicate fabric until the scraps fall off her body.

She gasps, but I see her eyes flare in pleasure.

"Sorry," I growl. But I'm not.

"You're buying me another pair."

"I'll buy you a dozen, and I'll rip them all off you."

"Deal," she says. I back her up until the back of her legs hit the raised bed.

I pick her up and gently set her on it. Her skin glows, dusty with freckles. Her curly hair spreads out around her, partially covering a dainty pink areola and tight nipple. My mouth waters with the need to taste those sweet tits. Her hips flare in a curve I want to worship all night.

I kneel and give her pussy a long lick. Her hips lift off the bed in response.

Her smell and taste make me crazy, but she tugs at my shoulders.

"Hey, big guy, wait." She moans at the teasing of my tongue. "Oh God, seriously, stop."

I move up over her, wiping my mouth. "What's wrong?" I ask.

"When you do that, I can't concentrate on anything else. And I need this not to be so one-sided. I want to make you crazy as well."

"Is that all? Poppy, we have all night. And I want to start by showing your pussy just how much I adore it."

"Oh, fine," she says grumpily. "Have at it, then."

I shake my head, holding back the laughter at her expression.

And I do as she says and have at her until she's moaning and grasping my hair, as I lick and suck and rub my stubble against the sweetness of her. When I add a finger and then another into her center, she screams. And I work my tongue and lips and fingers to make her shatter around me, and I wish it were my dick being grasped by her internal muscles.

We have all night, I remind myself.

And the next night.

And the next night.

And only a few more after that.

Poppy

He did it again. Made me come like never before. It's not fair. I wanted to start off by making *him* crazy this time. I'm the giver, not the taker. And here he is, giving and giving until I orgasm all over his face.

Stubborn man. Stubborn, gorgeous, sexy man whom I'm going to make pay.

Just as soon as I catch my breath.

I stretch sinuously.

His eyes light at my movement, and I'm thankful for the low lamp, even if it makes me feel self-conscious.

We lean on our sides, facing each other.

I'm naked except for those shoes, and though he's lost his coat, he's still fully dressed. The contrast is sexy. Like he's the master of me. We can play that later. But right now, I'm dying to see him naked.

"Take off your clothes," I order. Maybe I'll be the master.

His mouth hitches up. "Yes, ma'am." He unbuttons his shirt until it's hanging open.

I run my hand over his chest, reveling in his rippling muscles. My fingers follow a line of hair that leads into his pants. I unzip his zipper and push his trousers and underwear down with his help. He kicks them off.

I look down, and I can see his erection in its full… ahem…glory.

Oh.

Oh my.

Oh crap.

He notices my worried expression.

"It'll fit. I promise."

I bite my lip so I don't burst into a fit of nervous giggles.

I run my finger down his hard length. He sucks in a breath in response. I love how affected he is by just my touch. I love it because he affects me that same way, and I'd hate it if this were one-sided.

I lose myself in touching him, and soon, it's not enough. I need my mouth on him. I need to kiss and taste him everywhere, make him crazy for me.

I kiss down his chest, down the hard planes of his abs, counting each rib and muscle. His breath is tight and labored, and his skin is covered in a flush.

I did that. *Me.* I've made this incredible man moan and gasp and tremble with want.

It's addictive. I need to do more. So I give him another long, lingering lick, and he gets even more impossibly hard. I'm not sure I can fit him in my mouth, but I give it my best shot, swallowing as deeply as I can and using my hands on the rest of him.

"God, yes," he moans.

I try every trick I know, which unfortunately isn't many, to make him as feverish as he made me.

It doesn't take long before he pulls me off him.

He's panting now.

"What's wrong?" It's my turn to ask, kissing his nipple.

"I'm too close. I need to be inside you."

I need that as well. So badly. But I'm still a little hesitant about how this will work.

"I'm, uh… You're much bigger than…"

"What are you trying to say, Poppy?" he teases.

"I'm just trying to explain why we might not fit," I say. "Don't get cocky. Maybe bigger isn't better."

He laughs. "Oh, we'll fit. I intend to be buried in your tight, gorgeous pussy. But you're right. We need to do some TLC to ensure it's comfortable for you."

"What kind of TLC?"

"The kind that makes you very, very wet," he rumbles, and in one smooth motion, he twists us around so his face is between my legs again.

And he proceeds to make me very, very wet again, as planned. When I'm nearly incoherent with lust, he adds one finger, and then two, and then three, and uses them to stretch me. I'm riding his face, riding his fingers, racing toward the best orgasm of my life when he abruptly pulls away and kneels above me.

I give a hiss of dissatisfaction, like an angry cat.

He gifts me his small half smile. "Don't worry, love. I'll make it better," he soothes. "Now?" he asks, pushing, and he's right. Any trepidation has melted away. I need his massive, hard cock in me. I want every inch of him. I need to feel the burn of him, the pleasure-pain. I need it with every last breath.

"Now," I order with desperation.

He reaches behind him to his discarded pants and pulls out a condom, slipping it on. I didn't even think of that. I can't believe I forgot about everything, even safe sex. I'm on the pill, so maybe I could be forgiven for the lapse in judgment, but this is how crazy I am for him.

Then he's at my entrance, and I'm back to forgetting about everything else except needing him to fill me up.

He surges into me and then stops. I gaze into that handsome face, into those glacier eyes that look anything but cold now. They burn into mine. "Okay?" he asks, though I can see the tension that holding back is causing.

"O-okay."

He pushes in a fraction more. I wince at the stretch, and he stops immediately, checking in with me.

I nod, but instead of surging forward again, he puts a hand between us and luxuriously plays with my clit, teasing me as he kisses my ear, my neck, and down my breasts in soft kisses. I'm throbbing everywhere, feeling more filled up than I can manage and, at the same time, needing more.

I gasp as he slowly starts to move again, and I welcome that stretch until he's fully in me.

I grasp his muscled ass, moving restlessly.

"Easy, love," he groans, moving with slow, deep, steady strokes that drive me mad. He slips a finger between us and teases my clit, circling lightly in a way that pushes me higher, keeps me poised on the edge of climax.

I can tell how much he's holding back.

"Harder. I need all of you," I beg raggedly.

"Fuck, yes. Take it. Take all of me," he rasps and buries himself fully with one pounding movement. I stretch around him. The intensity is like nothing I've felt before, his cock hitting a spot that turns me mindless with want. He sets a driving, merciless pace, and I chant his name over and over to it. One of his hands plays with my nipple, the other with my clit, and his mouth licks and sucks at my neck while he fills me over and over.

He's everywhere, in me, around me. My mind and body are all so full of him. I go higher and higher until it's all too much, and I explode.

I cry out, and he swears and surges into me until he comes with a sound that I want to remember forever.

He flips us over, taking me with him so I lie, spent, on top of him. Even in this moment of release and ecstasy, he's considerate of his size. Reaching between us, he deals with the condom.

"That was..." I say, flailing for words.

"Yeah," he agrees.

"I'm so..."

"Perfect," he completes, and I get even more flushed with pleasure.

"You fit!" I say in amazement when I finally get my breath back.

"Told you," he mumbles.

"When I think of the time we've wasted. We could have been doing this all month. Why didn't we do this earlier?" I ask, thinking about all the orgasms I missed.

"You're the nanny. We're not even supposed to be doing this now."

"Psh. I'm only the temporary nanny. We wasted so much time." My heart constricts at the thought. All I want is to wring out every last second of time together. "You're off tomorrow, right?"

"Yes."

"Good. I have plans for us."

"What kinds of plans?" he asks as he circles my breasts with one of his fingers. My nipple tightens in response.

"It's snowing. We can go sledding and build a snowman. Belle will love it."

"Hmmm." he bends down to kiss my stomach. I'm amazed that after that orgasm, I'm still ready to go again. I was always more of a one-and-done kind of girl. But with Ronan, it's different. Everything's different.

"Sledding makes children very tired. Tired children tend to sleep through the night," I say as I feel his other hand making its way downward.

"Sledding is good."

"Yes," I say on a sigh, reaching for him. My eyes widen to find him already hard again.

Everything about Ronan is different. In all the best ways.

"So how many condoms fit in a suit pocket?" I ask. "Just out of curiosity."

"Not enough. But I have more in my drawer."

"Good," I say. "Very good."

"I'm glad you approve. Because I intend on having you all night long."

"Okay."

CHAPTER 29

7 DAYS TO CHRISTMAS

Ronan

I'VE BEEN FIGHTING MY ATTRACTION TO POPPY FOR THE ENTIRE three months since we first met, and the two months since she became our nanny. Throughout that time, I worried that if I gave in to my base urges, it could somehow destroy everything.

But I was wrong. It didn't ruin a thing. It only made everything so much better. And it won't hurt Belle because Poppy cares about her, regardless of what happens.

We couldn't get enough of each other last night, and I didn't want to leave. I wasn't used to that. Normally, I don't spend the night. Even with Belle's mom, who lasted a little longer than most.

But with Poppy, close wasn't enough. I always wanted more. Being with her felt like coming home, not to any home

I've ever known, but to the very best idea of it. It felt like hope. It felt like joy.

And when I was with her, I didn't want our time to end.

Not our nights. Nor our days.

The next morning, when the thin early light streamed in through the curtains, Poppy and I made love again, not having our fill of each other the night before, even though we'd barely slept.

We spent the morning in bed until it was time to get Belle.

We pick her up from Sasha's house to find her dressed in a Christmas sweater with a red beanie over messy, unbrushed hair.

"I'm ready for sledding!" she says. "Did you see the snow out there?"

We drive home, and after taking turns sledding on a small hill at the back of our property, we make a very ugly snowman and then walk back to the house. Belle runs up ahead. I grasp Poppy's hand to steady her when she slips. When I don't let go, she looks at me, startled. But I hold firmly. I know I shouldn't, but I can't help it.

Belle turns and sees us. She doesn't say anything, just runs back and grasps hold of my hand on the other side. I look down at her, and she smiles as bright as the fresh white snow glinting in the sun, while we all walk up the steps hand in hand. It's corny as hell, but I feel like the Grinch whose heart grew three sizes that day.

I wonder what would happen if Belle and I came back to Snowflake Harbor to visit when I get a break in my schedule in January. I have another movie lined up, but I plan to call my manager to see if I can get out of it so that Belle can enroll in school. It would beat having to have another nanny and tutor, following me to yet another set. I might not want to take a break in my career indefinitely, but I've been working nonstop for the last decade. I could take some time off.

"Want some hot cocoa, Belle?" Poppy asks.

"What about me?" I say. "Do I get some also?"

"Nope. But there's a delicious green smoothie waiting for you." Her eyes twinkle.

"Daddy, you can have some of mine," Belle says, looking at me with a worried expression, as if not having a cup of cocoa would be a travesty.

"Thank you, pumpkin," I say, touched.

We make it to the house and take off our boots, laughing and arguing good-naturedly, when I get a call from my manager.

"Ronan, we've got a problem," he says, sounding grim.

CHAPTER 30

7 DAYS TO CHRISTMAS

Poppy

I KNOW IT'S BAD THE INSTANT I SEE RONAN'S FACE. HE'S often quiet, sometimes grumpy, but rarely angry. His still waters are so deep, you aren't sure what's under the surface, but usually it all feels placid on top.

Not now.

I try to catch his eye to ask if he's okay, but he's entirely focused on the phone call as he walks out to the porch to talk.

I've promised Belle cocoa, and I need to order the pizza we planned, so I get started on heating the milk and place an order on the food delivery app. I know everyone's favorite toppings, though it's fifty-fifty whether Ronan will eat that many carbs and fat.

As I finish making the chocolate, I try to eavesdrop on his

conversation, just a little, but all I can make out are various swear words. I think I hear something about tabloids and paparazzi.

I herd Belle into the living room with our cups and turn on a Barbie Christmas movie. As she settles in, I check my phone for the first time today to distract myself.

It's blowing up.

I have messages from my mom, from Sadie, from my sister, and half the town.

What the heck.

I click on Sadie's message. She's forwarded me an article from a shady yet popular tabloid.

The headline reads, *Ronan Masters Caught in Scandal with Nannies.*

My stomach churns as I click on the link, and I see a photo of Ronan and me taken during our dance at the Christmas ball. Our arms are wrapped around each other. We look in lust. Heck, we look in love.

Judging by the story, the writer believes the lust part.

I tell myself that everything will be okay. No one knows anything. How could they? It only happened last night.

I read the next headline.

The Nanny Tells All. My Affair with Ronan Masters.

My mind spins. I never spoke to a reporter. We didn't have an affair, only a night. And how did they find out anyway? I haven't told anyone. Will Ronan think I talked to a reporter?

Panic bubbles. What if he doesn't believe me? I scroll down to see a cell phone photo taken of Ronan sleeping in bed. It's creepy and invasive.

I scroll farther and see a picture of Tiffany, the nanny Ronan fired, looking wholesome and pretty. And I realize with a small fraction of relief that the nanny tell-all the tabloid refers to isn't about me. It's about Tiffany. I speed-read. In the interview, she claims she had sex with Ronan.

It's a lie, of course. He fired her for taking photos of him and Belle. He told me that his manager had ensured she wouldn't go to the tabloids. His manager was obviously wrong.

But the image of Ronan dancing with me, the new nanny, looks bad. In the photo, it's obvious that I'm besotted, and he doesn't look indifferent either. When we were dancing, I hadn't realized just how low his hands were on my back, skimming my buttocks in my red dress. It's a gorgeous dress, the most beautiful I've ever worn, but no one seeing me in it would believe I'm a small-town teacher who normally lives in jeans and painting smocks.

It only gets worse, and like a car crash, I can't look away. Below the interview with Tiffany, I find an article that's all about me. It details my broken engagement, speculates how I want to trap Ronan, and decides that he's got a thing for nannies. It makes me, him, us—sound sordid.

Nausea rises. The door from the porch opens and closes, and I look up at Ronan. His eyes are stormy.

"Ronan, I—"

"I need to talk to you," he whispers in a hard voice, his eyes on Belle, who is curled up on the couch beneath a cream knitted blanket that looks like an Irish sweater. She's still facing the movie, but I suspect she's fallen asleep.

He turns and strides toward the kitchen. I follow him on legs made of jelly. My phone that contains the disastrous tabloid article and all the messages of concern is clasped tight in my hand.

He turns to me when he gets to the island and rubs his neck.

"We have to leave," he says. No emotion. No explanation.

"What?"

"Belle and I. We have to go. Now. Back to LA."

Panic shoots through me. "What? No. You said you're staying through Christmas."

"Things have changed."

"The article," I say.

"You saw."

"Several people forwarded it to me. Ronan, you have to understand. I had nothing to do with it."

He shoots me a fierce look. "Jesus, Poppy. I know that. Don't you think I know that? It was Tiffany. Apparently, the nondisclosure agreement and threats of a lawsuit weren't enough. My manager said he'd handled her, but he was clearly mistaken. *Fuck*. I'm not used to the press mattering."

"But it doesn't have to matter," I say. "Tiffany's lying, and the situation will die down. We can have our Christmas like we planned, like Belle is looking forward to. And then we'll go back to our normal lives. Only hire eighty-year-old nannies from now on. It will be okay."

He hunches his shoulders, his muscles taut. "If it were just that, we could get through it. But I got a call from Claire, Belle's mom."

"Oh," I say, tensing at what that could mean.

He looks out the window at the falling snow, where we were just playing and laughing, building snowmen. Not even twenty minutes ago, I'd been the happiest I've ever been, having fun with two of my favorite people and anticipating the thrill of another night with Ronan.

Now, it could all be wiped away as if we'd never had any of it.

"The article names her as Belle's mom and who she's dating. Her current billionaire boyfriend doesn't like the publicity. She decided she wants Belle back early so that she doesn't get caught in the tabloid crossfire. She says she made a mistake leaving Belle with me and she's on her way to LA to meet us and take her back to England."

"No." I'm not sure what I'm protesting, other than everything. "She can't."

My heart is breaking. For Belle. For him. And, yes, for me.

He blinks and clears his throat, then swings his gaze in my direction. The pain in his eyes devastates me. "She can. She may have left Belle with me, but she has custody. I have to go. I have to try everything I can to change Claire's mind. And not make the tabloids worse."

He doesn't say the rest of it. The tabloids will get worse if we're together. Being seen with one of the nannies will fuel the fire of the scandal.

I always knew we weren't forever. We lead completely different lives. He's in LA and I'm here. I'm an art teacher. He's a movie star. But I had hoped we'd have more time.

"What if I lose Belle?" he asks.

I launch myself into his arms, though he doesn't even sway, as steady as the giant sequoia in the yard. "I'm sorry, Ronan. I'm so sorry."

"Hey," he says. "It's not your fault." He pushes my hair back and looks into my eyes. "It's mine. I should have been more careful. I've been living this life for a long time, and I know how the tabloids work. I'm so damn sorry you got dragged into it. But Belle has to come first."

"I know. I understand." I want to say how disappointed she will be not to stay for Christmas. How devastated I am at the loss of our final week. I want to break down because I may never see Ronan or Belle again.

But I need to be strong for him, not make this any harder than it already is. He's dealing with the risk of losing his daughter. All I can do is let them go with grace and pray that he can gain at least partial custody, so that Belle won't be yanked from his life forever.

"Do you think Claire will be reasonable?"

"I don't know. I hired the best team of lawyers I could in LA. I'll be meeting with them as soon as I land. But this article isn't good. If she wants to play hardball, she's got ammunition now. She doesn't even want Belle. She just doesn't want to look like a bad mother. Or get bad press for that asshole she's dating."

I hug him as tight as I can, and he wraps his arms around me. I feel his lips on the top of my head. Then he tilts my chin up to meet his eyes.

"No matter what happens, I'll never regret meeting you, Poppy O'Brien. I'll never forget you. The way you hum when you paint. How you sigh when I kiss you. How I feel when you smile. The way you made me a better person." His lips curve up, though his eyes are sad.

I swallow past the lump in my throat, tears falling. "And I'll never regret meeting you, Ronan Masters. Even if you forgot the duct tape and can't escape elevators. I'll never forget how you taught me to stand up for myself. How you gave up your gym to make me an art room. How you made me feel beautiful. How you made me just *feel*, more than anyone else or anything else in the world."

He sweeps me in for a raw, rough kiss that might have been the beginning, but instead is the end.

Ronan

I CAN TASTE HER TEARS. I DON'T WANT TO RIP MY MOUTH FROM hers because then it will be time to walk away from Poppy.

It will mean breaking Belle's heart.

A voice inside me says it will mean breaking my heart as well. But that can't be true.

It's only been a few months. I don't fall in love. This is just lust, like, and affection.

So we kiss until I find the strength to push away.

She smiles at me. It's sad, but that damn dimple still shows.

"It'll be okay." I'm not sure if she's trying to convince herself or me. "It's just a little early."

I nod. That's the truth I need to remember.

Poppy was never mine. We were going to pack up in a week anyway. We were just pretending here, pretending in this temporary house that somehow felt real.

And now the fantasy has blown apart. But it felt so damn good while it lasted.

I didn't want to acknowledge just how precarious our time was. With Poppy.

And with Belle. I've just been fooling myself. I knew this would happen. That Belle would have to return to her life in England. It's why I hired the lawyers. It's why I tried to guard against loving her so completely. I'd hoped I could keep a distance, but Belle wormed her way into my heart with her little hand in mine, with every sweet moment and every fit of temper.

I'll figure it out later. But first, I have to do what I always do. Carry on. I need to pack us up. Have flights arranged to LA. Meet Belle's mom. And meet the lawyers.

The next right step is doing whatever is best for my daughter.

Regardless of what I want.

So I walk over to Belle, gently lift her in my arms to carry her upstairs to the bedroom she loves, the bedroom we decorated just for her, so that I can get her dressed for a plane ride and try to explain why we're leaving like thieves in the night.

"I'll start packing for her," Poppy says somberly. We're walking up the stairs when she stops me with a hand on my arm. "Hey, want to know a way to console a child who'll be upset about her canceled Christmas plans?"

"What?"

Her mouth tilts up. "Belle really wants a dog. You could adopt one that needs a home."

I bark out a laugh. I can't help it. Her idea is so unexpected.

"And what happens if Belle…" I ignore the panic that threatens to bubble up. "Goes back to London? What do I do with a dog then?"

"That part's easy. You love it. The dog isn't just for Belle, you know. I think you could use a friend as well."

"And what do I do with it when I'm working?"

"Movie stars can have pets too," she says. "They have more in their life than just work."

I'm overcome with a wave of feeling that almost knocks me to my knees. I can't name it. But it's sharp and bittersweet. Poppy's still here in my corner, even when her name is plastered all over the tabloids, making her look like she's been taken advantage of at best, a gold-digger at worst.

Yet she's still thinking of Belle and me.

"I'm sorry. For everything. My manager is hiring a PR agency to take care of some of the press. I'll do everything I can to set the record straight and get your name out of this. I have the house rented through the new year, so don't feel like you need to be out of here right away. Emma will get in touch with you, and we'll take care of everything, including your salary for the full time we were supposed to have."

Her smile falters. "I don't care about the money, Ronan."

"I don't mean that. I just want to make sure you're taken care of." Everything I say seems wrong. I try again, "You deserve all your dreams to come true. Take the studio. Stop saying yes to everyone but yourself. And don't settle for a life you don't want. Or for a man who doesn't treat you like you're the most precious person in the world."

She smiles, but the tears still glisten in her eyes. "Okay."

She looks down at Belle, who's still asleep in my arms. She brushes a hair out of her face. "Let's go upstairs and get her ready. We can do our best to set this up as a fun adventure for her."

"It won't be that without you, Poppy. You know that."

It's the most I'll admit to. The closest I dare get to what's in my heart. So I turn to take the stairs with the little girl in my arms. It's my job to protect her. And not for the first time, I wish things were as simple as they are in my movies. Where there's a good guy and a bad guy. Where with some muscles and, as Poppy claims, some duct tape, the good guy wins in the end. Wins the fight, saves the child, and gets the girl.

CHAPTER 31

5 DAYS TO CHRISTMAS

Ronan

"So you screwed the nanny," Sebastian says conversationally.

"Shh. How are you still alive?" Emma slaps Sebastian on the head. It's her signature slap, and I'm glad she did it because he wouldn't survive mine.

I can't even manage a glare.

"I told you there's something seriously wrong with him. He didn't even growl at me," Sebastian says.

"I don't growl," I growl.

"Grunt, then."

"You do grunt," Chase says. "And growl. He's got you there."

Sebastian, Emma, Chase, and Chase's girlfriend, Olivia, came by uninvited this morning and are crowded into the living room of my small house. It's on a bluff overlooking the Pacific, with a rugged expanse of private beach among the rocks. I bought it ages ago with one of my first paychecks. It's a far enough drive outside of LA that I don't have to worry about the paparazzi, which suits me.

The sudden move back to California has been confusing for Belle, and she's asked about Poppy a million times, which makes sense because I've thought about Poppy a million times.

But we've been trying our best.

Last night, when I read her a bedtime story, Belle asked me if I was sad. I didn't want to lie, so I said yes. And she said she was as well. But that she was happy she was still with me.

"Emma, can you set up an appointment with an interior decorator for me? Maybe tomorrow," I say.

"It's a few days before Christmas, Ronan. Really?"

"I want Belle to have a room she loves," I explain. "She's staying in my former office that I converted into a bedroom when she arrived, but I want something that feels more like hers." I don't say that I want her to feel like she did at the lake house in Snowflake Harbor. That would be impossible, but at least I can give her this—blue, sequins, and whatever else she wants. "I don't know how long she'll be here, so I want it done as soon as possible."

"Consider it done," Emma says.

I bite back panic at the thought of having to give Belle up. Claire and her lawyers have been playing hardball.

It's all my fault. Claire is back in our lives because I didn't manage Tiffany correctly. And because I let myself have Poppy, when I knew I should stay away from her. She was my daughter's nanny, temporary or not. It didn't matter that she was special or that she wanted me as much as I wanted her.

But I did whatever the fuck I wanted to do, to hell with the consequences. And now, we're all paying the price, Poppy included. I called a few people in Snowflake Harbor to arrange a Christmas gift to try to make it up to her, even if I can't fix this entirely.

"Hey, pass me that box of candy canes," Sebastian says as he places a gold ball on the Christmas tree that I put them to work to decorate.

"You can't put the ornaments on the tree before the lights are on." Emma unravels a string of lights. "What are you? A heathen?"

"Why are you all here again?" I ask.

"We're friends. We were in the neighborhood and thought we'd stop by," Chase says.

I snort. "My house is in the middle of nowhere."

"We wanted to make sure you and Belle were okay," Sebastian says. "And see if you needed anything."

"Sebastian's right. Friends stick together." Olivia adds a red ball to the tree and then looks at me. "Don't you want to save the decorating for Belle?"

"I have some ornaments planned for the two of us, but I want to surprise her with this. We already decorated a tree in Snowflake Harbor."

"It's really sweet, Ronan. You're a great dad," Olivia says.

Chase wraps an arm around her and kisses the top of her head.

"God," Sebastian says. "They're still disgustingly loved up, even after all this time."

"It's cute," Emma says.

"Who are you, woman? Are you going soft on me? I thought you hated PDA."

Emma ignores Sebastian. "So where's Belle? With a babysitter?"

I swallow, trying to ignore the acid in my stomach that's taken up residence since this whole thing started. "With her mom. They went out to lunch together."

"Holy shit. Why didn't you say anything?" Sebastian asks.

I shrug and help Emma with stringing the lights around the top of the tree.

"Did she tell you what she wants?" Emma asks.

I take a deep breath and try to center myself. It's a practice I learned in martial arts that's come in handy lately. "Claire's pissed about the scandal. Her boyfriend isn't happy that she and Belle are in the tabloids. The lawyers said that the nanny situation is a goldmine for Claire."

"Oh shit, Ronan," Chase says.

"All I care about is Belle. If Claire wants money, she can have as much as she wants."

"Whoa, well, maybe don't go overboard. Hope your lawyers aren't leading with that," Sebastian says.

"Has Belle indicated who she'd prefer to live with?"

I nod. "She wants to stay with me." When she begged me not to send her back to her mother, it broke my heart. She loves her mom. But she says that she didn't see her much when she lived with her. Belle spent most of her time with the nannies, which is ironic, considering she would love to do that if the nanny were Poppy.

We've just finished decorating when there's a knock at the door.

I open it to find Belle and Claire standing there. Claire is elegant as usual, in a simple black sheath of a dress, a cream coat, and a sleek bob.

"We're going to take a break from decorating, Ronan. We'll be on the porch," Emma says when she sees who is at the door. She herds Sebastian and Chase outside.

"Daddy," Belle cries, giving me a big smile. Relief is

evident on her face. Relief that she's back home with me and not on a plane to England with her mom. "You bought a tree! You decorated!"

I kneel down. "I did, pumpkin."

"I love it." She runs over to it. She gasps as she looks at an ornament I placed on a low branch. "A shell ornament!" she says.

I smile. "I collected some shells on the beach, and I thought we could make them into ornaments together."

"Just like Poppy would do," Belle says.

I nod, my chest feeling tight. "Just like Poppy would do."

Claire's eyes narrow and she frowns.

"Is that Sebastian out there? And Chase and Emma?" Belle asks.

"It is. Why don't you go and say hi while your mother and I talk."

She walks out but looks back at us worriedly. I try my best to smile, though my mouth feels like it will crack.

When she's gone, I turn to Claire. "What's up?" I ask as neutrally as I can manage. I don't want to antagonize her. I need to be smart. She's Belle's mom, which means that if I'm lucky enough to have a proper place in my daughter's life, we'll have a relationship for the rest of our lives. Lord help me.

"I want to talk about Belle."

"We've done that with our lawyers," I say.

"We did. And now I want to talk without the lawyers." She holds up an elegant arm, gold bracelets jangling. "Aren't you going to offer me anything? A glass of wine?

"I only have water."

She snorts. "Still the same. Sparkling?"

I force myself to keep my temper. "I have regular." I get a glass from the cupboard.

She sighs as if it aggrieves her but nods. I pour her a glass of water from the bottle in the fridge and pass it to her.

She fluffs her hair. "Don't look at me like that." She gives a brittle laugh.

"Like what?"

"Like I'm some kind of monster."

I try to stuff down my anger, but I can't help retorting, "Claire, you dropped a bombshell on me that I was a dad after lying about who Belle's father was for years, then you left her here with no prior notice, when she barely knew me. And now you've dragged us both back to LA the week of Christmas to meet with lawyers and forced us to cancel all our plans. You can try to jerk me around all you want. I can handle it. But Belle is just a little girl. I won't see her get hurt."

"So who is Poppy?"

I don't answer.

"All Belle could talk about is Poppy this, Poppy that."

"She was the..." I start to say "the nanny," but I trail off because that doesn't sound right. She was so much more. "She was a friend."

"Don't play dumb with me. She was Belle's nanny. I read the tabloid. She's the one you're screwing."

"If you know who she is, why ask?" I run a hand through my hair. "Leave Poppy out of it."

"I would," Claire says. "But Belle can't seem to," she snaps. Then she sighs. "Listen. I'm never going to be the mother of the year. I wasn't cut out to be a mom, and Belle was a mistake."

"She wasn't a damn mistake."

"An accident, then. Whatever you want to call it. Everything was fine. We'd broken up. We were never compatible."

"You mean I wasn't flashy enough for you, even if you liked that I was a celebrity."

She shrugs. "You and I both know we had nothing in common. I was already dating Howard by the time I found out about Belle. She could have been his. It wasn't until she was older and started to look like a mini-you that I realized the truth."

"What's the point?"

"The point is that I didn't purposely mislead you, even if I had my suspicions. I eventually came and told you about Belle."

"You took your time with that. And only after Howard divorced you and demanded a DNA test. You left Belle here with no warning for either of us and no notice about when you would come back."

"Yeah, well, I thought you two could get to know each other. No time like the present. Charles travels a lot for business. He wants a woman who can go with him. Our au pair quit. It seemed like the perfect solution."

"So why are you here then?"

"Because you couldn't keep your dick in your pants and you had to mess with the nannies. I didn't think you were the type, Ronan, but you *are* a man. If the tabloids hadn't dragged Belle and me into it, everything would have been fine. Charles is old money, the kind that considers that sort of celebrity culture a little tasteless. He told me I needed to deal with this situation."

"What do you want?"

"I want to work this out without our vulture lawyers getting everything. It's the least you can do after causing this scandal. If you're generous enough, in return, you can have primary custody of Belle. She seems happy with you, and believe it or not, I do want what's best for her. We can work out the visitation rights. Summers, holidays."

"You would give me Belle?" I ask, not daring to believe it.

"I had a long talk with her today, and it's no secret she'd prefer to live with you over going to a boarding school, which was always my plan for her. You may think I'm heartless, but I went off to boarding school at her age. However, if she'd rather live with you, that works for me as well. It saves me money and makes things simpler since Charles has no interest in raising someone else's child."

"And what do you want?" I know this won't be free.

"I want three things. First, I want money of my own. I learned the hard way after Howard that a woman needs her own money and can't rely on a man. I also want flexible visiting rights. And I want to control the PR narrative—I won't be painted as the bad mom who gave up her child. You'll be the asshole who practically stole my kid away with your movie-star money and power. And no more scandals, nanny or otherwise. I don't want Charles to have any reason to regret being with me. Do you want your daughter?"

"Yes," I say swiftly.

"If we play it right, this can be a win-win."

"Claire, I expect full custody of Belle."

She takes another sip of water. She sets it down delicately, tilts her head, and smiles.

"How much is it worth to you?"

CHAPTER 32

4 DAYS TO CHRISTMAS

Poppy

"It's yours," Conner holds out a set of keys.

"What?"

"The building."

"What do you mean, it's mine? I didn't put in an offer." I look around the former hardware store, at the large windows and the white walls.

"You didn't. But someone else did."

"Who?"

"Ronan Masters. He paid cash, over asking. His only stipulation was to make it happen before Christmas and to give you the keys."

"But why?"

Conner shrugs. "I just figured, with the photos and all, you two had a thing."

"No!" I cry. "I mean, I liked him. Like him. As a person. And, uh, a man. But you're telling me he bought me a building, Conner. *A building*."

"I'm well aware," Conner says. "And I can't even be irritated with the guy because I got a great commission."

"Why would you be irritated with him?"

"Come on. The guy hated me. He knew I liked you, and that I hoped maybe you and I would be an item. He was jealous."

"I can't accept this gift."

"You should. Maybe this is his way of making it up to you."

"Making what up to me?" Make up for breaking my heart?

"The tabloids and the gossip. All those internet articles trashing you, to start."

"Oh, those," I say. "Thanks for reminding me. Yeah, those suck."

"Everyone's talking about it. Though most of the town is on your side."

"Hmm, great." I've been trying to listen to Ronan's parting words and not care so much what other people think. Just focus on what I want. It's good timing, really, this lesson, considering I'm now known as Slutty Nanny #2.

Tiffany is Slutty Nanny #1, and she's working that position for all she's worth, riding her fifteen minutes of fame. Maybe the situation works if you want a life in LA and are trying to get famous. But being in Snowflake Harbor and possibly opening an art studio that relies on giving lessons to children is another situation entirely. Being known as the nanny who hooked up with her famous boss is not an asset.

But on the upside, if I want to have my studio, now I have a building.

If I accept it. Which I can't, of course. It's too much.

"Are you sure he didn't, you know, tell you anything about this? Maybe leave a note?"

That was the problem with a man who was more comfortable with silence than chattiness.

A chatty man would send a text or an email. Something. Anything. Explaining why he bought me a building.

Something like, "Hey, Poppy. Just wanted to tell you I left you a building. Think of it as a tip because you did such a great nanny job, and I'm super rich, so this is a rich-person-type tip. Totally normal. Nothing unusual here. And the building definitely isn't a tip for the great sex we had. Because that would make you a prostitute."

But noooo, I had to like a quiet guy. So he just leaves me with a cracked heart and a key to my dream studio and no other contact. Darn quiet, grumpy, wonderful man.

Why did he have to leave?

I feel a tear I didn't even realize I had shed track down my cheek. Conner looks scared.

"He did write a few things about it," he admits grudgingly.

"Really?" I say, practically jumping on him.

"He said..." He fiddles with his phone for a minute or two. "Here it is. He said this is his Christmas gift to you from Belle and him, and that you can't turn down a Christmas gift. But that you wouldn't want to take the building, and if you argued, to tell you that you can pay it forward by keeping on with your art lessons at the Kids Creativity Center. To take the studio for them. And that when he was younger, he wished he had someone in his corner like you. So this is his way of giving back. He said you can't turn down a gift for the kids and that you should just say thank you."

"Thank you," I whisper, even though Ronan is a whole world away—in Hollywood, of all places.

I try to stop the tears, but it's no use. I sniffle.

"He also said that he didn't want to force you into anything, so if you didn't want to accept his gift, that you could just consider this a rent-to-own lease. And that any rent you pay will go toward the Kids Creativity Center." Conner looks up. "He said it's your choice."

"Why does he have to be so damn perfect for me?"

Conner looks pained. He throws his hands up. "I'm successful. I own my own house. I have a great real estate business. I drive a Tesla, Poppy, *a Tesla*. I'm a nice guy. Did you know that I'm considered a catch in Snowflake Harbor?"

"I'm sure you are. You're very good-looking, also," I add. Positive reinforcement and all.

"Thank you."

"You're welcome."

"So why is it that I don't like any of those other girls throwing themselves at me? No, I had to like you, Poppy. I can't compete with a movie star who buys you a building."

I sigh. "He's wonderful, isn't he?"

"I mean, his muscles. I can't compete with those muscles."

"And those eyes."

"He's so tall," Conner says glumly.

"But you aren't competing. I don't have Ronan. He left me. He's gone. He's back in LA, and he doesn't plan on returning. Whatever we had was just short-term, and we didn't even get that. We didn't even get our last week."

"So you'll go out with me?"

I smile sadly. "Conner, you're a great guy. But you're right. I'm head over heels for Ronan. Even if there's no hope, it's going to take me a really long time to get over him. I may end up an old maid with lots of cats. But I know you'll find another girl with no problem." See? There, the compliment sandwich at work.

He nods and thinks for a minute. "You're right. Hey, do you think Sadie would go out with me?"

Damn. I wish I could cure my broken heart as easily as Conner just did.

But there's no cure. I've moped around Snowflake Harbor since they left, feeling lost. The worst part is not knowing how Belle and Ronan are doing. I've now got a sick little internet addiction. I'm on every *Wanderers* and Ronan Masters fan site to try to find any teeny tiny tidbit of gossip that could give me a clue. I had no idea Ronan had so many Tumblr accounts dedicated to his abs. I get it, though. He's got really great abs.

So far, I haven't gotten much information. There were some paparazzi photos of Ronan and Belle going grocery shopping. She looked so cute in the cart. It made me smile to know that they were still together, that Belle's mom hadn't taken her back immediately.

And then there were a bunch of photos of Ronan coming out of a meeting with a lot of men in suits. Belle's mom was there, looking glamorous in a black dress and oversized sunglasses. Belle wasn't with them. I wondered what the meeting was about. And I prayed that Ronan could keep Belle. For good.

I finally slammed my laptop shut and vowed not to go on to those sites again, especially when I still saw the horrible rumors about me when I did. The fact that I'm searching on creepy tabloids for any glimpse of Ronan tells me all I need to know.

It's over. I need to move on.

And apparently, I'm moving on with the keys to a new studio.

Ronan may not keep in touch well. But I can't fault him for his gift-giving skills.

Still, as much as I wish I could keep this insanely generous gift, I can't. It wouldn't be right. After Christmas, I vow to figure out a way to pay him back. Maybe with his rent-to-own lease suggestion. I do like the idea of my "mortgage" payment going to my kids at the center every month.

But if Ronan believes in me so much that he'd buy me a building, then I need to learn from that example. I need to make my own dreams come true, minus my one little dream of having Ronan and Belle for myself.

CHAPTER 33

4 DAYS TO CHRISTMAS

Ronan

I CAN'T FIGURE OUT THE BEST WAY TO SAY IT, SO I TELL BELLE the news while we're making dinner.

"Am I really going to live with you, Daddy?" Belle asks tremulously, as if she doesn't quite trust it.

I try to keep my voice steady, holding back my emotions. "Yes."

"Truly?" she asks.

"Truly," I say to Belle.

I'm paying lavishly to have the contracts and paperwork drawn up right away. It's my Christmas gift to us. There are still a lot of legal hoops to jump through, but I'm meeting Claire's demands, adding in even more incentives, and I now believe we'll get there. I never thought I'd be a dad. And I worried I wouldn't be good enough because I'd never had a functional family of my own to draw inspiration from, but Poppy taught me that I didn't have to be perfect. I just had to show up, day after day, and give this my everything. Give Belle my love.

Her smile matches mine, full of relief and joy.

"Yes!" she cries and punches her fist in the air.

Then she's in my arms, and I catch her up and spin her around. She laughs and laughs.

I set her back down, and I turn back to the stove. It's just pasta and a jarred sauce, but she likes it, especially when I add some cream, butter the noodles, and grate fresh Parmesan cheese on top. I'm on Christmas holiday, so I'm giving myself a break.

"Like Poppy's spaghetti," Belle says with satisfaction when I add the cheese.

Her hair is in a simple braid that I made this morning, wisps now sticking out of it. She's starting to lose her obsession with fancy hairstyles, thank God, and has switched to wearing cat-ear headbands. Every day. We're amassing a collection of them.

We also added a few more stuffed animals, including the corgi Poppy got Belle for Christmas. I let her open the gift on the plane back to LA. I know we should have waited until Christmas, but it was an emergency.

I haven't taken Poppy's advice, however. No live puppies have been acquired.

I'm still wrapping my head around the pet thing because our life will be nomadic for a while yet, though I've been working with my agent to get out of most of my current commitments. I'll still do the final *Wanderers* movies, but when the last one's done, I can pick my assignments more carefully, perhaps only selecting projects that shoot in the summer, so Belle won't miss school. Or maybe I'll do a television series on a set in LA. The future is wide open, and for once, I'm not walking it on my own.

It's Belle and me. We're a package deal.

We finish eating and clean up together. When we're done, I give her a high five. "It's me and you, kid," I say. "We make a good team."

She tilts her head.

"Only…does it have to be, Daddy?"

I laugh. "Not the puppy conversation again."

"I want a puppy. But I want Poppy more."

I turn on the dishwasher, trying to come up with something to say.

Something besides, *I want Poppy as well.* Because I do. But I can't risk another tabloid scandal if I start dating "the nanny" again. Claire made it clear that keeping scandal-free was a requirement of our arrangement continuing uncontested.

"Belle, Poppy lives in Snowflake Harbor. Her life is there. And we live in LA. She wouldn't want to be taken away from her family. She loves her town." And that part is true. Our lives couldn't be more different. She would hate Hollywood. Even if I could figure out a way to get around Claire and the tabloids, what we had was always meant to be temporary.

Plus, it's a stretch just to be enough for my daughter, risking my heart day in and day out. How do I risk it for two?

"But, Daddy, everyone says you're like a superhero. That you can do anything," she says with such simple faith. "And Poppy told me that when we love people, we try to help them be happy."

"She's right, honey."

"Well, I know you love me. And I know you love Poppy. And I know she loves both of us. I could tell when we said goodbye how sad she was we weren't going to be together. If you're a superhero, can't you do something so we can all be happy together?" she asks. "When I was scared to make new friends, Poppy said you have to face your fears and do what's right in your heart. And I just don't think being apart is what's right."

I'm just a single dad, with a kitchen towel in one hand and a child's apron in the other, at a loss for words because of a seven-year-old girl's wisdom.

Damn.

She has me there.

I'm not a superhero. Not really. But I am Ronan Masters, movie star. I don't often think of myself in that way. I like to pretend I'm normal, living as quietly and regularly as possible. I don't surround myself with models and mansions or have a team of people to do my every bidding or suck up to my every whim.

I've spent my life honing and then sheathing my power. Even before I was famous, I was always big. I never needed to flaunt my ability to kick ass. It was just there. If anything, I downplayed it.

Maybe now is the time to acknowledge my strength.

I'm rich, a little less than I was before paying off Belle's mom, but I'm still disgustingly rich.

I'm famous as hell.

I know a lot of people in high places who would love to do me favors. And so, yes, I have a lot of power.

And Belle nailed it. I'm afraid. After what happened with the tabloids, I'm gun-shy. I'm afraid to take another chance and lose Belle.

But there's more.

I'm afraid to risk my heart with Poppy. I know she wanted a night with me and a week with me. I know her soft heart fell for Belle. But after she's been splashed across the tabloids, does she really want more than just temporary with us?

She's so much better than I am. I'm taciturn. I'm grumpy. I'm quiet. I'm less of all that with Poppy, but I'll never be the fun, outgoing guy. That's okay. I'm fine with who I am. But that doesn't mean I'm the easiest person to live with.

I never thought of myself as a relationship guy.

But things change. And I've never shied away from a challenge before.

I get Belle ready for bed, read her a bedtime story, and then read her stuffed corgi a bedtime story. Finally, we say good night. She says good night to me. She says good night to her stuffed corgi. And she says good night to Poppy, wherever she is.

And throughout it all, my mind is only half there.

If I were my character in *The Wanderers,* this is the time that I'd be hatching the big heist to save the day and win the girl.

CHAPTER 34

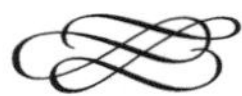

2 DAYS TO CHRISTMAS

Poppy

WHEN I GET THE KEYS, IT DOESN'T MATTER THAT IT'S ALMOST Christmas.

Like a little kid with a new toy, I want to set things up right away. So I have a painting party. And that's the thing about a party. Everyone wants to join.

At first, I just ask my parents and Sadie to help. I figure that everyone will be too busy getting ready for Christmas to have time for this.

But my parents called a few people, who called a few people, and suddenly I'm not just throwing a party. It's a full-blown rager, with half the town popping in to congratulate me or help out. It's possible they also heard who bought the building for me and are looking for gossip, but I don't want to attribute such neighborly behavior to questionable motives, so I push that out of my mind.

"Thanks for coming, Mom and Dad," I say for the dozenth time today. I look around at my friends and family, who came to help paint. I've done favors for all of them in the past, and it's nice to know they are willing to reciprocate as well. I'm still uncomfortable with people doing things for me, but that's something I'm trying to change.

My mom smiles. "Of course, honey. I wouldn't miss it. I brought my chocolate chip cookies. They're on the table over there, so everyone can dig in when they get hungry."

"Good brush technique," I tell her, watching her paint. I decided that Simply White was the perfect shade for the gallery room. As opposed to Super White or White Heron or Chantilly Lace or a gazillion other options. I'm a painter, and even I had no idea there could be so many versions of white.

"I've painted my share of walls in my day, darling. Your dad, however, is another story."

My dad is supposed to be taping off the crown molding, but instead is fighting with the tape, mangling it. I take the roll from him so he doesn't do more damage.

He shakes his head. "I'll be quality control. Inspire the troops."

"Sounds good, Dad." I kiss him. "I appreciate your help. I know this wasn't what you wanted me to do and that you're worried about me leaving a stable profession for something riskier."

He sighs. "I only want you happy. It's just that I know what it's like to be a starving artist, and I didn't want that for you. When I was younger, I wanted to be a musician."

"What?" I say, shocked.

He laughs. "I played guitar, but I wasn't very good. My parents talked me into staying in school and getting a practical degree. So I got my degree in education, and I've always been glad. The truth is, I'd be a terrible rock star."

"He really would," my mom says. "He'd be terrible at drinking and whoring and trashing hotel rooms. It must be exhausting. And he's not exaggerating about his guitar skills either. They weren't great."

I try to picture my dad onstage with a guitar. Try and fail.

"I wasn't that bad. I did go on the road for a while with a band."

"Oh my God. Is there photographic evidence? Do you have an album? A single? A mixtape? How did I not know this?" I ask.

"I hope any evidence has been burned," he says.

"There's a video somewhere. I'll find it for you." My mom grins.

"You have to. *Please.*"

"Being a musician or an artist sounds more romantic than in reality. I was thankful that I had something to fall back on. And I wanted the same thing for you. You're so good at being a teacher. I thought it made you happy."

"It did, Dad. It does. I'm still going to teach, just in my own studio."

He nods. "I was wrong to discourage you. Just because I wasn't comfortable taking a risk, doesn't mean you aren't."

"Well, I'm not exactly trying to be a rock star. Just open a painting studio," I say. "It's pretty tame as far as risks go."

"You'll be brilliant at it. You always put your whole heart into everything. It makes me worry that you'll break it sometimes. But it's also your superpower."

I give my dad a hug, careful not to get paint on him.

"Speaking of superpowers, how's that movie star of yours?" My mom winks at me.

"He's not mine."

"He bought you this place," she points out. "That's kind of a big thing."

"I'm paying him back. I didn't ask him to. He's just, I don't know, being nice."

"Nice is buying someone a fruit basket, not commercial real estate."

"And you told us he turned his gym into a painting room for you as well. Don't forget that," my dad says.

"I can't forget that. But that's just the problem. It's hard to forget someone like him. But we don't have a future. He's back home now. Living his superstar life."

"Hmmm," my mom says and turns back to her painting.

"Poppy! Fabulous studio. Well done." I turn to see Derek in a painting smock.

My mom holds up her hands. "Don't look at me," she says. "I didn't invite him."

"What are you doing here, Derek?"

"I heard you needed help. So here I am."

I snort.

"Where's Monique?"

"We broke up. She moved to New York."

"I'm sorry." It's a lie. But I'm not sure what else to say.

"It's okay. She wasn't right for me. I realized when she left that I missed you. I thought maybe we could try again."

I look him up and down, and I wonder what I ever saw in him, beyond our history and my aversion to change. We had fun when we were younger, and despite him being an idiot lately, I still have a fondness for him. But somewhere along the line, his innate tendency toward selfishness solidified. Being with me probably amplified it. I indulged his worst inclinations by being too accommodating, never pushing back.

"Thank you. But no," I say. Ronan would be so proud. I didn't even use the compliment sandwich.

"Excuse me?" He looks shocked.

"No," I say. "But thank you for your offer."

"Ronan Masters is gone," Derek says. "Are you holding out for him? Because he's not going to choose you over the supermodels he normally dates. I'm not saying that to be mean. It's just the truth."

"Derek?"

"Yes."

"Leave," I say.

My dad puffs up taller. "Yes. Derek. You heard Poppy. Leave. Or I'll make you. Just like Ronan did at our anniversary party."

"Yes. Leave," my mom adds. "We should never have tried to get you two back together. She's far better off without you. *And* far better than you."

A warm glow flows through me at their words and support. "Thanks, Mom. Thanks, Dad," I say. And then I turn to my dad, startled. "Ronan kicked Derek out of your anniversary party?"

"He did," my mom says. "It was very impressive."

"I didn't see that. But why didn't he say anything? Why didn't anyone tell me?"

"Apparently, Ronan wasn't pleased about some of the things Derek said about you," my dad elaborates. "But he managed the situation quietly. He didn't want to upset you. He knew you wouldn't want a scene at the party."

"Since that guy showed up here, you've all lost your damn minds. Fine," Derek grumbles. "I'm going. I have better things to do with my time, anyway."

My dad holds out his hand. "Leave the smock. We don't have enough."

I smile.

"Poppy." Sadie interrupts the scene, and I'm glad to focus on someone I like better than my ex.

"Sadie! Thanks so much for helping to arrange this. I know everyone is busy so close to Christmas. I really appreciate it."

"Of course, hon. We all love you. Everyone was happy to return the favor. But your sister just called me. She said she couldn't reach you. She's in town to see your studio, but she needs a ride from the inn, where she's staying."

"Rose is in town?" I turn to my mom. "Did you know Rose was here?"

"That's right! I was supposed to give her a ride. Oops. With all the excitement, I guess I forgot. And you know us, we always leave our phones at home."

"You never leave your phone at home," I say.

She shrugs.

"We're all kind of busy, dear. Do you think you could give your sister a ride?"

"But..." I wave my hands. "All these people are here for me. For my painting party. How can I leave?"

"How can you not, darling? It's your twin sister. Don't be so selfish. I'm busy painting, and your dad is taping."

My dad grabs the tape back and starts fiddling with it.

This is one of those times I should probably say no. *I must not people-please,* I tell myself.

"Poppy," Sadie says.

"Yes."

"Go to Holly Hill Inn. She's in Room 509."

There's something about the way she says it. And the way my parents are staring at me, that I decide I need to go to the inn. If nothing else than to figure out whatever it is they aren't telling me.

"Fine, I'm going. But not because I'm people-pleasing."

"Good girl," my dad says.

"Oh, darling," my mom calls to my departing back.

"What?" I say in exasperation.

"You might want to brush your hair. And put on some lipstick."

I HIT THE ELEVATOR BUTTON AT THE INN SEVERAL TIMES. AND a memory comes back to me.

"That won't make the elevator come any faster," Ronan said that night.

I close my eyes, and I try to recall everything about the night I met Ronan Masters.

I open my eyes at the moment the elevator arrives.

And I must be hallucinating because inside is the man I was imagining.

He's even larger than I remembered. His wide chest and shoulders stretch the seams of a navy sweater. Jeans encase those long legs. Days of wheat-gold stubble pepper his strong jaw. And his crystal blue eyes pin me with intense regard.

Did I dream so hard that I conjured him? Sort of like a manifestation, which is all the rage. Maybe it's all the rage because it works.

"Are you real?" I ask in an amazed whisper.

"Poppy, get in here."

"You're grumpy. So maybe you are real. Dream Ronan Masters would probably be sweet and kiss me."

"Poppy, get in here so I can kiss you." Ronan reaches over and grabs me by the waist.

"Eeep," I say as he pulls me to him until we're facing each

other in the elevator without even an inch between us.

He swoops down for a long, drawn-out, drugging kiss. Electricity shoots across my nerve endings, and I melt into him. Damn, I missed his strong arms and chest and, oh God, those lips.

When the kiss finally ends, I blink, trying to come out of the fog.

What was it I needed to ask him?

"What are you doing here? In the elevator?" I narrow my eyes in confusion. "Were you going up? Or down?"

He smiles. "I'm going anywhere you are."

I'm flummoxed. "I'm going to get Rose. Fifth floor."

He hits a button. But it's the emergency stop. I didn't even know elevators had those anymore.

"Rose isn't there." He flashes one of his rare smiles that overtakes his face. It makes me even more flustered.

"Where is she?"

"Back in New York, I imagine."

"Sadie and my parents told me to come and get her because…?"

"Because I told them to."

"Why?" I school my features. I've just had my heart destroyed. I can't risk hope.

"Because I wanted to talk to you."

"Hmm. You could have called."

"I'm an actor. I'm dramatic." His mouth curves.

"You're the least dramatic person I know."

"And yet, here we are. Maybe you inspire me, Lady in Red."

I look down at myself and remember I'm wearing a red shirt with a snowman on it. It's two days before Christmas, after all. But his comment reminds me of the dress. And the ball. And everything that happened after.

"What'd you want to tell me?" I ask, breathless.

His brow lifts. "I hired a public relations company to help us with our PR problem."

"*Our* problem?"

"Well, they didn't just trash me. They did the same to you."

I shrug. "It's fine. I live in a small town where everyone knows everyone. It was big news for a week, and then people moved on to who stole the Rudolph sign from Mrs. Kim's yard."

"The PR company gave me a choice between two strategies." He turns us until my back is against the mirrored panels of the elevator.

"What's the first?" I try hard to get my lungs to work.

He lifts a hand and traces the line of my face, which isn't helping with my breathing problem.

"The first is for me to never see you again. I could date a popular actress, and everyone would forget about any scandal."

"Oh." I really don't like that plan.

He traces my frown. "Want to hear Plan B?"

"Yes, please," I say against his finger.

"Plan B is to lean in to this. I come back to Snowflake Harbor. I bring Belle with me, and the three of us get photographed doing wholesome family things. Maybe we give a few select interviews. We act like we're in love. Completely, deeply, hopelessly in love."

He drags his finger down my neck and to the neckline of my shirt. I close my eyes. I'm concentrating on his words, truly, I am. But I'm having a hard time deciphering them.

"You're an actor," I say. "And, you know, I always like to help."

"The thing is, I don't have to act."

My eyes pop open. I push him away slightly, enough that I can breathe. Enough that I can think.

"What are you trying to say?" I whisper, afraid to hope.

"I'm trying to tell you I love you. And I'm doing a damn poor job of it."

"B-but you left. Belle's mom threatened to take her. I've been so worried. I needed to know what happened, if you had Belle still, if she was safe with you, if the two of you were happy, but I didn't want to risk someone finding out that I messaged you."

"She's staying with me. I have custody. Belle's mom and I worked out a deal."

"Oh my God," I cry and jump at him, engulfing him in a tight hug. My arms can't reach all the way around him, but I still give it everything I have. "I'm so happy for you—and for her. I'm so happy." I wipe away my tears.

"I wanted to talk to you. But Claire made our deal contingent on there being no more scandals."

"But even with the PR company, it's still going to be a big story if we're together," I say. "You can't risk that."

"That's what I thought at first. But then Belle gave me a lecture. You must have rubbed off on her. And I remembered that the only thing Claire likes more than money is society stature and clout. *Couture* magazine has promised to do an interview and photo spread of Claire and her home in England, naming her one of their Top Ten Women to Watch."

"But she's not famous, is she?"

"No. But Chase, Sebastian, and I all promised them exclusive interviews and a cover photo shoot with the three of us in exchange for it. And we called in a few other favors."

"But why would Chase and Sebastian do that?"

"Because they know how much you mean to me. And to Belle. And we need you in our lives. I may not be able to fight my way out of this with my fists. But I have friends I can call on and a lot of capital in Hollywood I've never put to use."

"So Claire is okay with this, even if it causes more publicity?"

"She is. Belle and I need you," Ronan says, desperation in his voice. "You make everything better. I want to wake up with you every morning and go to bed with you every night. I want to listen to every single one of your proclamations on the wonders of glitter glue, and I want to cut down whatever Charlie Brown tree you choose. And I want Belle to be there with us every step of the way and—Poppy, you have to stop crying now."

I laugh and sniff and wipe at my cheeks. "I'm trying. I can't help it. I'm a crier. I cry at dog food commercials and Christmas movies and those baby goat videos. If you love me, you're going to have to love my tears."

He kisses first one cheek, then the other, his lips catching the moisture. "I love all of you, even your tears, unless they're sad tears."

"These are super-happy tears, big guy. You know why?" I ask.

"Why?"

"Because I love you."

"Thank God." He picks me up and swings me around, and then he makes me even dizzier by kissing me.

I look up. There's still mistletoe above us, so we have to kiss. I think of that first night and my fantasy of having Ronan in the elevator, just the two of us.

"Babe," I say.

"Hmm." He kisses my ear.

"Want to find out what my panties say?"

"Hell yeah."

EPILOGUE

CHRISTMAS DAY—1 YEAR LATER

Ronan

I WAKE ON CHRISTMAS MORNING IN THE BEDROOM OF THE lake house, happier than I've ever been. Because I wake up in bed with Poppy. She kisses me. I groan and pretend to be annoyed.

"You keep me up all night, and you want more?"

She laughs. I settle her on top of me, letting my erection show her that I'm just kidding. I always want her. All day. All night.

"I can never have enough of you," I admit.

She leans down for a lingering kiss.

To my disappointment, she breaks it far too soon. "It's Christmas morning, and we have a little girl who's not going to wait for us to make love again before she starts banging on the door, demanding presents."

I groan. "It's still dark. And I was hoping for my own Christmas present. Now."

"I gave it to you last night." She grins. "Over and over."

"And I fucking loved it."

"We have a Christmas tree to light, a fire to start, and I have cinnamon buns to put in the oven."

But she moans as my hand strokes her, dipping in to feel how wet she is for me. I want to wake up to her, to this, every morning of my life. Not just the sex, though that's mind-blowing. But the warmth and love. The sweetness and support. The times when she drives me mad and the times she challenges me. I want it all—all of her.

Now.

"It won't take long to make you come," I urge.

She laughs, but it's breathless. "Oh yeah, is that a challenge?"

"It's whatever the hell you want it to be. Get on all fours," I say.

She does as instructed and turns back to look at me with a soft, eager smile and the sensual beauty of her steals my breath. Cinnamon curls flow around her. Freckles decorate the cream perfection of her skin. I've made it my mission for the last year to kiss every last one.

I don't know what I did in a past life to get Poppy. but I'm so damn grateful every day. Every hour.

We don't have much time, so I skip the preambles. Promising myself that I'll enjoy every inch of her tonight. I grasp her hips and dip two fingers into her. She cries out. And I reach and play with her breasts. She looks so sexy panting and writhing for me as I fuck her with my fingers, that I almost lose it, but I need more. I replace my hand with my mouth, circling her clit until she's moaning my name. I lick her languorously, thoroughly, over and over.

"Ronan, please, please."

"I love it when you beg."

I reward her by giving her faster teasing licks until she's as high as she can go, mindless with pleasure. My dick is painfully hard at the taste and feel of her.

"Come for me," I half order, half plead, desperate to be inside of her. I suck her clit and pinch her tight nipple at the same time. She cries out and explodes. I love that sound. I'll never get enough, and I can't wait any longer.

I position myself behind her and guide my cock lower, to her entrance, into that spot I'd just pleasured, the place that's all mine.

As I sink into her, I groan and swear. She feels too good. Too tight, too hot, too slick. I won't last long. I go deep and stroke slowly. For all my talk of fast, I want to savor this mindless joy. Her small, sharp gasps of pleasure, though, make me out of my mind.

"I need to see you," I moan. "I need to watch you when you come again."

I twist her until she's lying on the bed below me, and I hover over her.

"Hi," she whispers.

"Hey."

Her hand reaches out to push strands of my hair behind my ear. She cups my chin.

"Love," she says.

"Yeah?" Even through my frantic heartbeat and screaming erection, I'm undone by the soft way she says, 'love.'

"Get that gorgeous cock of yours back in me."

I grin and do as she instructs. I drive my dick into her and she thrusts her hips up with a gasp as I set a driving pace.

Her hands explore all of me, setting fire to everywhere she touches as she rains kisses across my chest.

We come together over and over, until it's all too much, the feel of her tits against me, the way she cries out each time I pound into her, the wild heat in her eyes. And then her silent scream at the end in ecstasy.

Her inner muscles grip my dick, and I come with a shout. My mind is mindless except for one thought repeating like a prayer. This is everything I'll ever want.

Minutes later, she's curled up on top of me, stroking my chest.

"Best. Present. Ever," she says. I can feel her smile on my skin.

"Best present ever," I murmur.

She lifts her head and I smile at the way a curl falls over one of her eyes. I brush it away with my finger.

"Come on, big guy, we can't lie in bed all day. We have other presents waiting. And I'm greedy."

She hops out of bed and throws on her Christmas pajamas that I stripped off her last night. She bought a matching pair for Belle and for me as well, but that was a step too far. So I dress in a green T-shirt and plaid pajama bottoms, my concession to the holiday.

"It's snowing." She stands at the window in the weak light of dawn. "For our second Christmas together." She smiles at me with shining eyes. "I didn't think I could be so happy."

I come up behind her and encircle her in my arms, lifting her hair and kissing that sweet spot on her neck. "Are you sure? I know it's been busy. With you opening your art studio and me juggling my movie commitments around Belle's school schedule. And our summer in California."

She turns in my arms. "How can you doubt it?" She looks at me with joy in her eyes. Something fierce and sweet twists in my gut.

I lean in to kiss her, wishing I could breathe in her smile

so it was with me always.

We break apart after long minutes. "Let's go downstairs before I change my mind and take you again," I growl.

We walk hand in hand, trying to be as quiet as we can on the creaking stairs. We know we only have minutes, so we work fast, getting things ready for Belle. We prepared almost everything the night before, looking up the Santa tracker on the internet, reading *'Twas the Night Before Christmas* to an excited, sleepy girl, putting all the gifts under the tree, and leaving out cookies for Santa and a carrot for Rudolph. All those little details that I never got to experience when I was a kid, but with Poppy's help, we can give them to Belle.

Twenty minutes later, we're kissing in the light of the oven with the smell of cinnamon buns wafting through the house when Belle races down the stairs and screams, "Presents!"

With a fire going, we open them all, one at a time, with each person taking a turn. I admit I got carried away with presents, so it takes a long time until the last gifts are opened.

Poppy gives me a painting of the three of us in front of the lake house. It's the best gift I've ever gotten, unless you count the gift of them and this Christmas.

"I have one last surprise," I say.

I lead them outside to the porch.

Three new Adirondack chairs with bows on them face the lake.

"They're so cute!" Belle says, running her hand over the smallest chair. "It's just my size." She plops into the kids chair.

"These are beautiful," Poppy says. "Thank you." She kisses me. "We can try them out. I'll bring some blankets and hot chocolate."

I give a ghost of a smile, nerves and hope warring in me.

"The gift isn't the chairs. It's the house. It's ours now."

She gasps. "How? Ronan! The owners said they'd never sell!"

"They apparently could be convinced." For a lot of money. And many signed photos of every celebrity I know in Hollywood. "I may have to travel, we may spend time away, but Snowflake Harbor is our home now. And you're our home."

Poppy holds a hand to her chest.

"Daddy," Belle whispers, tugging on my pants leg with impatience. "Now."

I go down on one knee, my hand shaking as I reach into my pocket and bring out a velvet box. "You aren't just my home. You're my heart too. I know nothing about my life is easy. My job comes with a lot of baggage. There will always be fans and paparazzi and reporters, and sometimes I'll have to be away to film. I'm not sure if I can ever give you a peaceful life. But I can give you all my heart and love. And if that isn't enough, I'm part of a pair. So there's also all Belle's love."

"I have lots and lots of love, Poppy!" Belle says.

Poppy laughs through her tears. "I know you do, darling."

"Tears, again?" I sigh and stand. "Happy tears?" I ask, hoping with everything in me.

"Of course, happy tears," she says. "Yes, I'll marry you. There was never even a question." She wipes her glistening eyes. "I love you so much." She launches herself at me, and I catch her easily and we kiss.

Belle stands on one of the chairs to get higher and join our hug, so I pick her up as well.

"I love our house. But as long as I'm with you and Belle, that's the only thing that matters." Poppy says.

I realize I'm still holding the ring box, so I unravel us

from our hug and put the ring on Poppy's finger. She admires it, watching it catch the light.

"It's a really, really big ring, Daddy." Belle looks at Poppy. "I helped him pick it out."

It is a really big ring. I might have gotten a little carried away. But I want the other guys to see that ring from Mars so they know that she's mine.

A car turns into the driveway.

I hear a car door slam and the sound of bickering. The sound of Poppy's parents bickering.

"Oops," she says. "They're early. I wanted to talk to you first."

"Early for what?" I ask.

"Well, I did a thing."

"What kind of thing?"

I hear a suspicious sound.

I glare. "Did I just hear a dog bark?" I ask. "Poppy, what did you do?"

"To be fair, it's not really a Christmas present. And technically I'm fostering, not adopting. The shelter was full, and he really needs a home until they find a permanent one. And I couldn't leave him at the shelter over Christmas. But we can adopt, if we decide we want to. And I'm pretty sure we'll want to," she trails off.

There's that sound again.

"It is! It's a dog!" Belle tears around the wraparound porch to the front.

Poppy smiles up at me impishly. "You love me."

"I do."

"And you know what? You'll love the puppy too."

The end

ALSO BY SARAH DEEHAM

IN THE FALLING FOR FAMOUS SERIES

Star-Crossed Letters, Olivia & Chase's story, is a celebrity pen-pal romance. One girl with a typewriter + one movie star = anonymous pen pals, a secret crush, and a steamy, slow-burn summer to risk it all.

Star-Crossed Crush is Ryder & Daisy's story. It's a celebrity romance featuring a small town, pet-sitting puppy hijinks, and a girl crushing on her brother's best friend (who just so happens to be a rock star).

& the FREE NOVELLA

Star-Crossed Darcy - Sign up for my newsletter and you'll get Star-Crossed Darcy, a free standalone novella in the Falling for Famous series. Star-Crossed Darcy is an enemies-to-lovers celebrity romance with a sassy fan-fiction author heroine and a hot Hollywood hero who plays *Pride & Prejudice*'s Darcy on a TV show.

ABOUT THE AUTHOR

Sarah Deeham is the author of sexy slow-burn romance novels to make readers smile and swoon. With a master's degree in writing and publishing, she got her start in writing as a freelance journalist, communications director, and an editorial director for a public relations agency. She is an American expat living overseas and currently makes her home in Kuala Lumpur with her husband, two children, and lazy golden retriever. Sign up for her newsletter at www.sarahdeeham.com, for free stories, new release updates, and all the fun.

Printed in Great Britain
by Amazon

32387694R00193